NICK MIRAGLIA

A MAN'S WASTED LIFE
COMES FULL CIRCLE

THE
DOLPHIN
IN ME

COPYRIGHT

Contents

CHAPTER 1

REGRETS

Marco Ricci sat in his wheelchair overlooking the ocean from his veranda. The sky was blue with white, puffy clouds scattered here and there, and all the palm trees gently swayed in the breeze. The beautiful plants and flowers and the beautiful sound of the waves had a calming effect on him. The sun shone brightly, and the warmth through the window felt wonderful on his old body. Off in distance, a pod of dolphins was jumping out of the water.

Looking back on his life, he felt regret. He had taken every opportunity, legal or not, to make a vast amount of money. His actions contributed to a part of the earth's environmental problems. Starting out as a fisherman working on his boat, it didn't take long to figure out he wouldn't be making the money he wanted, so he planned a scheme using the boat as a front. During the night, he would go to the industrial factories and pick up barrels of hazardous and toxic waste. He dumped them while fishing. It changed his life. So much money came in that he bought two more boats, both doing the same thing.

He was so busy making money he didn't have any time for his wife or son. His wife was the main family influence for his son, David. She never knew what her husband did, nor did she ever question about the money that he brought home. She supported David in his true love, which was painting.

Marco ridiculed his wife over their son's desire to be a painter. It got to a point where she would hide all of his paintings and all of the materials he used. Suddenly, she died from a massive heart attack. David never had a good father and son relationship, and he was angry over the death of his mother and the lack of a family. Shortly after his mother's death, Marco shipped him off to boarding school.

All the money in the world could not help him get out of his wheelchair. Looking back over his life, he was filled with regrets, and he was alone, paying his penance for his sins.

Every day, he sat looking out over the water, hoping to see something that would help pass the time. The only thing that brought a smile to his face was a pod of dolphins that would travel by at the same time every day. He would daydream, *What would it be like to be a dolphin? Not a care in the world, jumping so high I could almost touch the clouds, in and out of water and spinning like a top.* When the pod was out of sight, the daydream would end with the realization that he was back in his wheelchair.

CHAPTER 2

TOO LATE

Upon completion of private school and graduation from college, David returned home with a PHD in chemistry, but he never forgot his true love of painting. After a failed attempt at the family business, David had a falling out with his father. The main reason was the business itself. After he found out what his father doing, they argued constantly about how the business was run. David wanted to recycle hazardous and toxic material into clean energy, but his dad didn't want anything to do with it. The falling out got so bad that David left the company. They had not spoken to each other for over a year. During that time, unknown to David, his father had a paralyzing stroke. After his stroke, while he still had the capability of communicating, he told the business attorney, Frank Goldstein, that he was not to let his son David know of his condition. He was a stubborn man that always got his way. As the months went by, his condition got worse, and after another stroke, he lost the ability to speak. But he still had the full function of his brain and knew what was going on. Frank realized that his client and friend was slipping away, and though he knew he would be breaking the attorney-client privilege, he felt he should try to get David to see his father before he passed on. Although Frank did not approve of the way the business was run, he was paid well for his services, and they had become friends for many years.

Knowing of the fall out, Frank decided to go to David and try to get him to come back home and see his dad for the last time. But instead of a phone call, he did it in person. Frank had known David since before his mother died and was very fond of him. So off to Maine Frank went on the next flight with a heavy heart. After renting a car at the airport, he headed for David's house. Walking up to the front door, before he could even knock, he heard a voice from behind him say, "Hello, Frank! What brings you this way? Is my father in jail yet?"

Frank turned his head and said, "Hello, David." Frank then explained why he had not called earlier when his father first went down with the stroke. "Your father didn't want any sympathy from any-one, especially after your last talk with him. He was a proud man and wouldn't allow anyone to know he was ill. I'm breaking your father's trust by disclos-ing his condition." After a moment of silence, Da-vid had a look on his face as if he knew what he should do. Then Frank said, "David, you need to do the right thing, and that's come back with me and try to make peace with your father because you don't want to go through life with any regrets. His condition is bad, and we don't have much time."

"I'll get my things, and I'll be right down." He turned and headed up the stairs to his room.

David and Frank were off on the next flight to his father's home in Florida. The next day, when they arrived at his father's house, Flo, the maid, whom he had known since childhood, met them at the front door. "Hello, Master David. I'm glad that you came home."

"Hello, Flo. It's been a long time."

"Too long if you are asking me." Flo was never shy on making her opinions known. She turned to Frank. "Hello, Mr. Goldstein."

"Hello, Flo."

Flo said, "I'll have Stephen take your bags up to your room." Stephen had been the butler and driver for his dad for a long time. Flo then told Mr. Goldstein that his office had called and that the day nurse had gone to the store. Flo then turned to David. "Your father is on the back porch, overlooking the ocean as he does every day. That's the only thing that seems to make him happy."

As Frank and David walked to the back porch, David could not help but to reflect back on his childhood. All he ever wanted from his father was to have a good father-son relationship. When they arrived, the smell of the warm, tropical salt air filled the room. Along the side of the porch, under the shade, he could see the wheelchair with his father sitting in it. The back of his head was all that was visible. David looked and thought to himself how hard it must be for his father. He had always been such a tall and proud man, walking with such confidence and holding his head up in pride, and he was confined to a wheelchair. Seeing the pain that his dad suffered and remembering what he had done, everything that had transpired between them seemed to disappear. An eerie feeling crept over David as if something was not quite right. He touched Frank's arm, and they hurried closer. When he was in front of his father. They could see the cold, blank look in his open eyes which had been staring out at the ocean. David said, "Dad! It's David. Answer me." He shook his dad, hoping to wake him up but to no avail. His skin was cold to the touch. David stood there unable to move.

Frank quickly checked for a pulse and then said, "David, I'm sorry. He's gone."

David became even more frozen, unable to speak. After a while, he looked at Frank and said, "Even though we had our differences and didn't get along with each other at all, he was still my father. This is how my life has always been with him. We never really got to know each other."

CHAPTER 3

REALIZATION

Marco had fallen into the deepest sleep he had ever had, and then there was the brightest flash of light, and the next thing he knew, he was flying through the air, landing in the water, and diving to the depths in seconds only to be airborne again. *This is what Michael Jordan must've felt on his way to the hoop.*

He kept doing that until he could hardly take a breath. He kept waiting for someone to wake him up, but something was very different about his "dream." He felt the wetness of the water over his skin. He felt the warm, tropical air when he broke the water and returned. He never had a dream like that before. He realized it was not a dream!

In his mind, he thought, *What just happened? Where am I? What am I going to do?* He kept repeating all those questions over and over again.

Okay, he said in his mind. *Settle down. One thing at a time. First, I'm in the water. No one is around me in any direction. I'm not paralyzed. I'm not in a wheelchair. I must've fallen off a boat. I have no clothes on!* Then as he looked at his hand, he could only see a fin. He quickly turned his body to check his feet. The shocking realization was he had been reincarnated as a dolphin!

Is this God's way of paying me back for what I've done? All he knew was what he was experiencing...and he had better start figuring out how to survive or he would be one dead dolphin. And…dying was not an option.

In the background, he could make out a series of tones and clicks. Following the sounds seemed to be the most logical thing to do.

While following the sounds, it was time to check out his new body. With little effort, he leapt from one wave to another, and the tones and clicks became more clear. He plunged deep into the ocean and then came up out of the water as high as he could to get a better bird's-eye view. There they were! A pod of dolphins. As he got closer to the pod, there were clicks and tones all around him.

He listened. It seemed as if there was a sense to the series of noises. His mind was full of the same thoughts. "Food here." He quickly realized that he understood them. The entire dolphin pod surrounded a school of baitfish like a band of Indians surrounding a wagon train. As each dolphin would go into the circle to feed, the other dolphins would keep the school of fish packed tightly, and each took their turn feeding. As soon as the feeding was done, the dolphins scattered. The organization was something to see.

With that type of organization and a higher form of intelligence, he thought there must be a way to communicate with the dolphins. When he got closer to the pod, they would drift away from him. One more attempt to get close to the dolphins was met with the same result. All of a sudden, a lone dolphin broke from the pack and headed right toward him. He cleared his mind of all thought in order to get a clearer communication with the dolphin. The dolphin clicked at him, "Stay away! Stay away, spotted one."

Not to provoke the dolphin, he turned off to the left and swam away, keeping his distance. It was a clear warning. He thought to himself. *Why did the dolphin pack reject me? Did the dolphin call me spotted one?*

To answer those questions, he figured that maybe if he jumped high enough before he re-entered back into the water, he could have a clear reflection of what he looked like. It took a couple of times for him to realize that, yes, he was a dolphin, and there was a white star between his eyes and in front of his blowhole that made him completely different looking than the other dolphins in the pod.

The pod began the same series of clicks and tones. "Food here," and they were gone again. He was getting a little hungry, so he decided to stay far enough away to not disturb the pod but still eat his first dolphin meal.

The clicking and tones sounded a call. "Danger." He jumped out of the water for a better look. The dolphin pod was in real danger. A purse seine fishing boat was closing its nets with the pod of dolphins hopelessly trapped inside the circle of death.

When he fished for tuna, it was a common practice to wrap the whole pod of dolphins because wherever fishermen found the dolphins, they would find the tuna, and unfortunately, the byproduct of catching tuna would be that some dolphins would get tangled in the net and drown.

The closer he got to the fishing boat, he could see the back of the boat and the name. The *Angelina* was his first boat. He still could remember the crew and how they all rejoiced when they used the dolphins to find the school of tuna. When they found the school, they would drop the small boat into the water and let out the net. The small boat would then drive around the tuna and dolphins, pulling in the bottom of the net to entrap all within its death trap.

To keep the fish from getting out before the small boat completely circled, they would throw underwater explosives the size of a cherry overboard. The explosions would scare the fish back into the net until it was completely closed off, encapsulating all fish and dolphins in the net.

He could still remember Pablo picking the cherry bombs from the basket and then lighting them with his cigar and throwing them overboard. While he swam closer to the little boat, all he could think of was how could he stop them from closing the trap.

With a couple of flips of his tail, he was at Mach speed, jumping the net and landing in the center of the trap and clearing his mind of all thoughts except "Follow me."

He used the appropriate clicks and tone sounds through his blowhole, but as he got closer, he knew the small boat was just a moment away from closing the net.

He could feel the percussion of the explosive ringing in his head. Clearing the water for a better look, he could see one man taking them from a basket at his feet and throwing them into the opening between the small boat and the mother fishing boat. The only option left was to slow the little boat down. Without time to think, he dove down really deep so that he could jump as high as possible. Aiming at the front of the small boat, he jumped right at the fisherman who was throwing the explosives. Marco hit him just as he lit one. The man fell over the bow of the boat, landing in the water. The lit explosive fell into the basket, which ignited all the unlit explosives.

All hell broke loose with the basket exploding in all directions. The driver of the boat dove in the water to get away. On the other side of the net, Marco kept repeating, "Follow me! Follow me!" As he turned to look at the results, the small boat was dead in the water with two men hanging onto the side of it. He could see the pod of dolphins making their way through the opening between the two boats to open water.

Once in open water, the dolphins slowly worked their way north. There was no celebration of escape or joy. It was another escape in the daily life of a dolphin. He was in the middle of the pod. No longer was he an outsider. He had been accepted by the dolphins as part of their family. Clearing his head of any thoughts other than the sounds the other dolphins were making, he kept hearing the same clicks and tones repeating. "Is he the one?" As the dolphins communicated back and forth to each other, he was approached by the same dolphin that just hours earlier had chased him away. Swimming next to him, he repeated what he'd been hearing from the other dolphins. "Are you the chosen one, spotted one?"

Clearing his head again, trying to think like a dolphin, not as a human, he responded with, "Who is the chosen one?"

"It has been spoken about the chosen one who would come and would know all about humans and would bridge the gap between the sea mammals and the humans so we could live together in harmony."

He replied, "I know the ways of the human, and I can communicate with them, but the ways of the sea mammals I don't know even though I am a dolphin."

They traveled on their way north. He listened to the entire problem the dolphins had with pollution of the water that not only affected their survival but eventually human life as well. Also, he learned how the dolphins and other sea mammals had tried to show the humans what they had done by committing suicide by beaching themselves on the beach. But nothing had changed because the dolphin could not communicate to humans what their problems were. Traveling north, he heard a different sound like a dog crying with long tones. A pod of humpback whales appeared. "Are you the chosen one?" asked a whale.

"I know the ways of the humans," he replied again. The whales began telling him of all their problems and that it was for the good of the creatures and all mankind for the humans to clean up what they had done to the ocean as well as the earth. Marco listened, and he realized what his mission was. He was "The Chosen One." He was paying a penance for his sins against nature to bridge the gap between humans and sea animals.

Turning south, they came to an area where an alarm was sounded. "Danger, bad water." He went to see, and a cold chill ran up his spine. There were drums of leaking hazardous material, the same drums that he had dumped while working on his first boat. He closed his head of all thoughts so as not to give away his sins.

As they headed south again, he decided that he must leave the pod to make contact with humans on his own. He explained to the dolphin that he must go and that he would be making contact with the humans, and at the right time, he would meet up with them again.

The dolphin pod stayed with him until they could see the lights of the city. Saying his goodbyes, he was again on his own, but he had a real purpose.

CHAPTER 4

MEETING AARON

That morning, he reached a group of private sport boats anchored off the coast. Marco popped his head out of the water to get the attention of the people on the boat. But all that came out were dolphin noises, and the people on board threw fish at him and tried to touch him. Going from boat to boat with the same result, Marco was depressed to say the least. How was he going to communicate when he could only speak like a dolphin?

He continued swimming until he reached a small cove where a house sat next to a small pier. At the end of the pier, Marco saw a young boy fishing with a Miami Dolphins cap on his head. Marco thought to himself that a boy so young might have the imagination to make it possible to find a way to communicate with him.

Marco knew he should take it slowly so the boy wouldn't be scared. He popped up next to the pier. The boy looked up at him with a dejected look. It was not at all what he expected. He began making dolphin noises and nodding his head. Then the boy said, "Hi, Mr. Dolphin." There was no excitement in his voice. Then he said, "There are no fish here. I've been here every day for nothing."

With one flick of his tail, Marco went under the pier and scattered up a group of fish so fast that four or five popped up on the pier. The boy ran to catch all of them and put them in a bucket he had next to him. Marco looked up to see all the action. When the boy bent over to pick up the flopping fish, his Miami cap fell off, exposing his bald head.

Marco's heart sank. It looked like the tell-tale sign of someone going through chemotherapy for cancer, but to see the boy filled with joy and excitement in his voice was heart-lifting.

The boy then said, "Thank you, Mr. Dolphin. Wait until I tell my mom!" The kid picked up a cell phone in a plastic case and dialed the phone number. "Mom, come down to the pier." The last thing Marco wanted was the mother to see him with her boy. He was afraid of the mother being overprotective. She might be frightened, and he would lose his opportunity to communicate. He decided to leave for the moment.

Just when he saw the boy's mother, Nicole, running toward him, Marco dove underneath the pier. That way he wouldn't be seen, but he could still hear everything. Nicole noticed how her son kept looking back at the pier, and she gave a quick look but saw nothing. That was a good start. Marco decided to give it one more try the next day.

"Are you all right, Aaron?" She was bent over, out of breath. Her long, brown hair covered her eyes after the long run to the end of the pier.

"Yes, but look what I have." He showed his mother the bucket of fish.

"Aaron, when you called me, you scared me half to death." She pulled her long hair from her face, and he could see frustration in her eyes.

"I'm sorry, Mom. I know the only time I'm to use it is when I need help, but Mom, there was a dolphin right here."

"All right, that's enough excitement for today. Let's go back to the house." Nicole took his hand as they walked back to the house. Aaron, carrying the bucket of fish, kept looking back at the pier with every other step they took.

"I'll be back tomorrow, Mr. Dolphin!" She looked back but couldn't see anything.

That night, he was filled with what had transpired during the day and all the problems yet to come. First, how could he communicate with the boy? Secondly, would the boy's mother be a problem by being an over-protective mother? One thing he had going for him was a young boy's imagination that might help. He had to take it slow and easy if he wanted his plan to work.

After Aaron and his mother were at home, Nicole could not help but feel the excitement of the day's events. Not to spoil the moment, she put the fish in a bag in the refrigerator, knowing that as soon as her husband got home, Aaron would want to display them for his dad.

"Mom, can I use the computer?"

"Sure, Aaron, but let's take a bath first and get these fishy clothes off."

After the bath, he went right to the computer, looking up all the information he could find on dolphins while his mother was preparing dinner. When he heard his father, John, pull the car into the driveway, he ran to the door. The excitement of the day began again, and Aaron's face filled with joy.

"Dad! I have something to show you! Come with me!" Aaron brought his father to the refrigerator to look at the fish. He looked, overtaken by his son's excitement. It was just as if he had hit a home run to win the game. He did not have any friends because they had only lived in the neighborhood a few weeks, and after his last visit with Dr. Bailey, his oncologist, things were not looking good for Aaron. The chemotherapy had not stopped the cancer from spreading.

After dinner, Aaron questioned his dad on what he knew about dolphins. John replied that all animals of the ocean are wild, even when they appear to be harmless.

Nicole said, "A few more minutes and it's off to bed with you."

"Yes, Aaron. You had a big day today."

After Aaron was in bed, both of his parents remarked on how he looked so happy and excited. After the last visit with Dr. Bailey, there was not too much to look forward to. John questioned Nicole about the dolphin.

"I didn't see anything. I don't know if it's Aaron's imagination or what."

John looked over at Nicole. "Let's allow Aaron to keep doing what he was doing down at the pier. It seemed to make him feel good and happy."

CHAPTER 5

BREAKING THE CODE

That morning at breakfast, Aaron couldn't wait to go back to the pier. John had already gone to work. Nicole had put sunscreen all over his body and put the cell phone in its plastic case and reminded him that it was to be used only in emergencies and not to frighten her into thinking something was wrong.

"Okay, Mom," Aaron replied with a smile on his face.

Aaron came down to the pier. Marco could see him with his cap on and carrying his pole in one hand and the bucket in the other.

Marco waited a minute until Aaron was settled in so Nicole couldn't see him.

Marco popped up just behind Aaron, making a couple of dolphin tones and splashing him with a little water. The boy turned quickly and with excitement in his voice said, "Mr. Dolphin, I knew you would come back."

Marco nodded his head as to communicate with the boy. He understood! The boy said, "Wait right here. I want my mom to see you."

Then the boy turned back to the house. Marco shook his head back and forth, expressing no. Full of excitement, the boy kept going. Marco could only stop him by disappearing under the pier.

Aaron reached the start of the pier, turned around, and stopped, not seeing Marco. He headed

23

back to the end of the pier. As he reached the end, Marco popped up again.

"There you are!" he said. "Don't you want to meet my mom? She's really nice."

Marco shook his head.

The boy put his hands on his hips and said, "Okay, it'll be our little secret." Marco quickly nodded his head up and down to answer yes.

Then to gain the trust of the boy, he pitched a small plastic bottle at him as if to play catch. He nodded his head up and down. Little did Aaron know that it was the first day of school between a boy and a dolphin.

Aaron threw the bottle not very far, and Marco was able to quickly pick it off in mid-air.

Swimming back to Aaron, he flipped it back so he could catch it, but at the same time keeping his eyes on the house to make sure Nicole did not see them playing.

After three hours of playing catch, Marco noticed a lobster fishing boat coming into the cove. Aaron saw it too and said, "They come every day to check their traps," but Marco didn't want to take a chance, so he slipped back underneath the pier.

Marco stayed under the pier not to be seen by the fisherman. Aaron picked up his pole as if he was fishing. The boat went by. The boy waved to the fishermen, and they waved back asking, "How's the fishing?" Aaron gave them a thumbs up.

After the boat left the cove, Aaron called out to Marco. "They're gone." He grabbed the plastic bottle and threw it again. As Marco returned the bottle, he looked up to see Aaron's mother was walking to the start of the pier. He didn't want Aaron to throw the water bottle. Instead he shook his head back and forth. Back under the pier he went. Aaron, seeing his mom approaching, understood why the dolphin disappeared.

"Aaron, it's time to get cleaned up for lunch," Nicole called from halfway to the pier.

"Be right there, Mom." Aaron then bent over to pick up his fishing pole and bucket. He whispered, "I'll be back after lunch."

Marco gave a couple of clicks to let him know that he understood. Aaron and Nicole walked to the house. Marco could hear Aaron's mother ask if he had seen the dolphin. Aaron gave a sigh and said, "No, Mom, not today."

Marco thought to himself, *Good job, Aaron.* The boy was on the same page.

After Aaron returned to the house with his mother for lunch, Marco began planning his next step with him. He needed to get away from the view of his mother and also anyone else that might see them.

A small rowboat tied to the end of the pier would be a way to get the boy closer without his mother coming down. How to get Aaron to understand was going to be a problem.

After lunch, Aaron came back down to the end of the pier with his fishing pole and bucket. The boy put down the bucket, reached inside, and pulled out a tennis ball.

Marco popped up from underneath the pier. Aaron said, "I got us a ball." He threw the ball farther than he had the plastic bottle.

They played catch for about two hours. Then instead of throwing it to him, Marco flipped it in the rowboat that was tied to side of the pier. Aaron had a puzzled look on his face as to why the ball was thrown into the boat. He climbed down into the boat to return the ball and quickly threw it again.

Again, Marco returned the ball to the boat. Aaron again climbed down and threw the ball back. That time he stayed in the boat. Marco then returned to him, and instead of throwing the ball, Marco just held it in his mouth in hopes that he would take it. Marco let Aaron take the ball from his mouth as he ran his other hand over the dolphin.

Marco kept still. He could see the boy's eyes light up with excitement. He rolled over like a dog would do, gaining Aaron's trust.

Marco went to the front of the boat where a rope hung off the bow. He grabbed the rope and pulled the boat away from the pier until it was stopped by the line attached to the dock cleat. He stopped, moved it out away from the pier, and repeated it again. He was trying to let Aaron know he wanted him to take the rowboat out away from the pier so they could interact without being noticed by his mother.

Aaron had a confused look on his face and asked, "Do you want me to take the boat out?"

Marco nodded his head up-and-down.

"I have to ask my mom and dad if I can take it out. Okay?" Again Marco nodded his head yes.

They played catch in the boat for couple of hours. Then Aaron's cell phone that was strapped to his belt rang.

"It must be my mom." He reached into the plastic bag. "Hello...hi, Mom." Marco could hear Nicole say that she couldn't see Aaron from the house and had to call to check up on him.

"I'm down in the rowboat cleaning it up. Can I take it out?"

"Not today, Aaron. It's time for you to come up to the house and finish your homework and get cleaned up for dinner."

"But, Mom, can I take it out tomorrow?" Aaron asked.

"We'll see. I'll talk to your dad about it when he gets home."

"Okay, I'll be right there." Aaron turned off the phone and climbed out of the boat.

A thought came to Marco. *Is it possible to use my high frequency sound to activate the phone?* With all his concentration, he gave it a try. Aaron's phone beeped as if someone was calling him. He looked at his phone with a puzzled look.

"I bet it's my mom trying to call me again." Marco quickly shook his head back-and-forth. Aaron looked at him again with a puzzled face. "Was that you?"

Marco quickly nodded his head up and down, but Aaron still had a puzzled look on his face. Then Marco did it again and again. Aaron did not respond.

Aaron called his mom. He dialed the number. Marco listened to the tones to get familiar with the phone.

"Sorry, Mom, did you just try to call me?"

"No."

"Okay, I'll be right up. Goodbye."

Marco beeped the phone again.

Aaron looked at him, "That's you?"

Again, he nodded his head up-and-down, making the usual noises and then toned it again and again.

"Wow, that's neat!" He picked up his fishing p[ole and bucket. "I better go now before my mom gets mad. I'll ask her if I can use the rowboat tomorrow. Okay?"

Marco nodded his head yes. And just for good measure, he toned again. Aaron smiled and then left to walk home. What a day! He was on the brink of how to communicate.

It was then Marco's turn to do his homework. He tried to remember the letters and numbers on the phone. He thought, *Let's see. One and zero are blank*, so he could use number 1 to say yes and number 0 to say no. That was a way of making a connection to Aaron.

The excitement grew. He realized Aaron was making his way into his heart. He remembered his own son and how he never took the time to even play catch with him because he was always chasing the almighty dollar. Once their relationship was out of his control, he finally understood.

Aaron put his fishing pole and bucket away.

"What, no fish?" Nicole looked in the bucket.

Aaron thought that was a good time to bring up the rowboat. "Mom, can I take out the boat tomorrow? All the fish are offshore, and there's no more under the pier."

"Well, I don't know."

"I'll be careful, Mom. Please?" pleaded Aaron.

"Wait until your father gets home, and we will discuss it. Now off you go upstairs to take your bath."

He ran up the stairs. Nicole was glad to see him so full of energy, excitement, and happiness. But she didn't want him to take the boat out alone. She would go with him, but she got seasick, so that was not an option.

Afraid of hurting his feelings, she let her husband make the decision. He came downstairs from his bath, and before his father got home, he asked his mom if he could use the computer.

"Sure, but do your homework first." She was happy for the new interest with the computer, but as soon as John's car hit the driveway, he was at the front door.

"Hi, Dad! Mom said if it was all right with you, I could take the rowboat out." His father had not even had a chance to put his keys or briefcase down.

Nicole gave her husband a kiss. "Hi, honey."

"Can I, Dad? Can I?" he pleaded.

"We'll talk about it a little later." Aaron went back to the computer.

John sat in his reclining chair, going over the mail.

Nicole came back from the kitchen with a drink. She handed it to John and asked, "How did your day go, hon?"

He tossed the mail on the end table. "Thank you for the drink. This new position is really a challenge, but I like challenges. What's going on with you today? Why is Aaron so suddenly interested in the rowboat?"

Then Nicole explained that Aaron told her there were no fish under the pier. "I'm happy for Aaron's new interest in fishing, but I'm concerned with letting him take out the boat alone."

"I know how hard it is for you. I'm sorry I can't help you with Aaron or the house. The new position is really demanding, but I'm turning the corner now. I know we're still in boxes, but let's take our time with Aaron and not let this move get to us." He stepped out of the chair to give his wife a hug. "I'm so happy to see Aaron not depressed. He even looks better since our move. I think Aaron has adjusted better than we have. I think he'll be all right with the rowboat. He has the cell in the waterproof case. We'll put a life vest on him and give him specific boundaries not to venture out of the cove. You can call him on the cell anytime you want to check up on him."

"I guess it'll be all right."

"I'll go to the garage and get the oars and life vest and get the boat ready," said John.

"Don't be too long. Dinner will be ready in an hour."

John went to search for Aaron. He found him at the computer and could not help but notice that he wasn't playing games but was reading about dolphins. "What is so interesting?"

"I'd like to know more about dolphins. In fact, it says here that dolphins use sonar to find things. I don't know how that works."

John placed his hand on his son's shoulder, looking at the computer. "Well, after dinner we'll go online and check it out, but if you still want to use

30

the boat tomorrow, we have one hour until dinner to get the boat ready."

"Great! Thanks, Dad." Off to the garage they went.

In the garage were wall-to-wall unpacked boxes as a result of the move. Aaron's dad stepped over a group of boxes and found the oars and life vests. "Let 's see if we can find the one that fits. Picking through the safety vests, they found one just the right size.

"Why do I have to wear this, Dad? I can swim."

"I know you can swim like a fish, but it's important for your safety, and it will ease your mother's concern."

"Okay." He tried on a vest to make sure it fit.

"Let's go to the boat now and check it out."

Walking down to the pier, Aaron looked up at his dad. "Can dolphins talk to us?"

"Dolphins have their own language."

"You mean like people?" asked Aaron.

"Yes," replied his father. "But it's their own language."

"Do you think the dolphins can talk to us?" Aaron asked.

"Maybe someday, but it will take a breakthrough in technology. Aaron looked all around for the dolphin in hopes to show his dad, but he wasn't there. John stepped into the boat. Aaron handed down the oars to him. Putting the oars in the locks, he made sure they were secure. "Do you want to give it a try?"

"Dad, do you remember summer camp?"

"Yes, you were quite the oarsman. So what you're saying is you don't need practice." He patted Aaron on the back. "We'd better get back to the house then. Your mother will be wondering if we got lost in the garage." As they walked back to the house, John asked, "Do you want to go fishing this weekend?"

"Sure, Dad. That would be great!" Aaron started running back to the house, pulling his dad along.

As they reached the house, Aaron still donned his orange life vest. His mom said, "Here comes my little sailor. Is this a fashion statement or dinner attire? Everyone laughed. "Okay, let me take the vest from you, and we'll put it next to your fishing pole and cell."

After dinner, Aaron dragged his dad to the computer.

"Okay, what was the question you had about dolphins?"

"It was their sonar, Dad." Aaron looked at the computer. They found a section on how dolphins can locate things even when their eyes were covered. As they read on, they learned dolphins used high-frequency sound waves that hit an object and bounced back, giving them a complete size, shape, and distance in seconds. "Boy! They must be smart," said Aaron. "According to this, dolphins have the same-sized brain as humans. The dolphins could be even smarter than us."

"Maybe, son."

"Could the dolphins use their high-frequency sound waves to call us on a cell phone?"

His dad, looking at Aaron and knowing that his son was serious about the answer replied, "We will never know, Aaron. Maybe high frequency sound waves might be the same frequency as a dolphin sonar, but the technology is not in place yet to talk to them. Maybe one day, but that's a very good question."

"Dad, you know that when I grow up, I would like to work with dolphins."

John pulled a chair up next to Aaron. "Maybe you'll be the first one with the breaking technology. Time for bed now."

As Aaron headed upstairs, he turned to his dad. Remember, fishing this weekend."

"You got it, son." He reached over to give him a kiss goodnight.

The next morning, Aaron was up early. As he ate breakfast with his dad, he was reminded to stay in the cove and if he needed help to call his mom on his cell phone and to "Leave some fish for us to catch this weekend."

Aaron's mother interjected, "And wear your life vest. I packed a snack and something to drink in a small cooler."

"Okay, Mom. Don't worry."

John kissed Nicole goodbye and gave his son a hug and said, "Good luck fishing."

"Thanks, Dad."

When Aaron reached the pier, Marco could see Nicole with him. Reflecting back on his life, he could see the same relationship that his wife shared with his son, David. When Aaron rowed away from the pier, he could see the concern in her eyes. She watched until Aaron was in the middle of the cove, and only when Aaron stopped to fish did she go back to the house. The whole time, Marco stayed out of sight until Nicole was at home. When Marco popped up next to the boat, he could see the excitement in Aaron's face.

"Hi, Mr. Dolphin. I knew that you would be here." Marco came close enough to let Aaron pet him. Then Aaron's cell rang. "Is that you?" He looked at Marco who shook his head no. Aaron answered the phone, "Hi, Mom. Everything is all right."

"Call me back to see if the phone works in the cove."

Aaron let out a sigh, looked over at Marco, and shrugged his shoulders. "But, Mom, you're talking to me now! Okay, I'll call you." Aaron hung up the phone. He told Marco that his mother wanted him to test the phone and to call her right then, so he dialed the number. Marco listened to the tone and watched the numbers Aaron punched. "Okay, Mom, the phone works great."

When he hung up, he asked Marco if he understood what he was saying. Marco nodded yes. Aaron then asked him to go around the boat. He went around the boat as Aaron asked. Then he asked him to go around the boat backward. Marco did a 360 flip which answered Aaron's question. "Wow, you do understand," he said with a smile on his face. Marco nodded his head and for good measure toned him. He picked up the phone, checking to make sure it wasn't his mom, and said, "You're right. It's you!"

He then cleared the line. Marco reached over the bow rail with his head poking at the phone.

"Do you want me to call someone?"

He shook his head no. He came out of the water again and hit another number.

Aaron wiped the water off the cell and put it in a plastic case. "I can't get it wet. I think you want me to push the numbers on the phone. Is that it?"

He nodded yes.

"Okay, here it goes."

Marco listened to the tones that the different numbers made. It was like a code. If Marco could repeat the number, he could spell out a word. Marco reflected back to his first boat before G.P.S. He had to program his electric by using numbers to spell out words like a phone key board.

Aaron cleared the numbers and asked, "Do you want to hear them again?" Marco nodded yes. He ran through the numbers again as Marco watched and listened to the different tones each numbers made.

Marco thought of something simple at first. I can spell "hi" using buttons on the phone. One 4 would be G; two 4s would be H; then I could use star for space, and three 4s would be I. The coded numbers would be 44*444. He toned the coded numbers to Aaron's cell.

Aaron quickly grabbed the phone but really looked confused over the numbers. He said, "I'll ask my dad tonight. He is really smart. Don't worry. I won't tell him anything about you."

Marco nodded his head yes.

In the distance, a lobster boat was working its way into the cove as it did every day. As they got closer, Marco dropped underneath the boat. Aaron quickly grabbed his fishing pole as if he was fishing.

The boat got closer, and Aaron waved to the fisherman. They sounded their air horn and waved back. Marco could hear the sounds of the motor as it passed by, so he popped up to get a quick look to see if it was safe. The boat was far enough away that the men could not see him. He splashed some water on Aaron to lighten things up and give him some playtime. Aaron laughed and then grabbed the ball that was in the boat and threw it so Marco could catch it. During their playtime, the phone rang. He asked Marco, "Is that you?" He shook his head no, so Aaron answered the call.

"Okay, Mom. I'll start working my way home." He put it back in the plastic case. "My mom said it's time to go home, but I'll be back tomorrow." Marco nodded his head yes. While Aaron rowed back toward the pier, Marco quickly swam down to find the biggest fish he could catch and threw it in Aaron's boat.

He could hear Aaron laughing as he rowed back to the pier where Nicole was relieved he was home safely.

"How did my fisherman do today?" With a huge smile, he held up a big bass. "Wow, wait until your dad sees that!"

Walking back to the house, Aaron's mom felt the excitement with Aaron's new hobby. Not only was he very happy, but it seemed like his health was getting stronger. The dark circles under his eyes were gone, the troubled breathing was gone, and he was starting to grow back his hair. She couldn't figure out why all the changes were occurring—maybe the fresh salt air had something to do with it. Once they got to the house, it was off to take a bath before dinner.

After his bath, Aaron asked his mom if he could use the computer. Knowing what time his dad usually got home, he waited at the front door for him. "Hi, Dad, can you help me to break a code?"

"Sure, son, but can I at least get in the front door and say hi to your mom?" As he walked toward the kitchen, he gave his wife a hug and kiss.

She said to Aaron. "You didn't tell your dad about the big fish you caught today."

"Oh yeah, Dad, I got a big bass today!" He showed his dad a picture he'd taken of the fish with his phone.

"That's great. I hope you save some fish for this weekend. Remember, we're going fishing."

"I've got just the spot!" A smile spread across his face.

"Okay, time for dinner. We're having fresh fish tonight thanks to our son."

After dinner, Aaron wasted no time in asking his dad a way to solve the code that the dolphin had given him.

"Okay, Dad, here's a question for you. If you only have a phone and you wanted to tell somebody something, and you can't text or email them. How would you do it?"

His dad opened his eyes big. "Wow, what a question! Let's see if I got this right. All I have is the phone, and I want to tell somebody something?"

Aaron quickly added, "And you can't talk using the phone."

His dad then said, "You could start with numbers and letters on the phone. If I use the letters and the numbers together to form a word that might be a way."

"How does that work?"

John picked up the phone on the desk, got a pencil and paper, and with a phone, started writing down numbers and letters of the phone showing Aaron how to do it. "When you see at the end of a commercial, it might say call 1-800-123-PETS or whatever they are selling. In this case, pets would be 7387. It makes it easier for the consumer to remember than 7387.

Aaron then asked, "So, if I had 44*444 what would that be?" His dad showed him that 44 on a phone might be H, and the star would be a space for the next letter which could be I.

"Then 44*444 would be Hi. That's cool. Thanks, Dad." John heard the excitement in his voice when he figured out the code question.

Nicole came into the computer room where they were working and said, "Okay, F.B.I. agents who broke the code, one of you is being requested to go to bed."

"Okay, Mom." Aaron kissed his mom and dad goodnight, went to the table, took the paper they were working on the code with him, and went right to bed.

John and Nicole looked at each other with a puzzled look. "What was that all about?" Nicole asked.

"I don't know, but it's nice to see Aaron so happy." He then turned to Nicole and said, "I'd sure like to break your code tonight." They both started laughing, something that had been lacking for the last couple of months since they found out about Aaron's condition getting worse.

The next morning, Aaron was up bright and early, having breakfast before heading off to the boat. He brought the paper with code and pencil that they worked on the night before along with his fishing pole and lunch pail.

Aaron rowed out to the middle of the cove, excited that he broke the code, and he waited for Marco to pop up. The lobster boat was already in the cove, and as they drove by, Aaron waved back to the fishermen as he had done every morning.

Knowing Marco would not come to him until the boat cleared the area, he pretended that he was fishing. The excitement of breaking the code was the only thing on his mind. It wasn't until the boat was far enough away that Marco popped up next to him.

"Hi, Mr. Dolphin. I got some great news. My dad and I broke the code. Hi to you," he said with a big smile.

Marco toned his phone "Yes." Marco quickly dove deep enough to get the speed he needed to get airborne and did a 360 flip. Aaron was standing up in the boat, applauding him. Marco went back to Aaron to give him a high-five.

All of a sudden, Marco was thrown into the side of the boat so hard that the impact knocked the oar up, hitting Aaron in the head and knocking him into the water. Marco quickly swam away. He noticed a warm, burning feeling and that the water was red around him. Also, he had a pain in his side. He quickly checked to see if Aaron was okay! Aaron lay motionless. The life vest was keeping his head out of the water.

Marco guessed that he must've gotten attacked by a shark, and Aaron was laying in the water unconscious and bleeding from his head. He swam for Aaron and grabbed him by his orange safety vest and pulled him to shore, knowing that the shark would be coming back to finish them off.

He could feel the burning in his side, but his concern was to get Aaron close enough to shore as soon as possible so he would not drown and be out of the shark's reach.

His heart was saddened for the bump on Aaron's head as he lay unconscious. He was able to push him high enough out of the water so he wouldn't drown. He needed to keep the shark away from Aaron, so he began to travel away from him with a trail of blood following him. He needed to get help.

He remembered that Aaron had his waterproof plastic cell on his life vest. Clearing his head, trying to remember the tone Aaron used to call his mother, he repeatedly kept trying to call her.

At the house, Aaron's mother was washing the breakfast dishes when her phone rang. Looking at the number, she saw that it was Aaron.

All of a sudden, her heart sank in her chest.

"Aaron, are you okay?" she asked, but the other end of the line was silent. Nicole looked out the kitchen window. Seeing the rowboat upside down, she dropped her cell in the kitchen sink and ran out of the house.

Marco traveled in shallow water to keep out of the reach of the shark, a trail of red water behind him. He reached within 100 yards of the pier where he could see Aaron's mother running down the beach, crying hysterically. She could see Aaron's bright orange safety vest on shore and the boat up-side down.

She ran down the beach. She saw Marco moving along the shore, but Aaron was the object of her attention. As she reached Aaron, a young couple walking on the beach came to her aide as she held him in her arms. "Help me; help me!"

The young couple immediately called 911 on their cell. Nicole held her child in her arms, waiting for the paramedics to arrive. When Aaron started to come around, she asked the young couple if she could borrow their phone to call her husband. As the paramedics arrived and were checking Aaron out, he gained full consciousness.

The first words out of his mouth were "Where's my dolphin?"

The paramedics looked confused, knowing that he suffered a mild concussion, so they played along with him. "He swam away," replied one of the paramedics.

"I want to get up and see him."

"Settle down, son; you've got a pretty nasty bump on your head," a paramedic told him.

The young couple, Dennis and Karen, handed Nicole their phone, and she called Aaron's father. She told her husband, "There was a boating accident. Aaron capsized the rowboat and hit his head. The paramedics say he is okay, but they're going to take him to the hospital for further evaluation."

"I will meet you there," John said, trying to calm down Nicole.

Nicole thanked Karen and Dennis for all their help. Then she left with the paramedics to the hospital, not letting go of her son's hand.

Marco slowly worked his way to the pier, staying in shallow water to avoid the shark and hoping that Aaron was all right. He beached himself under the shade of the pier because he was so tired.

Looking around, he could hear a boat's motors. What he didn't realize was all of the events were going on in full view of the fisherman on the lobster boat. The fishermen took the rowboat in tow, knowing where Aaron lived, and tied it to the dock.

Seeing the spreading blood from underneath the pier, two fishermen jumped out of the boat and wrapped Marco up, carrying him back to the boat where they put him on the swim step. Marco looked up at the fishermen, and by the look in their eyes, he could see they were good men.

The first mate, Charlie, bound Marco's wound to stop the bleeding. He gently said, "We'll get you help. Just relax."

Captain Sam kept pouring water over Marco's skin. He said, "I've never seen markings on a dolphin like this. Looks like he has a star on his forehead." Captain Sam then retrieved the marine radio to call Sea Land and said, "We have a wounded dolphin, and he needs help."

The Sea Land dispatch operator replied, "We have a research vessel named *Sea Odyssey* in the area. We'll contact her. Over and out."

Then over the marine radio, Marco heard, "This is Dr. Mary Olsen of the research vessel, *Sea Odyssey*. I hear you have a dolphin with a major wound. Apply pressure and keep him wet. What is your location?"

Captain Sam gave longitude and latitude to the *Sea Odyssey* and told her, "We're heading your way to save time. The dolphin is in bad shape."

Dr. Olsen replied, "Thank you. We are at full throttle and should be there shortly."

Marco was slipping in and out of consciousness, but he felt that he was in good hands. His mission was to stay alive.

Sea Odyssey finally arrived and pulled up next to the lobster boat so they could transfer him over to the research vessel. That was the first time Marco saw Dr. Mary. She kept saying, "You're in good hands now. We will take care of you."

Dr. Mary quickly set up an IV and asked the crew, "What happened?"

"We were pulling up a trap when we saw this dolphin save a little boy and push him to shore. We know where the little boy lives, so we took his boat back to the pier in front of his house. There was a lot of blood under the pier. That's where we found him. It looks like a shark got him."

"I've heard that dolphins have done things like that, but I've never heard of it firsthand. We've got a hero. How's the little boy?"

"We saw people on shore helping, and an ambulance showed up. As far as we could see, he looked okay," said Captain Sam.

"That's great. Now we have to get this guy fixed up." Dr. Mary checked out his wound. "I think I found the problem." She grabbed some hemostats and closed off one artery that was pumping the blood out. "He's lost a lot of blood. I hope he can make it once we get him to Sea Land. We'll have a better chance there. I'll call Sea Land to get all the preparations ready for the dolphin when we get there. Time is of the essence." She thanked Sam and Charlie for doing such a good job of slowing down the bleeding and told them they might've saved the dolphin's life.

On the way to the hospital, Aaron kept asking about the dolphin.

Aaron's mom said, "I'll have your dad check on the dolphin when he goes home." She was trying to settle Aaron down.

At the hospital, the doctor came in, introduced himself as Dr. Allen, and said that he needed to run some X-rays and tests. He told Nicole, "When Aaron's tests are done, we can come get you in the waiting room."

While Nicole was in the waiting room, John came running in, looking for his family. John hugged his wife, and she started crying again. She kept saying, "I knew we shouldn't have let him go out in the boat."

After a while, Dr. Allen came out of the emergency room and introduced himself to John. He let them know Aaron's X-rays came back negative except for a bump on his head, but he wanted to keep him overnight. With a puzzled look on his face he said, "According to our records, he was diagnosed with cancer. How long has he been in remission?"

Both of Aaron's parents looked at each other with surprise. John said, "Aaron was diagnosed with terminal cancer. Even the chemotherapy treatments failed."

"Well, not according to the test we just ran. Who is Aaron's oncologist?"

"Dr. Bailey," both parents said together.

"I ran into Dr. Bailey about an hour ago. Let me see if he's still here. I'll be right back, but you can go in and see Aaron."

"Let's not get our hopes up until we talk to Dr. Bailey," John said, holding his wife. Nicole started crying again, but this time it was cries of hope.

As both parents went to Aaron's room, they were wiping the tears from their eyes. Aaron was lying in bed and looked up at them.

"I'm sorry, Mom and Dad. I don't know what happened! I was playing with the dolphin. The next thing I knew, I was on the beach with Mom."

"I'm glad you had enough thought to use the phone to call your mom."

"But, Dad, I didn't call."

"Then how did your mom receive the call?"

"It was my friend, the dolphin!" exclaimed Aaron.

The door opened, and Dr. Bailey walked in and said, "I hear you've got a little bump on your head." He examined Aaron, checking his pupils and the bump on his head. "They're going to keep him overnight just to make sure everything is fine," he told them.

Dr. Bailey asked the parents to step outside for a quick chat. He told them, "In all my years of medical practice, I have never seen results change so quickly. The tests show that Aaron's cancer is in remission. There is no medical explanation for it. I'm going to run more tests while he is in the hospital. There must be something triggering the antibodies to fight the cancer cells. Whatever you are doing, keep it up," he said with a smile. "I'm so happy for him. I'd like to follow up with Aaron on what is causing the change."

Both parents started crying and hugging each other with tears of joy. Nicole turned and gave Dr. Bailey a hug, saying, "Thank you; thank you."

Dr. Bailey said, "I didn't do anything except bring you good news."

After Dr. Bailey left, they both went into the room to see Aaron. The first thing out of Aaron's mouth was, "Can we go home now?"

"First thing in the morning when we know you're all right. We want you to get some rest now. I'll stay with you all night." Nicole gave him a hug.

"Dad, will you check the end of the pier when you get home tonight? Please, Dad. Please. I'm afraid something might have happened to the dolphin."

John leaned over to give him a goodnight kiss and said, "I'll see you in the morning."

Walking with his wife, they left the room.

"I'll go home, secure the boat back on the pier, and lock up the house and meet you back here later."

"There's no need for both of us to stay here. I'll stay here with Aaron, and you go home and get some sleep. When I was running down the beach, I saw a dolphin with a blood trail in the water. See if you see anything. Maybe that is the dolphin Aaron is so worried about."

"All right, I'll see you first thing in the morning." John gave her a hug and said, "I can't believe it. Aaron is in remission!" Holding back the tears, he walked down the hall.

When John got home, he saw the back door wide open and the phone at the bottom of the sink. He could not help but think what was going through his wife's mind when she saw Aaron on the beach with the boat upside down. What about the phone call? Who called?

The front doorbell rang. The young couple, Dennis and Karen, introduced themselves. They explained they were the couple that helped Nicole on the beach and had called him. "We came by to see how Aaron was and to return the life vest and the cell phone that was clipped to it."

"Thank you. Aaron was doing fine. Did you happen to see a hurt dolphin on the beach?"

They both looked at each other and Dennis said, "No, there was a lot of blood in the water, but we thought it might have come from your son."

"Do you remember what time you called 911?"

Dennis looked up his call history. "I called 911 at 11:00 a.m.

Karen handed John Aaron's life vest and cell phone that was clipped to it. John thanked them again for their help.

After the young couple left, John removed the phone from the waterproof case. He opened the phone up and checked the call history, and sure enough, there was a phone call made at 10:46 a.m. to his wife's phone.

Who made the call? He then checked Nicole's phone that was in the sink. It confirmed that it came from Aaron's phone. *Maybe he called before he went unconscious and doesn't remember?*

He walked down and checked the rowboat, making sure it was secure. He looked all around to see if he could find any evidence of a hurt dolphin. Finding nothing, he picked up the oars that were in the boat and brought them back to the house.

At Sea Land, the research vessel carrying the wounded dolphin arrived. Mary quickly took charge. "Okay, guys, let's get him right into the operating room, stat."

In the operating room, she was able to repair a severed artery and stitched up the dolphin. "Let's get him into the treatment pool. The next twelve hours are crucial."

They brought him into the pool. She changed from her operating gown into a wetsuit and jumped in. They lowered the dolphin into the water, supervised by Mary.

"Make sure to keep the wound and his blowhole clear of any water, but we need to keep him wet. He's still sedated. Let's put him into the sling. I don't want him thrashing around when he wakes up."

Marco slowly regained consciousness. He looked up, saw Mary, and knew he was in good hands as she held him up in her arms. He could hear her. "I think he's waking up. Make sure he doesn't thrash around," she instructed the other two people in the pool with her. Hearing her instructions, he lay quietly in the sling with her arms around him, letting out a chirp to let her know he was awake.

He could hear Mary say, "Good boy. Take it easy now. We've got you all fixed up." He chirped a tone twice.

"Quite the little talker." To let her know that he understood, he chirped three more times. That time she burst out laughing. "I think we're all going to get along just fine with you."

Little did she know that was her first day of school with Marco just as he'd done with Aaron. While relaxed in her arms, he could not help but think of Aaron, hoping that he was all right and that he was missed.

He was so close to communicating with him, and now he would have to start all over with an adult. To make things worse, she was a doctor and marine biologist with a scientific background and would never believe a dolphin could actually talk.

If Marco behaved like a normal dolphin, she would treat him like one. By changing his behavior, she would know he was different. Marco's plan was not to act like a dolphin. Mary spent the first twelve hours with him and only left for lack of sleep.

The next morning, Marco saw Mary step into the pool, dressed in her wetsuit. He immediately started chirping. Zoe, her long-time assistant, stated, "That's the first noise he's made the whole time I've been in the water with him."

"That's my new boyfriend." Then she asked Zoe how he was doing. Zoe, who was never short for words, said, "His breathing seems to be a little shallow and laborious." Mary immediately examined him and with her stethoscope listened to his lungs.

Marco could hear her explaining to Zoe that there was some fluid around one lung and that she would have to remove it. He could see a long needle, and then two other people jumped in the water to hold him down.

"I have to get the fluid out from around the lung." He just lay there as she pulled out the fluid. He felt as if someone took 100 pounds of weight off his chest.

Mary checked his breathing and said, "His breathing is clear." The help in the pool clapped their hands. Mary then said, "The next six to eight hours will tell if this worked. If the fluid returns, we will have to go back in to fix it. Thank you for all the help." Marco gave Mary and the assistants some chirps and tones as to thank them. Mary laughed at him and said, "He just said thank you too. I have to make my rounds. Call me, Zoe, on my cell immediately if anything changes." Marco looked at her as she stepped out of the pool with a plastic waterproof case holding her cell. He immediately thought about Aaron and how they used his phone to communicate, but because so many people were around, he chose not to.

The six hours passed, and Mary returned to the pool. "How is he doing, Zoe?"

"He has been resting with no noise or activity and breathing normally." Mary entered the treatment pool. Marco turned his head so he could see her and then gave her a chirp sound.

Zoe quickly looked over. "Boy, he sure reacts to you."

"That's my guy." She went over to Marco. "Are you hungry?"

He nodded yes.

Mary turned to the Zoe with a surprised look on her face. "I wonder if he has been trained by another park and then freed like the program we have. I swear, sometimes I think he knows what we are saying."

"I know he's not one of ours. Look at the marking on his forehead. That is something you would remember." Zoe pointed to the star.

"I'm going to feed him now and then try to let him swim without any assistance."

She stepped back three or four steps away from Marco. She told Zoe to let him go. Instead of swimming right for the sardine she was holding, Marco went straight to Mary and rubbed his head against her body as if to say thank you. Then he turned and ate the sardine in her hand. She couldn't believe it. Neither person had ever experienced dolphin behavior like that. Mary and Zoe looked at each other in amazement.

After feeding him more sardines, Mary said, "Let's see how he swims by himself. Let's try something." She had a whistle around her neck. She waved her hands in a circular motion and then blew the whistle. Marco knew what she was up to. She was trying to figure out if he had been trained before. He didn't want her to think that, so he did nothing. Instead he went up to her and rubbed his head against her body.

This had her really confused, but he didn't want her to think he was a normal dolphin. She stepped out of the pool and told Zoe to let him swim and just keep an eye on him. She was going to make some calls to the other parks.

As Mary walked away from the treatment pool, Marco lifted his head as high as he could and gave her a couple of chirps. He could see her shake her head, turn her head toward him, and then shake her head again.

About two hours later, she returned to the pool. "I called everyone I could that is involved in dolphin training and nobody has lost or freed any dolphin with a star on its forehead," she told Zoe. As soon as Marco heard her, he swam close to her.

"He has been swimming slowly around in circles," Zoe said, holding a sardine. "I've tried to feed him, but he wouldn't eat at all.

Mary reached into her pouch and pulled out a sardine and then handed it to Marco, and he ate it. "I guess it's just you and me, big guy. Zoe, the babysitting time is over. It's all right to leave him alone." Zoe got out of the pool. "I'll keep checking in on him since he won't let anybody else feed him." Mary was about to leave, so Marco gave her a couple of chirps. "I'll see you a little later for dinner."

He nodded. She chuckled as she walked away.

While circling the pool, Marco was alone again and reflected back on what had transpired in the last week. He couldn't help thinking about Aaron. He remembered the bump on his head as he lay motionless in the water. He hoped Aaron's medical help was as good as his was. Aaron's fight for his life against cancer weighed heavily on Marco's heart. The only saving grace was Aaron's smile, and Marco thought he gave the boy a purpose to live.

For the short few days they were together, Aaron had touched his heart as well.

CHAPTER 6

SEPARATION

Back at the hospital, John walked into the room where Nicole was reading to Aaron.

"Dad! Did you see the dolphin?" Aaron sat up, hoping to hear good news.

"No, son, but I bet he's waiting until you come home."

"Yeah, he is on the shy side, but you have to meet him."

John walked up to the bed and gave his son a hug. "Well, you'll be out of the hospital soon, and I haven't forgotten about our fishing trip." Nicole wasn't crazy about another row boat outing.

"What time do I get to go home?"

John sat on the side of the bed. "I'll check with the doctor now."

Down the hall, Aaron's dad ran into Dr. Bailey. He saw John, walked up, and shook his hand. "I was just looking over Dr. Allen's tests and the other tests that we ran last night, and still, I can't believe the change in Aaron. His cancer is in complete re-mission."

That brought out a smile from John.

"After the chemo failed, it looked hopeless. But now, this is wonderful! I practice medicine for moments like this." As they entered Aaron's room, Dr. Bailey greeted Nicole. "I confirm Dr. Allen's results. After running my tests last night, they all came to the same conclusion that Aaron's cancer is in complete remission."

"Does that mean I can grow hair again?" Everyone in the room laughed.

"I still need to find out what caused the changes."

John excused himself and said, "I have to find out when Aaron can go home." Dr. Bailey told him that he would make a call and have all of them out within the hour.

Back at the Sea Land treatment pool, Mary would come by about three times a day to check on Marco and feed him. He would go right to her and do anything she wanted for as long as she told him to. That way it was voice communication. He wanted so much to communicate with her, but how could he break through when she was always in a wet suit with no cell.

He would always stay close to her when she was in the pool. He was doing everything he could not to act like a dolphin.

Late that night, Mary came by the pool. As she reached over to rub his head, he noticed she was not in her wet suit, and he could see a cell in one hand. She greeted him with "How's my guy doing? I was a little lonely, so I came to see my favorite guy. Seeing you doing so well makes me feel good inside."

Marco nodded his head.

"You are not like any other dolphin that I've had. You're quite a character." He knew it was his chance.

"Now, I'm going to be gone for about a week at a seminar, so I want you to behave while I'm gone."

He shook his head no.

She chuckled and said, "I swear, sometimes I think you understand what I'm saying."

Marco knew that he was finally getting somewhere, so he nodded his head.

"See what I mean." As she stepped away from the pool, Marco toned her cell. He could see her look at it. He could see her clear the phone. He immediately toned it three more times.

She then took a long look at it, seeing 44*444. She cleared her phone again and again. He immediately toned 44*444. The whole time he was chirping like a dog howling at the moon.

The night watchman walked by. "Working late, Dr. Mary?"

"Hi, Joe. Yes, I'll be gone for a week. I'm double-checking on our new dolphin—the one making all the racket!"

"That's funny. Every night I make my rounds, I never hear from him."

"We have this thing going on. By the way, Joe, are you having phone reception problems in this area?"

Joe pulled out his phone. "Mine's working fine. Do you need to use my phone to make a call?"

"No, just one more thing I've got to do before I go to the seminar."

Mary came by that morning in the normal wet suit attire. She stepped into the pool. He quickly went to her side, rubbing her. "You are the most affectionate guy!" she said. "It's time to check you out." Putting on her stethoscope, she checked his lungs. "Well your lungs are clear. Let's see how the shark bite is healing....That looks good. Looks like your vacation is just about over, and you'll be working for your keep."

He quickly shook his head no. She was now used to him coming up with yes and no responses to her questions and just went along with it. "No talking back now. It has been over a month. I'm going to be gone for a week, so you behave yourself."

He heard her talking to Zoe, saying that she would be gone on the research vessel for a seminar for a week. Zoe would be in charge while Mary was gone. "If anything comes up, give me a call. And keep an eye on this one." As she left the pool, she looked back at him saying, "Goodbye, big guy. Behave yourself." He gave her a couple of chirps. She put her hands over her ears as if say, I'm not listening. She kept walking away.

CHAPTER 7

DEPRESSION

Back from the hospital, the first thing Aaron did was to run to the end of the pier, looking for the dolphin. He called, only having his voice fall on deaf ears. Aaron's parents could only watch painfully. When his dad couldn't take it any longer, he walked out to the end of the pier to be with Aaron.

"Any sign of the dolphin?" He sat at the end of the pier, giving a hug to his son.

"No, Dad, I hope he's all right." He looked back at John.

"Maybe in the morning we will look again. We'd better get to the house. It's getting late."

For the next month, every day, he would go sit at the end of the pier, hoping to see the dolphin again. Every day his mom's heart would ache a little more seeing her son's depression grow. The sparkle in his eyes was gone. Aaron didn't even want to be on the computer anymore. As the condition became even worse, it was time to get his blood work done before they took him to see Dr. Bailey.

That next afternoon, Dr. Bailey called Aaron's parents into his office. "Mr. and Mrs. Sullivan, I don't know how to explain what has happened with Aaron's remission. I'm sorry to say that Aaron's cancer has come back as fast as it went away. After his accident...all the tests I ran...I couldn't explain how quickly he went into remission, and now I can't explain how it came back so aggressively. All my research came up with no medical explanation for it. Has anything changed at home?"

Nicole was crying so much that she couldn't talk. John told him of Aaron's affection for a dolphin that was in the cove. But after he returned from the hospital, the dolphin had not returned. Aaron would go out every day looking for him. That was when his depression started. "What can be done?"

"Aaron's cancer has advanced so fast that any treatment would be more painful than helpful," explained Dr. Bailey. "I would make him as comfortable as possible. I'm going to contact the Make A Wish Foundation to help him."

"I can't believe there is nothing we can do! He was in remission! He was doing so well." Nicole collapsed, crying uncontrollably.

John held Nicole until the crying subsided. "We must be strong for Aaron."

"I knew this day would come, but when he went into remission, it gave us new hope." She blotted the tears from her face.

"It's now Aaron's time. We must think of what is best for him. He is waiting for us now. Remember that we need to be strong." As they held each other, they walked out of the doctor's office.

The next day, a call came from Make A Wish Foundation. They wanted to meet with Aaron and help him to cope with his depression. The caller asked, "Is there anything that Aaron would like to see or do?"

"He has expressed a real interest in dolphins," Nicole suggested.

"Would he like to spend a couple of days at Sea Land? We can make the arrangements where he could actually feed the dolphins."

"I know that he would love that." Nicole did everything she could to not cry.

CHAPTER 8

REUNION

At the pool, all Marco could do was wait for Mary to return. Zoe repeatedly tried to make him respond to commands with no response from him. He decided to hold out until Mary's return from her seminar.

Finally, one morning, there was Mary standing next to the pool with her hands on her hips, saying, "I hear you've been a bad boy since I've been gone."

She jumped into the pool. Seeing that she was back, he nodded his head and made all kinds of noise. Then he swam next to her, rubbing his body against hers. She was overwhelmed with his response and said, "Well, I'm glad you're still my guy and haven't forgotten me." She checked the wound and was amazed how fast be had recovered. "I think we will move you to the outside pool where you'll be with the other dolphins."

When Marco entered the main pool, he could see the grandstands and three side pens with small gates. While he swam around the big pool, he could see Mary on the outside. He could see the three pens and hear the tones and clicking from the other dolphins. As he went over to them, he heard Mary say, "Okay, open up the pens." He quickly realized she wanted to see how he reacted with the other dolphins.

The other dolphins were approaching him, and he could hear their comments. He answered them with "I'm the chosen one, and I am trying to communicate with the humans so they know our problems and help to resolve them."

The other dolphins responded, "What can we do?"

"Nothing right now, but I'll tell you when you can help."

Swimming around the pool, the three other dolphins followed him as if he was their leader. He swam to Mary who was standing on the platform. The other dolphins followed. As he popped up next to her, he could see Mary use her whistle to instruct the other dolphins to go. They ignored her command. Again, she whistled a command for the dolphins to leave with the same result. Marco nodded his head, and with his voice command, the dolphins left and went back to their pens.

She rested her hands on her hips, completely dumbfounded.

"I don't believe it." She told the other trainers to close the three pens to the other dolphins.

"That's enough of that!" Mary began to walk around the pool toward an open, small pen. Marco followed her, seeing the frustration on her face as she sat on the edge of the small pen with her feet in the water. As he entered, he could hear the pen close behind him. He popped up in between her legs and nodded his head.

"You are the strangest dolphin I've ever seen or worked with. I'm going to have to work with you a little more to find out what's up with you." He nodded his head.

Marco could see the grandstands around the pool still filling with people, and Mary sarcastically said, "The show must go on."

The three pens next to him opened, and the three dolphins went right to his pen gate. He signaled the dolphins to do what the trainers told them to do.

He watched the dolphins perform each part of their act and heard the crowd cheer. He noticed on the far end of the pool a little boy with a green Miami Dolphins cap with one of the trainers. On the public speaker system an announcement was made. "Aaron, from Make A Wish Foundation, is going to feed the dolphins from the platform."

He could not believe what he was hearing. It was Aaron all right, and he was okay. Marco's heart was racing in his chest. Knowing that he had to reach Aaron, he needed help. He called the three dolphins that were performing. With the help of the other three dolphins, they were able to lift the gate to his pen, releasing him so he could get to Aaron. He could see the dolphin trainers blowing their whistles to get the dolphins back into the pens. With a couple of flips of his tail, he was airborne, touching Aaron's hand while he was still holding the sardine he was to feed the dolphins with. Aaron recognized Marco immediately because of the white star on his face.

Mary quickly ran to the other trainers to get the little boy away from the dolphins but not before Marco was able to pop up next to him. When Aaron saw him, he started crying. He kept calling, "Mr. Dolphin." The trainers quickly grabbed Aaron off the platform because of all the commotion and the efforts to get all the dolphins back in their cages. The ushers holding him on the platform took him away. The crowd cheered as if it was part of the performance.

The public announcer said, "Thank you, folks, very much. Please exit to your left." The speaker knew what happened was not part of the act.

Mary quickly called Marco to the small pen. For the first time, he ignored her because he was looking for Aaron in the crowd of people. He continued looking for him until the last people left the stadium.

Aaron, being led out by one of the ushers, kept asking to see the dolphin again. Nicole and John came to him. Instead of excitement, they found him crying.

"What's wrong, Aaron? "

"I found the dolphin from the cove, and they won't let me see him."

The ushers told John and Nicole they were having problems with the dolphin, so Aaron wouldn't be allowed to see him again. "We're sorry. There is another dolphin display in the next underground pool if you want to see them."

"I want to see my dolphin," Aaron said, still crying.

"Again, I'm sorry. Maybe tomorrow you can see him." The usher led them out of the area.

John and Nicole were beside themselves, seeing how sad their son was, and tried to get him to look at the other dolphins in the outside ponds. However, he showed no interest in any other dolphins.

"Mom, Dad, can we go back to the hotel now? I'm tired."

The hotel, which was part of the Sea Land facility, was but a short tram ride. After they got off the tram, they went straight to their rooms.

Aaron lay on the bed. Nicole told him to take a nap and that she would wake him for dinner. Both of his parents were drained over what had happened. "Maybe we should rest also." John closed the bedroom door. They sat on the bed and turned the television on and stretched out. Within five minutes they were both sound asleep.

Waiting in his room until the coast was clear, Aaron slipped out of the hotel. He knew the stamp from the morning visit would let him back into Sea Land. He was going to find his dolphin no matter what. He approached the main dolphin exhibit, but the sign said closed. He slid between the gate, looked into the main pool, and walked to the small pen, which was empty. Little did he know that Mary had moved the dolphin back to the treatment pool inside the building after all the trouble he had caused during the dolphins' show.

Just as he was looking into the empty small pen, Joe, the night security guard, caught him.

"I'm sorry, son. This area is closed. Where are your parents?"

"I want to see my dolphin!" Aaron yelled.

When he tried to escape the security guard, he lost his hat, exposing his bald head. The security guard called for help on his portable radio.

Mary heard the call. She was just around the corner. When she reached the security guard, she asked, "What's going on here?"

"I want to see my dolphin."

In a soothing voice, Mary was able to calm him down and then asked where his parents were.

"If I tell you, will you let me see my dolphin?"

Noticing the boy's bald head, she asked, "Are you the boy from Make A Wish Foundation that was feeding the dolphin at the show?"

"Yes, and that's my dolphin!"

"How do you know he is your dolphin?"

"He lived in the cove at my house...and the mark on his face that looks like a star."

Mary agreed to show him the dolphin, but she had to call his parents first. He agreed, and she called his room.

John, awakened by the phone, said, "Hello."

"Mr. Sullivan, I'm Dr. Mary Cole, head veterinarian at Sea Land. Your son, Aaron, is here with us. He is safe, but we need you to come down to the security office to pick him up."

"He is where?" Nicole went to check for him. She came back saying that Aaron was gone.

"He's at the dolphin show, Nicole....We are so sorry, Dr. Cole. We will be right there. Thank you."

"Can I see my dolphin now?" Aaron said.

She put on Aaron's hat, smiled, and headed to the pool where the dolphin was.

CHAPTER 9

DISCOVERY

Marco could see Mary coming to the pool with a little boy. *Could that be Aaron?* As they got closer, he could see his Miami Dolphins hat. It was Aaron holding her hand. Marco nodded his head with excitement as he came running up to the pool. Mary held him back from getting too close to the edge. He couldn't help but notice that the dark circles around his eyes were back like when they first met in the cove.

"It's my dolphin! Hi, Mr. Dolphin! " he cried. Marco nodded his head, making all the noise he could and pushing himself high so he could to see Aaron.

Mary was amazed at the reaction.

"How do you communicate with him? He understands you. Ask him a question," said Aaron.

She looked at Marco. "Do you understand what we are saying?"

Marco nodded.

"He also can use a cell," Aaron exclaimed. "The dolphin can tone your cell phone."

"In what way?" She put her phone in her hand, so Marco could see it.

"Put any number of fingers up."

She held up four fingers. Then her phone toned. As she looked at her phone, the number four lit up. "I've been having trouble with this phone before."

"Maybe he was trying to call you."

Mary was still not convinced.

Looking at Marco, Aaron said, "Okay, without hand signals, what does five times six equal?"

Immediately her phone display read the number 30. Mary stood there with her mouth open. "What else have you done with him?"

"We play catch." He moved closer to the edge, so he could touch Marco. That time Mary let him go.

"I mean what other communication?" The intercom came on, paging Dr. Mary to the security office. "That should be your parents."

"Does that mean I have to go now?"

She smiled at him. "Let me talk to your parents. Maybe you can stay and help me." They started to walk away.

"That'll be great." His eyes lit up.

As they walked, he turned back and said, "I'll be back, Mr. Dolphin."

Marco then toned Mary's phone. She looked at her screen and showed it to Aaron.

"Means yes."

She chuckled and shook her head. They reached the security office, and Nicole came running up to hold her son. "I'm sorry, Mom and Dad, but I found my dolphin."

"Aaron, I know you want to see the dolphin again, but we have to do things together. You can't sneak out like this." Nicole held him.

"I was afraid you wouldn't believe. But it's the same dolphin that I was telling you about. Tell them, Dr. Mary."

"Hi, I'm Dr. Mary Cole, head veterinarian for Sea Land."

"I'm John, and this my wife, Nicole. We are so sorry for all the problems that our son has caused."

"There is a particular dolphin that your son has a special relationship with. You have to see this for yourself."

They all walked back to the pool where the dolphin was. Aaron asked how the dolphin had gotten to Sea Land. Mary explained that the fishermen on a lobster boat found him under a pier in a cove not far from Sea Land. The dolphin got bit by a shark.

According to the crew on the boat, they saw a dolphin save a little boy's life by pushing him onto the shore.

John and Nicole stopped dead in their tracks. Mary looked back at them with a puzzled look.

John said, "That little boy was Aaron." We never knew the details, but he was unconscious, lying on the beach with a bump on his head."

"I was running down the beach to Aaron. I remember seeing a dolphin in shallow water, bleeding," Nicole said.

Mary was beginning to understand the relationship between the boy and the dolphin.

When they reached the pool, Aaron quickly said to the dolphin, "I want you to meet my mom and dad."

Mary received a message on her screen. She un-derstood how the dolphin communicated using the phone. She looked at the screen and told Aaron it was the same numbers that kept coming up on her phone—44*444.

John got all choked up. "Son, tell Mary what it means."

"It's a code using the numbers to spell out a word. It spells hi. My dad and I broke the code."

Mary asked the parents if it was possible that they could stay for a couple more days so Aaron could work with her with the dolphin. Seeing Aaron reunited with the dolphin, the parents were thinking maybe that was the cure for cancer for their son. It worked before.

They agreed, and then Mary said, "We will all meet here in the morning at 9:00. I'll make the arrangements for you to get a pass to come straight here. Just go to security."

After all the goodbyes, everybody left, leaving just Marco and Mary. She reached over and stroked his head and said, "I knew there was something special about you, and I can't wait to find out what it is. See you in the morning."

The next morning, Mary met with everyone, and while they walked to the pool, she asked, "Are you ready to work now?"

Aaron was all smiles. "Okay."

"Now, let's start from the beginning when you first saw the dolphin."

He relayed the whole story up until he was unconscious. Writing down his story, she stopped when he explained how his cancer went into remission when he was with the dolphin and that after the accident, his cancer came back.

Mary, blotting her eyes from listening to his story, looked at him and said, "It has been proven that dolphins do have a healing effect on people, and this guy is a very special dolphin."

John interjected after listening to his son. "Dr. Bailey, his oncologist, said he has never seen such a radical change from cancer to remission back to cancer. We are hoping that reunion with the dolphin might put him back in remission." John wiped his face.

Mary got up to give everyone a hug. Words were hard to come by, but she continued, "I think there is a high power working here that has brought Aaron and the dolphin together. I can't see but a happy ending to this story." After all the eyes cleared up. She continued her questions. "How did the dolphin use the tones?"

"He listened to all the tones at least twice. Then he rang numbers," said Aaron.

"Okay, Aaron, let's see what we can do with him now."

Marco was listening to the whole conversation. She asked him to use the phone to answer. She then asked if he understood what they were saying and to ring number 1 for yes on the phone and the number 0 for no. Mary also pushed number 1 and number 0, so he could hear the difference in the tones. He rang number 1.

"Next question. Did someone teach you?"

No...the number 0 lit up.

"Can you communicate using the land line or cell phone?"

Number 1 lit up.

"How?"

Marco then dialed up the number 44 33 555 555 and 666.

"Maybe I can help," said John. "The number represents an alphanumeric system. That means that each number represents a letter. Number 4 would be G, H or I. Looking at the cell phone, the double 44 would be H. In that case, he is saying hello. Everyone cheered the results. Marco nodded his head.

Overwhelmed, Mary said, "What a breakthrough!"

John then said, "We need to link up the cell tones to an alphanumeric program that would display in real time."

"How do we do that?" Mary asked with a confused look on her face.

"I work in this field and specialize in making computer programs. I'll go back to my office where I have everything I need to make the program. I should have it done by tomorrow mid-morning if I leave now."

"Thank you, Mr. Sullivan,"

"It's John and Nicole. May we call you Dr. Mary or Mary?"

"Mary will be fine. I get Dr. Mary enough here."

CHAPTER 10

IT'S A MIRACLE

Morning came and everyone patiently waited. John finally arrived and said, "We will be online and ready in moments." He then passed out Bluetooth headphones to everyone and a laptop computer. "We need to keep this under wraps."

Marco was waiting patiently to tell his story.

"I added a computer voice to the alphanumeric program. You can read it on the computer or listen to a voice. It will come over only as fast as the dolphin can transmit. Are we ready?"

Marco started to communicate, "Hello, Aaron! Thank you for being here. Without you, I wouldn't be able to get my message out. You are my friend forever. Thank you, Dr. Mary, for saving my life.

"What I'm about to tell you is really hard to believe, and I'm not proud of it. Not long ago, I was a dying man. I don't know if I died or what happened, but somehow I became a dolphin for my sins against nature. I have been given a second chance at redemption for my sins. I have learned from the sea mammals that my mission is to bridge the gap between the sea creatures and man so we can live in harmony once more.

"To do that, I need your help. Mary, I need you to reach my son, David Ricci, and I need you to bring him to me. I have to clean up the mess that I have made, and he is the key. Time is very important. He lives in Seaport, Maine. Mary, I have to warn you my son was very bitter toward me, but I know he has a good heart. I can't express how important it is and how difficult it will be. But if anyone can bring him to me, it's you."

The next thing, Mary was on a plane heading for Seaport, Maine, with little more than a name and address of one David Ricci. While on the plane, she went over what had happened in the past 24 hours, trying to go over how to answer the questions that would be asked by David. She thought to say, "Let's see. Your deceased dad, who you were very bitter toward and have not spoken to in over a year, is now a dolphin. And the best part is, I have to take you to him in Florida where he wants to talk to you on a phone." How was she going to pull that off? Mission impossible.

She drove the rental car from the airport to a cozy seaside town. A Google search gave her directions to his home and some personal information about him. David Ricci graduated with a PhD from MIT, and, because of his outstanding accomplishments in chemistry, he was offered a professorship. That was unheard of for a graduate student to be offered a professorship at MIT.

She drove up to a small house that looked over the bay with a great view, something one might see on a postcard. After knocking on the front door with no response, she heard power tools coming from the back yard. She walked around and saw a tall, young, muscular, shirtless man sanding a sailboat.

To not startle him, she patiently waited for him to stop sanding.

"Hello, I'm looking for David Ricci."

As David turned to look, he saw a very attractive, tall, young lady asking for him.

"Yes, I am David. Can I help you?" He put down the power sander.

"Yes, you can. My name is Dr. Mary Cole, head veterinarian of Sea Land. I need to talk to you about Marco Ricci, your father."

He quickly changed the subject. "Would like to have something to drink?"

"Sure." She followed him to the front door which he opened for her as she walked inside the house.

"I have iced tea, coffee, or water."

"Iced tea would be great. Thank you."

"Can you excuse me for a minute while I get the sawdust off?...Unless you prefer sawdust in your iced tea instead of sugar." He smiled.

She chuckled too. "I don't know. I never had sawdust in my iced tea before. Maybe you could start a new drink. But take your time."

"I'll just clean up and be right back." He walked back to the other side of the house.

Looking around the room, she was trying to find something that could help her define David. His home was immaculate with everything in its place. She couldn't help but notice a painting on the wall. It was a mother holding a young boy on her lap. The boy held a paint brush in one hand and palette in the other. The colors and the facial expressions on the mother and child were breathtaking. It told a story without a word spoken. Next to that painting was another of a man looking out to a stormy ocean, but the man had no face.

In between the two paintings was a PhD diploma from MIT for chemistry. Drawn back to the paintings with the boy and the mother and the man with no face, it appeared it was the same artist. David walked in after getting cleaned up and putting on a shirt.

Mary said, "I couldn't help but notice the two paintings—breathtaking and powerful—leaving me to figure out what the story is behind the painting. Who is the artist? These paintings are incredible." She continued looking at the amazing details.

He walked over to the refrigerator, pulled out a pitcher of iced tea, and poured two glasses. As he handed the drink to her, he said, "This is my mother holding me on her lap while I'm painting. And she was a major influence in my life."

"You've captured the love of a mother for her son in her facial expression. It is so powerful."

"And the one of a man with no face? This is my father, whom I never knew because he would not let anyone know him."

"Why does the sea look so angry?"

"His defiance against nature. I'm afraid that is not why you are here, Dr. Cole."

"No, it's just the opposite." She turned her head, looking up at him. "It's Mary. May I call you David?"

"Yes." A confused look was on his face.

"What I'm about to tell you defies logic and any scientific reasoning. You might want to sit down for this." She sat down on the couch as David sat next to her. "I'm working with a special dolphin that was rescued by the crew of a lobster boat after surviving a shark attack. I was on the research vessel *Sea Odyssey* from Sea Land and spoke directly to the fishermen. This dolphin saved a little boy's life despite a nasty blow to the head and a fall into the ocean and pushed him to shore to keep him safe from the shark. This dolphin is so very different than any other dolphin I have ever worked with. We tried to work with him into our dolphins' show with other dolphins, but he disrupted the whole show and had to be put in a separate pen. A little boy from Make A Wish Foundation, suffering from cancer, was supposed to feed a dolphin during the show. During the show, the other dolphins went to the dolphin that I was working with and opened up his pen so he could get to the little boy. The boy and the dolphin share a special bond that I didn't know at the time."

"I'm sorry, Mary, but what does that have to do with my father?" he asked with a puzzled look.

"I'm sorry for the long explanation, but unless you fully know all the facts, you will not understand. Please listen with your heart," she said. "Later that afternoon, the little boy from Make A Wish broke into the dolphin area alone. The security officer who caught him notified me.

"The little boy wouldn't give us the information on where his parents were unless we took him to see his dolphin. When his parents arrived, I found out the little boy who was rescued by the dolphin was their son. Seeing the boy and the dolphin respond to each other, it was obvious. Then the little boy said he communicated through a cellphone with the dolphin."

He was still having a hard time understanding what that had to with his late father.

She explained how alphanumeric numbers and letters on a cell spelled out words by the dolphin using high frequency sounds. She also told him the little boy's father made a computer program that translated in real time what the dolphin was saying.

She took his hand and told him, "The dolphin told a story of how he was a man who was changed into a dolphin for his sins against nature, and that his mission was to bridge the gap between man and sea animals so they could live in harmony again. I'm a scientist first. I spend my life proving things to be either true or false. The dolphin is your father. I talked to your father through the computer, and he told me where I could find you and that he needed your help."

David stood up and started walking around the room, ending up in front of the painting of the man with no face. "Do you realize what you're saying? I was there when he passed. Even if what you are saying is true, my father never wanted to talk to me when he was alive. Why would he want to talk to me when he is dead or in another life form?"

Mary walked up to David as he was staring at the picture of the man with no face and said, "I know it's hard for you to believe, and if I was in your position, I would feel the same way. All I'm asking is for you to see for yourself, and then maybe you can finally put a face on the painting."

He turned to her and said, "I'm sorry you came all this way for nothing."

Mary tried her best to convince him. "I don't know what went on with you and your father, but you have a chance for a do-over in your relationship with him. Don't carry the bitterness inside for the rest of your life when you have a chance to let it go. Have you ever wished you could have told someone how you feel before they died? But they passed before you had a chance? You have that chance."

Mary realized that there was no way he would come back with her. She handed him her card and said, "Call me if you change your mind. Your father gave one message to give to you. He said he needs your help to clean up his mess."

"My father never needed anyone, much less me."

"He said you would be bitter, but I didn't know how bitter. It was nice meeting you." Then she walked out the door.

David watched as Mary pulled out of the drive. Some of what she said hit home. Could it be true that his father was now a dolphin for his past indiscretions?

All he ever wanted was relationship with his father. It weighed heavily on his heart. It was only a couple of months before that Frank was at David's home, trying to get him to see and talk to his father before he died. Then Mary showed up, telling him that he still had a chance at a relationship with his father if not only to say his goodbyes. He had to go to Florida to settle his dad's estate. He was justifying it, but the only way to find answers was to go to Sea Land.

Sitting on the plane heading back to Florida, Mary wondered what she could have done to change his mind. How was she going to explain to Marco why she was not returning with his son? What happened with David and his father's relationship that caused such bitterness? Maybe the dolphin would explain more. There were a lot of questions to be answered.

The next morning, Mary was greeted by sad looks. Everyone knew that she didn't bring David back. Mary went to the pool and put on the headphones. "I'm sorry. David is so bitter that he wouldn't come."

"I know, Mary. I was never much of a father figure, and I was never there when he needed me."

Marco was about to talk again. He saw Mary turn quickly to see Joe, the security guard, standing with David. He said, "Dr. Mary, this gentleman said it's important that he speak with you."

Mary walked over and greeted him with a hug. "You came! Thank you." She then told Joe, "It's okay. Thank you."

"You're right. I had to see this for myself." He walked to the pool, looking at the dolphin.

Mary explained how they were linked to the computer and to a voice recognition program. She handed him the headsets and said, "Your father's computerized voice will come over the computer and headsets." She then went over to John, Nicole, and Aaron, giving David and his father some privacy.

David could not take his eyes off of the dolphin.

"Yes, David, it's me. I want to say first that I am so sorry for not being there when you needed me...or for your mother. I wish I could turn back time and be more of a father to you...and a friend. I know I have left deep scars on your heart. All I can do is ask for your forgiveness."

Tears ran down his cheeks. He reached over and rubbed his father's head. "Thank you, Dad. That's all I ever wanted from you," He wiped the tears from his eyes. They continued pouring their emotions out, healing old wounds.

"David, could you get everyone to put their headphones back on. I need to explain to everyone what is happening."

When everyone was around the computer, Marco said, "I have so much more to tell you, but time is of the essence. I need your help. You need to bring Frank Goldstein to me. I need to go over how to deal with the business I was involved in with some really bad guys. I'm afraid that they might want to buy the business. I don't want them to continue doing what I did."

"How can I get Frank over here to talk to a dolphin that is my father?"

"I would talk to Mary about how to do that. She got you here."

"Mary, now, how are we going to get me out of here? The last thing we want is someone to find out that you have a talking dolphin."

"Sea Land has a release program for sea mammals that are untrainable. After your performance in the show the other day, they would be happy to get rid of you. I will get that ball rolling, but where will you go?"

"Back to the cove at Aaron's house." That brought a smile to Aaron.

"But how will we be able communicate without the computer we are using at Sea Land?"

John stepped in to say, "That won't be a problem. By the time you release him, I will have a cell phone application that will do the same thing."

Marco then said, "We all have something to do, and time is of the essence." He asked John, "Can I speak to you privately for a minute?"

"Sure." John put on the headphone and disconnected the other voice connection.

"Is it possible to make a program that could translate English to dolphin language?"

"Yes, once I have the baseline of all the tones to alphabet, the computer can do all the rest. Why?"

"So, if Mary had a speaker and microphone under water, she could talk to the other dolphins and listen to what they were saying?"

"Yes, if the dolphins choose to talk to her, but they would at least understand her," John replied.

"Can you do that for me?" asked Marco.

"Yes, I will be here in the morning with a waterproof microphone and speaker. Once I get the baseline, I can finish it in my office."

"I have been given a gift, and if something were to happen to me, it would die with me. I would like to pass this gift on to Mary. I know she will carry on my mission."

After leaving Sea Land, David immediately called Frank Goldstein, his dad's attorney.

"Hello, Frank, how are you doing?"

"Fine, David, I'm glad you called. I have an offer on your father's business."

"Good timing. I'm in Florida. Are you free this afternoon? I have something to go over with you."

"Yes, I'll be in all day."

"I'll come to your office in about an hour if that's all right?"

"Great. It'll be good to see you again."

David hung up. He had an hour to think of how he was going to get Frank to see his father. He called Mary.

"Hello, this is Dr. Mary Cole. Can I help you?"

"Yes, you can. This is David. Do you have any suggestions on how I can get my dad's attorney to Sea Land to talk to a dolphin that was a former client?"

"Now you know what I went through." She chuckled. "What if you said you were looking to make an investment on voice recognition for dolphins and what you needed was his advice. We'll set up a fake demonstration and have your father explain why he is a dolphin."

"You're amazing. I think that will work."

"You owe me one," she said, laughing. "I will let security know that you'll be coming by with a Frank Goldstein."

"Will you let my dad know what we are doing? Thank you again. What would I have done without your help?"

"Now you owe me twice. Go get him."

David arrived at Frank's office, and Frank met him with an embrace and said, "How are you doing? I'm glad you came by. I have some papers for you to sign. Please have a seat. We have the business in escrow awaiting your signature." He handed David the paperwork.

"I'll be going over it tonight. Thank you, Frank....I have something else to talk to you about also. There is an investment that I'm looking into with Dr. Mary Cole of Sea Land. She needs some investors. She has a breakthrough in voice recognition with sea mammals. They are setting up a demonstration for us today, and I need your advice as to whether this would be a good investment."

"Sure, David, I would be glad to help."

"The appointment is scheduled for five o'clock. Go to the security gate and tell them who you are. Dr. Mary Cole will come get you and bring you back to the demonstration area."

As he walked David to the door, Frank said, "I'll see you there."

"Thanks for coming on such short notice. I really appreciate it, Frank."

David made sure that he got an early start to go over with his dad and Mary about how they were going to show the demonstration to Frank.

While they were going over what to do, Mary got a call from security. "We have a Frank Goldstein at our office to see you, Dr. Mary."

"Okay, Joe, I will be right there."

"I'll go along with you, Mary. It will put Frank at ease to see a familiar face." He walked with her to the security office.

Marco noticed the way that David and Mary looked and acted with each other. There was a spark between them. It made him feel good inside. He realized his priorities were all screwed up and he should have worried more about his son and wife. It was sad that he had die to realize it. He felt that David couldn't find a nicer person.

When they arrived at the security office, Frank was talking to Joe.

"Hello, Frank. I want to introduce you to Dr. Mary Cole, head of the project."

"Glad to meet you, Dr. Cole. David said you have a breakthrough in communication with dolphins."

"Yes, we have. It's quite amazing." They walked to the demonstration area. "Mr. Goldstein, I will be hooking you up with a set of headphones and a computer screen. The dolphin in the pool will then answer any question. The question and answer will show up on the computer screen and a computer voice through your headphones."

"It's pretty amazing, Frank. I've done it."

After Frank was hooked up to the headphones, Mary turned the computer screen in full view for him. The whole time Frank never stopped looking at Marco. Then Mary instructed him to ask a question and look directly at the dolphin so he could hear.

"Okay, hello, dolphin. What is your name?"

"Hello, Frank. It's your old friend, Marco Ricci."

Hearing what Marco said, Frank took off his headphones, turned to David, and said, "Okay, David, you got me."

"This is no joke. That's my dad. Ask him a question that only you and my dad know."

"All right, what is the combination for the safe only you and I know about?" He put his headphones back on.

"1-23-44. My birthday, Frank. Remember I told you why I picked it? I wouldn't forget it."

Frank took off his headset again and looked at Marco, looked at David, and then back at Marco again, and with a panicked look on his face, said, "What the hell! David, you were there when we found your father dead."

"Frank put the headphones back on and listen to what Dad has to say. He will explain the whole thing to you." David put his hand on Frank's shoulder and handed him back the headphones.

"Old friend, I know this is hard to believe. It's hard for me to believe that I'm a dolphin and talking to you. I believe I've changed into a dolphin to redeem myself for my sins against nature. I know you disapproved of my business tactics along with David, and now I'm paying for it. I have been given a second chance to clean up my mess and make things right. You know of my dealings with some real shady characters.

"David has read me the proposal you have to sell the business which is in escrow. These are the same people that will continue the same practices I had been doing, dumping the chemical waste into the ocean. I need your help. Here is a list of things that I need to get done."

Marco continued. "First, stop the sale of the business. Then, my first boat, the *Angelina*, must be converted for the retrieval of chemical waste—supervised by David. The other boat will be converted into a research vessel for a rehabilitation center."

Frank furiously took notes. "Make sure my servant and driver, Flo and Stephen, are well taken care of. Sell all the stocks and bonds. From the sales of all the accounts, I want to have a research center built for all sea animals under the supervision of Dr. Mary Cole. David will oversee all the above with your help."

Frank wrote all the information down. "This is a project I'll be glad to help with. I'd better get going. I have a lot do. I have a lot more questions that I need answered, but we can get to them later. I need to get this escrow stopped before I do anything else."

"Frank, I know I can trust you not to tell anyone about this."

"You know I won't." Frank took off the headphones. "It's good to talk to you again, but can you do something about your voice? I think I'm talking to a computer." Frank laughed.

Mary walked over, grasped his hand, and said, "Sorry for how we got you here, but how else could we have done it?"

"You did a damn good job. I'm sure I'll be seeing you all again soon."

Then David shook Frank's hand and said, "I know how you feel. It will take a couple of days to sink in."

"You're right. It wasn't amazing; it was a miracle." He walked out with Mary, shaking his head in wonderment.

Mary returned from letting Frank out with a sheepish grin on her face. "Good job, you two."

David and Mary gave high fives to each other while putting on their headphones.

"Don't want to break up the celebration, but you two need to figure out when I'm getting out of here."

"How about let's work on our game plan over dinner?" David asked Mary.

"That'll be great. I'll text you my address, and you can pick me up around eight o'clock. I've got just the place."

With a big smile, he said, "Looking forward to it."

While driving to Mary's place, David felt the excitement of spending some time with Mary without all of the problems that were yet to come. It had been a long time since he had butterflies in his stomach, which he had while knocking on the door.

The door opened. "Hello, David. Come in."

His eyes grew big, and he could hear his heart start racing. She looked gorgeous. Her long, blonde hair fell on her shoulders. Her short skirt and blouse accentuated her figure. He had never seen her with her hair down and without a pants suit, wetsuit, or doctor's scrubs on. Without even thinking, he spoke out, "You look gorgeous!"

"Why, thank you." Then Mary offered David something to drink. "Would you like a glass of wine, or would you prefer iced tea with sawdust." They both started laughing. She went to get the wine out of the refrigerator. He couldn't keep his eyes off her. It was only until she came back with the glass that David had a chance to look around. Her nice townhome made him feel right at home. The view from her living room showed the boats in the harbor.

David complimented her on her place and how comfortable it felt. Then he asked, "What does a Dr. Mary Cole do when she is not working?"

"It seems like I am either at Sea Land or I am on their research vessel. But in those few moments, I love to walk through the marina. I guess seeing the boats gives me the yearning to be at sea, my first home."

David, looking into her big, blue eyes, could see the love for the sea in the way her face lit up.

"Have you ever been out on a sailboat?"

"You know, I never have. Growing up, my dad had a power boat. It was either water skiing or fishing."

"When you are on a sailboat with the warm summer wind filling the mainsail and feeling the power of the wind push the boat through the gentle rolling swell, you smell the ocean mist as the hull pushes through the water. With a sailboat with no motor on, all you hear is the wind on the sail. I feel like I am one with nature. No phones, no scheduling, and no worries. That is my therapy. When things get settled down, I would like to take you out in my sailboat."

"That sounds wonderful. I would really like that, David. Thank you, especially the thing about no cell. Maybe we could visit your dad," she said laughing.

"Or invite Frank. Poor Frank, I don't think he's ever had a vacation."

"After what we did to him yesterday, I think he might need a vacation."

"Did you see the look on his face when he found out that my dad was a dolphin."

Mary took a sip of wine, and not missing a chance to kid David, said, "Almost the look on your face when you found out." She started laughing.

"Okay, you got me on that one."

"Are you hungry yet?" She then started to stand up from the couch.

"Sure, where are we going?"

"There is an Italian restaurant within walking distance."

While they walked to the restaurant, the conversation flowed. They talked about everything but the release of the dolphin. After dinner and two bottles of wine, they made their way back to Mary's place. She fumbled for her keys to open the front door. They fell to the ground. She bent down to retrieve them at the same time David did, and they bumped heads.

He held her up from falling. As they both started to stand up, they engaged in an intimate kiss. Mary dropped her keys again as the kiss lingered. He drew her closer by putting his arms around her, and she, with her hands free, ran her fingers through his hair until they melted into one. After the kiss, David, being the gentlemen, reached down and picked up her keys and handed them to her.

She unlocked the door and said, "I need to drop my keys more often!" They both laughed. "Where did all the time go? We never talked about the plans on how we are going to release your dad."

"Too much vino," he expressed.

"Tell you what. I will make dinner for us here tomorrow night. We can go over plans to release your dad even though it won't be for a couple of days."

"That would be wonderful. I haven't had a home-cooked meal in a long time."

"Don't get too excited on the home-cooked meal until after you've eaten it." She put her hands on his hips.

"I'm sure it's going to be delicious. No pressure."

With her keys still in her hands, she dropped them. Hearing them hit the floor, he turned his head.

She put both of her hands behind his head, pulling him in for another intimate kiss. After the kiss, she said, "Whoops!" They both laughed. "I had a great time with you tonight."

"It was nice being with you." Holding her tight, he gave a short kiss goodnight.

The next morning, Marco greeted Mary. Putting on her headphones, she said, "We are breaking you out of here tomorrow morning." Then she went over how the release was going to happen and how they had to stay pretty much with Sea Land protocol so as not to draw any attention.

"We'd better not use the computer to communicate after today. We have a satellite probe attached to you that will last about three to four days, and then it will fall off. Once you reach the location where the hazardous material is located, circle the area at least five times so we can get a fix.

"Remember, you only have three to four days before the satellite probe falls off. You need to locate the area as soon as possible, and don't eat any fish in the area. We will meet you back at the cove at Aaron's house at the end of the pier. And don't cause any problems." Then she said, "By the way, you have a nice son. You should really be proud of him."

"It was my wife, Angelina, that gave David what you are seeing, but thank you. Have you and David worked out logistics for tomorrow?"

"We are working on it."

"I want to thank you for saving my life. I know not being able to let any of your colleagues know what we have done speaks of your integrity. If this got out that you can communicate with dolphins, it would cause a major problem if it got in the wrong hands."

He went on to explain how Frank Goldstein was in the process of buying the property next to Aaron. "On that property, we are going to build a sea animal rescue facility where you can retrieve and release back to the ocean all of God's sea creatures. It will also be an educational center that will bring human and sea creatures back in harmony again. Educating our young children is the key to our future. We will also have a U-shaped pier stretching out into the cove where the dolphins will come to interact with the young children—especially the handicapped and the ones fighting cancer. All this will be under your and David's control."

He continued, "I have a special gift for you. I have had John secretly working on a program that will allow you to communicate with any dolphins or whales by laptop or cell. If they need help or you need to find out what's wrong with them, they will talk to you because you speak their language. If they ask you how you know their language, tell them the 'chosen one' gave you the gift." As Marco spoke to her, tears were flowing from her eyes. Marco then said, "I will only ask one thing. If something happens to me, you will finish my mission, so I can die in peace."

Mary was so emotional all she could do was nod her head up and down. Just then, David came by.

Not wanting him to see her crying, she excused herself. David put on the headphones and immediately asked, "What's wrong with Mary?"

"Everything's fine. She just got a little emotional. How is everything going on your end?"

"I'm working with a marine architect on converting the fishing boat to retrieve the hazardous materials. Also, I have some contacts at MIT for a grant to help us with the conversion. I have been working on a project for more than a year that will recycle hazardous waste to clean energy. And MIT just got the grant for funding the project for another year."

"I am happy and proud of you. I only wish I would have listened to you when you asked me to stop the dumping of the hazardous waste in the ocean. I remember you asked me to do the same project, and I told you it was a waste of time and would never work. I'm so sorry, son."

"That's okay, Dad. You are making up for it, and look at you now in the process of recycling it."

"I'm so proud of you, and I know your mother would be beaming with joy."

"I know, Dad. There's not a day that goes by that I don't think of her," David replied. "I have a meeting with Frank on the business that we are stopping."

"Be careful because you'll be dealing with some bad dudes." He watched David leave. He could only watch and pray that everything would work out.

David, arriving at Frank's office, walked into the room where two guys were standing next to Frank. "Sorry, David, they wanted to meet you in person."

Frank started to stand up. He was quickly pushed back down into the chair."

Then one of them said, "I don't think we've been formerly introduced. My name is Al Luca, and this is my brother Max. You might have seen it on the contract that you forgot to sign. We had a deal and gave you a deposit check."

"I tried to give them the deposit check back, but they wouldn't take it." Frank again tried to stand up only to be pushed down again.

"Look, we are not selling the company. This is not a legal contract because I haven't signed it, nor has any money exchanged hands."

"You know, you're nothing like your old man. He worked with us."

Al walked up to David. Taking his hand and patting David on the shoulder, he said, "Tell ya what I'm going to do. Because me and your old man where good friends, we're going to pretend that there was a misunderstanding. I'll be back next week, and I'm sure you will have a change of heart." They walked out the door, leaving Frank and David alone.

"I'm sorry. We need to talk to your father."

"They're releasing him to the ocean tomorrow morning, and they're getting him ready now. We have no way to communicate with him until we meet him back in the cove in three to four days. They gave us a week. Don't worry, Frank."

David was excited, driving to Mary's place for dinner. But in the back of his mind was the meeting with the Luca brothers. He didn't want to hold back anything from her, but at the same time, he didn't want her involved for her own safety. Clearing his mind so as not to show that something was wrong, he rang the doorbell. Mary opened the door and all negative thoughts disappeared. Her smile was contagious, and her sense of humor was next to none.

He started to walk in.

She pulled him in close and gave him a kiss. "Hello, David. I'm sorry I don't have my keys to drop."

"Now that's the type of hello I'm talking about." Still in each other's arms, he looked into her blue eyes and said, "You really know how to brighten my day."

"Wait 'til after you eat and see if you feel the same way." Then she asked him to pour a couple glasses of wine while she finished dinner.

Walking to the refrigerator, David could smell something cooking. While pouring the wine, he asked, "Is that beef stroganoff I'm smelling?"

"Yes, it's supposed to be."

While she stirred the sauce, he put one arm around her waist and his other hand on her hand, helping her. Then he gave a kiss on her neck. She dropped the stirring spatula and turned around, engaging him in a romantic kiss after which she said, "You're trying to sabotage supper, aren't you?"

He just smiled.

"Go sit down. It's time to eat."

He went to the dining room table that was lit with candles. Placing the wine down, he then went back to the kitchen where she handed him two plates of food. She walked to the table; he pulled her chair back as she sat down.

"Thank you, David."

David handed her a wine glass and said, "Yes, madam, don't forget to tip your waiter."

She, in her most sexy voice, said, "I'm planning on it."

David took a bite and said, "Mary, this is really good."

She took a bite and said, "It's not bad, especially after somebody tried to sabotage it. Not that I'm complaining." Then she said, "We'd better go over tomorrow's release."

David took another bite and agreed.

"The *Sea Odyssey* will be taking your father and releasing him in an area where we see dolphins. A satellite probe will be attached to him so we will be able to monitor three or four days of activity. I told your father once he found the dumping area that he was to circle the area at least five times, so we can ascertain the exact location. We are then going to meet him in the cove where Aaron's house is. John will download the cellphone application that will allow us to communicate with your father. Then we will be waiting for your father to return back to the cove."

"Do you need my help?"

"No, the less attention the better off we will be. I'm trying to keep this as much a normal release as possible."

"Okay, my dad gave me plenty of things to do." Then David went on to explain how they were converting two of his dad's first fishing boats to a hazardous retrieving vessel and how he got a grant from MIT to help with the conversion.

"What will happen with the hazardous waste?"

"That is the best part that I've been working on for over a year now. It's a program that will recycle the material into clean energy. We just got our grant for the program renewed for another year. We are ready for the first testing."

Mary, looking at David, was overtaken with emotion. As she fanned her eyes before her mascara could run, she said, "Must be something in your family's genes. Your father did that to me earlier."

"What was that all about?"

"Your father gave me a gift. John is making a computer program that will allow me to communicate with the dolphins and whales in their language. I'll be able to ask them where they are hurt or what they need. He gave me this gift and made me promise that if something ever happened to him that we would carry on his mission so humans and sea mammals will be able to live in harmony together again. He told me he could die in peace knowing it was in good hands. If they ask how I know of their language, your father told me to tell them 'the chosen one' gave me the gift."

No matter how much she fanned her eyes, the tears started flowing. He immediately got out of his chair and held her in his arms until she stopped crying.

"That was the best gift anyone could ever give another. That's why I became a marine biologist." She started again. David felt the tears of joy she was feeling without a word being spoken. His eyes became full as well as they bonded in joy together.

After the last deep breath was taken, they turned to each other and kissed, but it was not a passionate or intimate kiss; it was a loving kiss—a kiss that said more than a few moments of passion would mean. It was at that moment their souls bonded into one, and the real meaning of soulmates became understood. Not a word was spoken as if not to ruin the moment. The only pause was for another loving kiss.

Finally, she started to laugh because his face was full of her eye make-up. He looked at her with a puzzled look, but then realized her mascara had rubbed off and there was nowhere for it to go but on his face.

"I think the camouflage look is in." They both broke out laughing.

David, being a gentleman, so as to not take advantage of the situation, told her that he had to leave.

"I have to fly to MIT early in the morning to get the recycling testing ready. You also have a big day tomorrow."

"How about we have dinner at my house tomorrow night, and you can tell me how everything went with the release."

Not wanting him to leave, she just nodded her head. After a short kiss goodbye, he left. She sat in the living room couch, thinking over what had just happened. *Could this be what true love is?* She never had that close of a feeling as she had shared with David. She kept going over in her mind the feelings and bonding that they shared with each other.

She got a text message. The first thing that came into her mind was something went wrong at Sea Land. She picked up and read the message—not from work but from David.

"I miss you already. I would have called but time goes by so fast when I'm talking with you that we won't get any sleep, and you have a big day tomorrow. PS, if you need a shoulder to cry on, you have my number."

While she was laughing, she was texting him back. "And you have such a nice shoulder to cry on."

His phone toned, with another text message from her. All it said was, "Whoops." Immediately, he started laughing. He knew she would come up with something. He reflected back on when she purposely dropped her keys. He messaged her back, "Got it." Her response was "Sweet dreams." He knew that she had worked her way into his heart. While driving home with a big smile, he reviewed every intimate detail of the night's events. He was looking forward to dreams about his sweet Mary.

CHAPTER 11

GETTING READY

The next morning, Mary came by the pool with a glow on her face. Marco couldn't talk to her, but seeing how she was around David, he knew romance was in the air. As she jumped into the pool, no one was around, so she gently stroked Marco's head with both of her hands and said, "You sure have a nice son." Then she explained that the truck would be there in a few minutes. She told him, "The hoist will put you in the truck and drive you to the boat. I will be right here with you." Then she gave Marco a kiss on his forehead and said, "Behave yourself and act like a dolphin. I'll see you in a couple of days in the cove. Remember the plan—at least five times around the area." Marco nodded his head.

She attached the satellite probe to his dorsal fin. Zoe, along with group assistants, jumped into the pool. After they lowered the hoist into the water, Marco could hear Mary shout instructions to her assistants driving him to the boat. Again, he was lowered into the pool on the boat—the same boat that brought him to Sea Land. Mary was right there by his side.

When they reached the area where they saw a pod of dolphins, Marco was then lowered into the water. With one last stroke of her hand on his head, she said, "Okay, now you are free." He swam away, jumping into the air, and headed for the pod of dolphins. He could hear everyone on the boat cheering.

Once Marco reached the pod, he was back into dolphin mode. They already knew who he was. He proceeded to tell them that in the cove there was going to be a building with a pier where they could get help if they are hurt and where they could communicate with the humans. He said, "No longer do you have to beach yourself on the sand for help."

How do I tell them when to go to the cove? Thinking like a dolphin, he knew using the moon phase would accomplish it.

"In two moons, a pier in the cove will be built where we can interact with the children of the humans. They are the key to bridging the gap, so we can live in harmony again."

He told the pod that they needed to go to the bad water area where a boat would be coming to pick up all the things that were making the water toxic and unsafe. They understood and headed to the area of hazardous chemicals he had dropped over the years.

Back on the *Sea Odyssey*, Mary had binoculars and was watching Marco interact with the dolphins. "Is the satellite picking up the dolphin?"

Zoe replied, "Everything is working fine. This is one of the easiest releases that we have ever had."

Mary smiled and told the crew, "Good job, everyone." Then she clapped her hands in appreciation to the crew, and the crew joined in. Then she said, "Okay, we are done here. Let's go home."

She gave a sigh of relief. Everything had gone off without a problem. Excited about how the release went, she sent a message to David. "Your dad is free, and everything went according to plan. Looking forward to tonight."

He responded back, "Don't forget to bring your keys." She started laughing. He then sent his address and the code to the front gate.

"Seven o'clock, and bring your bathing suit."

"Was that a birthday suit or bathing suit?"

With a smile on his face, he replied. "Both."

That evening, when she arrived at David's house, she noticed a black car parked across the street with two guys inside. After she pulled up to the gate and saw the for-sale sign, it started to make sense. They were probably looking to buy the house. The car drove away as she dialed the code to get in. The gate opened to a beautiful home high on a bluff overlooking the ocean. Walking up to ten-foot-high glass front doors, she could see David walking toward her. Holding her keys in her hand, her heart started racing. The door opened. David was holding a set of keys in his hand too. They both immediately broke out laughing. Then they embraced into intermittent kisses.

She walked into the house and was overwhelmed with the home.

"Why would you sell this house?"

"There are too many bad memories. Plus, the sale of the house would go toward construction of the rescue center we're going to build in the cove." Then taking her hand, they went into the kitchen. "Close your eyes. I have something for you." He guided her to the kitchen table and said, "Okay, open up your eyes."

There on the table was an artist rendition he had made of what the rescue center would look like with the u-shaped pier. Off to the side was a man looking down on the cove with a smile on his face. She recognized the drawing had his father overlooking the cove. She was overwhelmed with emotions. She started fanning her eyes to not cry and then hugged David, burying her head in his chest. "I promised myself not to cry tonight. I even put on waterproof eye make-up."

"I got a call from Frank. It's official. We closed on the property today," he told her. "Now you are in charge of how you want the inside to look like. I have the name and number of the architect. Just tell him what you want."

"You know all of my life this has been my dream!" she blotted her eyes.

"A dream come true now....Yesterday, it got emotional, and I forgot to tell you about the *Angelina*. It was my father's first fishing boat...named after my mother. It is to be used for the chemical retrieval. My father's second boat, *Davede*, he wants to be used as your new research vessel." She reached over, holding his face with tears still flowing.

"I can't believe it is all happening...and so fast. What you and your father have done for me I will never forget."

She then looked over the drawing of her dream in front of her. It was overwhelming, especially to see Marco looking down on it with a smile. She turned her head, looking up at David. "Promise me that we will build a statue of your dad overlooking the cove."

He just nodded his head and pulled her closer, saying, "I've got to finish dinner."

She asked if she could help.

"Yes, you can pour us some wine. We need to celebrate."

"I'll drink to that." She went to the refrigerator, poured two glasses, and handed one to him while he put final touches on dinner.

"How did you learn to cook eggplant parmesan?"

"I used to watch my mother go through the tedious process that it takes to really make it good. She would tell me all the time to watch carefully as she would go through each step with me, from making the sauce from scratch to how to bread and fry the eggplant." He took a sip, then said, "Every time I make it, I think of her looking over my shoulder, making sure that I didn't make any mistakes. It was her signature dish. People would always ask her for the recipe. She would say she didn't have one...that she would just add a little bit of this and a little bit of that. I think she didn't want anyone to know. That's why she wanted me to be by her side when she made it, so in her own way she passed it down to me."

David took another sip of wine and started to pour the sauce over the eggplant. Mary stepped behind David, putting an arm around his chest and her other hand on his arm to help pour the sauce. She pulled him in tight with her body implanted in his back and her hand rubbing his chest. David's knees buckled. He said, "That's not fair!"

"What goes around comes around." He turned around, grabbed her, and pulled her in so her feet were off the ground and her breasts pushed into his chest. He then gave her a passionate kiss. After the kiss, she said, "Wow, what's for dessert?" She laughed.

"You."

"Yummy. I can't wait."

"Now, without any further interruption, I need to put this in the oven. Dinner will be served in one hour." He took her hand and walked out to the pool where they sat and enjoyed each other's company.

As they were sitting, looking up at the stars, she snuggled her head onto his chest. "I wonder what your father is doing right now in the dark of the night?"

"You're the expert on dolphins." He then looked down at her.

"You're right. Did you know that they can sleep while swimming by shutting off one half of their brain so it can rest and then switching over to rest the other side? But, when we have more time with your father, he will give us so much more knowledge of what we don't know about dolphins."

He moved her and slowly stood up. "It's time for dinner."

They sat down. She took one bite, and she said, "This is to die for. The flavors are just exploding in my mouth. This is fabulous."

"Thank you. I'm glad you like it."

"I don't like...I love it. Would you teach me how to make it?"

"Well, maybe. Can I trust you to keep it a secret?"

She playfully punched him in the shoulder. "Let's see. Your dad is a dolphin, and I, a marine biologist, have kept that a secret. Give me a break."

"Okay, I guess you have a point,"

After dinner, she took David's hand. Walking him over to the couch and sitting him down, she asked, "Do you trust me?"

"Yes, of course."

"Close your eyes and don't open them until I say to." He shut his eyes. She gently pushed him down until he was lying flat on the couch with his hands above his head. She straddled him and slowly unbuttoned his shirt to expose his chest. She pulled her halter top off exposing her breasts and ran her long, blonde hair over his chest. She kissed both sides of his neck, and in doing so, her chest brushed over his. She could feel his chest quivering and knew he was getting aroused as she straddled him. She then worked her way up from his neck and gave him a short kiss on his lips.

He started to respond to the kiss, but she said, "Keep your eyes closed." She put her finger on his lips to quiet him. She took his hands that were behind his head and placed them on her breasts. Then she said, "Your dessert is being served." He opened his eyes. Seeing how beautiful she looked, her breasts in his hands, he gave her an intimate kiss that turned into wild, passionate lovemaking.

After they finished, both of them just lay there, holding each other. Looking at the clothes all over the living room, they both started laughing. Then she rolled over on top of his chest and said, "Can I have seconds on dessert?"

He smiled and said, "You sure can, but I think we might need more room!" He picked her up and carried her to the bedroom.

The next morning, they were still embraced in each other's arms with her head buried into his chest. The only thing that woke them up was the bright morning sun glaring through the window. He opened his eyes. Looking down, seeing her cuddled in his arms, he almost had to pinch himself to make sure it was really happening. She turned and looked at him and with a smile and said, "Good morning!"

"A very good morning...I'll go downstairs and see what I can stir up for breakfast. I wasn't expecting any company, so I don't know what's in the refrigerator."

Then she said, "I wouldn't mind having a small piece of eggplant."

"I do have coffee."

"I would kill for a cup. Thank you. I'll be right down."

He went to the kitchen, turned on the coffee maker, and opened the refrigerator, pulling out a couple of pieces of leftovers from dinner. By then, she came downstairs in one of his shirts. He gave out a wolf whistle, and she did a pirouette with her hands up in the air. The end of David's shirt barely covered her behind.

She said, "Sorry I had to use one of your shirts. All of my clothes are down here in the living room." As she picked up each garment, she said, "Whoops, whoops, whoops." He started laughing and then handed her a cup. "Just what I need." She put her arm around him and took a sip. While they were waiting for the microwave to signal the egg-plant was done, she stared chanting "Duh, dah, duh, dah, duh, dah, dah" as if they were in a game show waiting to answer the question. Seeing him shaking his head, Mary said, "What? Two adults staring at a microwave waiting for a chime to ring?" She had a way of making life fun.

"That's what I like about you. You have a quick wit and a great sense of humor."

"At work sometimes it gets so crazy that when I get away from being Dr. Mary and just be me with-out all the pressure and problems that come with the job, I kind of let loose a little. Like being here with you, you allow me to be just me no matter how cra-zy I get. Thank you for that."

"If it was anything like last night, my pleasure," he answered with his eyes wide open, showing his approval.

After finishing the coffee and eggplant, she ex-cused herself as she took her clothes to the bath-room. She returned, looking as beautiful as she did the evening before. "Wow, you look great, but I still liked you better in my shirt."

"I'm sure you did," she replied. "I need to go home and change. I have to be at Sea Land to re-view your dad's progress on the computer and do all the data and paperwork." Then she asked, "What have you got going on today?"

"I have a meeting with the marine architect to finish up on the hazardous material retrieval on the boats. Then later this afternoon, I have to fly back to MIT. We are doing the first test today. I'm planning on meeting you at the cove in a couple of days."

"I'll call you later today and let you know what your dad's ETA in the cove is." She then gave him a hug and kiss and said, "I'll see you in a couple of days."

He was holding her as he gently whispered, "That was really nice, waking up with you in my arms."

"And all the stuff before wasn't bad either." Then they both laughed.

While she drove down the driveway and through the gate, she noticed the same black car across the street from his house. She immediately called.

"Miss me already?"

"Oh, yes, but that's not what I'm calling about." She then went on to explain. "When I pulled in yesterday, there was a black car with two guys across the street, but they drove away. I didn't think much of it, seeing the house had a for-sale sign. I figured people were looking at it to buy. Then this morning, the same car was parked across the street with two men in it. You might call the police to have them checked out. They may be casing the house to rob it. Please be careful, David."

He thanked her. Then he walked outside, and not seeing any black car in front or at the side of the house, he said to her, "They're gone."

"Just be careful," she told him in a concerned manner.

After leaving his house, she returned home for a quick shower and a change of clothes. She then headed off to Sea land. Looking at the data with Zoe, she could see where Marco traveled and then circled five times in the area of the hazardous material. Zoe asked why the dolphin was circling. Mary replied, "That's a good thing. It means that he's working with the other dolphins to capture the baitfish."

She asked Zoe how long he had traveled until he made the five circles. Zoe made some calculations and indicated about twelve hours. That gave her a good idea of an ETA for Marco to return to the cove. She instructed Zoe to keep track of the dolphin until the satellite probe came off.

David was at a meeting either with the marine architect or on a flight back to MIT. She stepped outside to text him that his dad's ETA would be around twelve the next day and she was looking forward to seeing him at the cove. She added that she needed a hug and maybe a kiss…a lot of kisses.

She made her rounds at Sea Land, trying to get as much done as possible so she would have the next day off when she met him at the cove.

She called Nicole and John, giving them the update and the ETA of David's dad. She also reminded them to make sure to keep everything quiet. Then John asked Mary to come a little early so he could install the app on her phone and still have time to show her how to use it before the dolphins come into the cove.

"How much time do you need?"

"It should be ten-to-fifteen minutes."

Aaron, overhearing that his dolphin would be in the cove at twelve noon, got all excited about the thought of seeing the dolphin again. It had been a couple of days since he was able to see him before his release, and he was worried about him returning back to the cove.

John reminded his son not to tell anyone about the dolphin. Aaron answered, "I know, Dad. Can I go outside? I want to check to see if he came early."

Aaron went running out the door. Nicole reminded him not to be too late because he needed to do his homework. They were happy to see Aaron so happy and full of life again. Aaron had an appointment with his oncologist soon.

They prayed that being reunited with the dolphin would put his cancer back into the remission stage. They had prepared themselves for the worst, but seeing Aaron so happy, they could not help but have a ray of hope.

John told Nicole he had to go back to the office to finish up on the new program. John could see his son looking out to sea for the dolphin. It inspired him to make sure that everything was ready to go for the next afternoon so they could finish up any loose ends.

He was looking forward to seeing the expression on Mary's face when she was presented with the dolphin language program (DLP). It was all possible because David's father gave them baseline data for the DLP. Communication would be the bridge between humans and sea animals, and they were about to make that happen. John was also aware of the problems if it got into the wrong hands with military and foreign governments. John was planning on putting a retina display to open the DLP program. Retina display would make it impossible for anyone to hack into it.

CHAPTER 12

POD OF DOLPHINS IS COMING

When the dolphin pod finally reached the hazardous material area, Marco told them to stay in one spot while he circled, so he could keep his bearing as he went around the area five times. As Marco swam, he was reliving over and over again each time he dumped hazardous material drums into the ocean. Each circle was a painful reminder of what he had done. After the last circle, Marco told the dolphins to follow him to the cove. He wanted them to see where to go if they needed him or if they were hurt.

They traveled the long way to the cove, so he had a lot of time to think. He thought that Aaron would be waiting for him to play catch as they did at Sea Land while he was waiting to be released. He remembered as if it was like the first trip when he met Aaron at the end of the pier.

Now he was bringing Aaron a whole pod of dolphins. He could not wait to see his face. At the same time, he couldn't forget what the poor kid was going through. But Aaron was looking better every day he saw him. Maybe the same bonding that stopped the cancer the first time would work its magic again.

He also considered what Aaron had said at Sea Land when they were trying to come up with a name to call him instead of "Mr. Dolphin" and how he never knew his grandmother who died before he was born nor his grandfather who died of the same cancer Aaron had.

Aaron asked, "Can I call you grandpa?"

Marco's heart just melted, but not to hurt Aaron's parents' feelings, he told him "In Italian, grandpa is nono. How about that?"

He quickly said, "Yes."

Marco turned his thoughts to David. Would the same thing happen to him? If things worked out with Mary and they had a child, would he be around to see it?

After his mission was done, what would become of him? Would the gift die when the mission was over? Would he be allowed to pass in peace? But enough of dying, he still had a lot of work to do.

CHAPTER 13

MARY DID IT

That afternoon after completing the first round of testing at the MIT lab, every test thereafter went better than David anticipated, which meant that he could go back to Florida and meet Mary at the cove without any delay. He left his assistant to analyze the data. He then stopped by his home to pick up more clothes before leaving in the morning. Sitting in the living room where Mary sat, trying to get him back to see his father, he was inspired to call her from the land line at his home.

Mary's phone rang, but because she didn't recognize the number, she said, "This Is Dr. Mary Cole. Can I help you?"

"Yes, you can."

Recognizing David's voice right away, she said, "Okay, David, you got me. I didn't recognize the phone number. I should have known by area code."

"I'm at my house, sitting on my couch, thinking of you and that day you tried to get me to go with you to Florida to see my father."

"For future reference, what was the contributing factor that made you come to Florida in case I ever have to do that again?"

"To be honest with you, what you said hit home...and curiosity, but there was also something very special about you. I couldn't put my finger on it. Anyway, I just wanted to let you know I was thinking about you."

"Thank you. That's sweet of you. While you're there, paint your father's face on the painting and bring it home for the sculptor to use."

"That is something I'll be happy to do. I'm going to miss waking up with you in my arms in the morning."

"Well, I guess you'd better get yourself back if you want any more." That got David's attention.

"I really would like that. I'll see you tomorrow at noon."

David wanted to say I love you, but it wasn't the appropriate time yet. Those words were very special to him. Too many people say "love you" and "I love you too" as a way of saying goodbye. The feeling, however, that he shared with her, he had never felt before with anyone. He thought, *Is this love? If it's not love, I don't know what love is.* Everything was happening so fast he didn't want to scare her off.

It was about 11:30 a.m. when Mary arrived at Aaron's home and was greeted by John and Nicole. She asked where Aaron was.

Nicole said, "Aaron has been waiting on the end of the pier all morning."

John greeted Mary and then said, "Please give me your phone, and I'll download the DLP app."

John did his work while Nicole and Mary talked about Aaron's condition. Nicole said, "His spirits and happiness are back to when he first met the dolphin. After the roller coaster of emotions we went through when he went into remission and then regressed back into cancer, now we're waiting for his oncologist appointment next week, hoping for good news."

She started to cry. Mary reached out and held her in her arms. She then told her, "I believe that God has his hand in this, and Aaron is the key to his plan. The dolphin has been given a gift not only to communicate with us, but to heal us. I believe with all my heart that something good will come of this. If it was not for Aaron, all of this would not have happened. Aaron found his dolphin at Sea Land, and now we're all here. Something more powerful is making this happen."

"Everyone is doing something except me," expressed Nicole.

Mary said, "You could help me coordinate with Make A Wish when we open the center."

"I would really like that!"

Just then, David pulled up in the driveway, and Mary excitedly went out to greet him. They walked into the house, and David was greeted by John and Nicole. John gave Mary back her phone along with a new laptop with an underwater microphone that plugged into it. "You can thank David for the laptop and me for DLP," said John.

Mary reached out to John and gave him a hug with tears in her eyes. She went to David who was holding a tissue for her. She took his tissue and gave him a hug too. "Let's go down, and I'll show you how it works," John said, taking the laptop from her.

They all went out to the end of pier where Aaron was standing. The first thing out of Aaron's mouth was "He's not here yet. Do you think something might've happened to him?"

Mary tried to explain that he was traveling a long way and he might be a little late.

It was getting closer to one o'clock, and there was no sign of the dolphin. Mary started to become concerned but didn't want to say anything or show any emotion that might upset Aaron any more than he already was. She took out her cell and walked away from everyone to call Zoe to track the location of the dolphin.

The phone started to ring. Aaron started to yell, "Look! What is that?"

Mary turned to look and knew immediately. "It's David's dad, and he's brought some friends!" Everyone hugged each other while the pod came closer to the end of the pier. John put the waterproof mic in the water and turned on the laptop.

CHAPTER 14

MEETING THE POD OF DOLPHINS

Marco turned into the cove; he could see everyone standing on the end of the pier applauding. When he got closer, he could see Aaron standing there with the tennis ball in his hand. As he got even closer, Aaron threw the ball. Not to disappoint him, Marco jumped high into the air, caught the ball, and flipped it back to him. Then he heard John say, "Let's try the phone app." He nodded and swam next to the underwater microphone. John asked, "How was your trip?"

A return voice said, "It was a long trip, but we made it!"

John told him that he was going to use the new DLP to show Mary.

Marco's voice came on the laptop and on the handheld. "Okay, let's see how it works." John handed the laptop to Mary, showing her how to work the program. David looked over his shoulder to watch and learn also. Mary again thanked John for the wonderful gift he had given her.

"I want to introduce you to my friends," Marco said. Over the screen, it read out, "I want you to talk to my friends."

John told Mary, "Like in any language, there are some words that aren't used. They will understand, but keep it simple."

"Dr. Mary is the one that I gave the gift to," Marco told the pod. As he spoke to the pod, Mary was reading and hearing what he said in real time.

She said, "If you are hurt or need help, you can come here, and I will help you."

"Hurt where to go?" asked one of the dolphins.

"A new pier will be here at the far end of the cove in two moons," she replied, remembering how Marco told her earlier in the week about using the moons.

"Very good, Mary," Marco replied. "They understood what you said." Marco then told the pod if they needed help before the pier was done to come to the pier and Aaron would get Dr. Mary to help them.

Marco talked to the pod while Mary read and listened to what he was saying over her laptop. Marco told them to go back to the ocean and he would be in touch with them. He told them to say goodbye. The pod all together jumped in unison and did the dolphin shuffle.

"That was so cool!" Aaron said.

Mary explained, "When a pod of dolphins signals danger, the pod takes off in unison at top speed, doing what fishermen called the dolphin shuffle. That's what you just witnessed."

Mary was so happy she handed the laptop to John, ran over to Marco with both hands on his head, and gave him a kiss. "Thank you, thank you, Marco."

Just then she got a call. Zoe explained there was an emergency back at Sea Land. "I have to go back to work," she said. She gave everyone a hug and asked David to call her later.

John told Mary that he had to put retina identification on the laptop and cell, but she needed to come to his office for the retina scan of her eyes.

She said she would the next day and asked John to text her his office address.

After Mary left, David went over to his father, and using the laptop, he said, "Dad, we have a problem." He went over what had happened at Frank's office and how they gave him a week to sign the escrow papers or else.

"This is serious. These guys are bad dudes. I have seen what they would do if they don't get their way." There was a long pause before he spoke again. "What I'm about to tell you is embarrassing, and I'm not proud of it. I got involved with the Luca Brothers who were dealing with drug trafficking. The money was so good, I didn't consider the consequences. Frank didn't even know about it. I am so sorry to have put you in this dangerous position. We need to deal with this right away. Call Frank. Have him go to my office, and in my floor safe, he will find large envelopes with the Luca brothers' names written on them. In the envelopes, you will find all the documents, tapes, and photographs to put them away forever, but I have to make sure that this doesn't come back on you or Frank. The police are not an option. We have to do it ourselves, and I know just how to do it. Set up a meeting tomorrow night at 8:00 p.m. at the *Angelina*. Set up the laptop on the boat so I will be able to communicate with the Luca brothers."

After talking to Frank, David told his dad he was going to a meeting at his old office.

"There is a duplicate copy in the safe for Senator Johnson to be delivered to him if something goes wrong. Leave that copy in the safe and take the other copy with you to the meeting with the Luca brothers. I'm going to leave now, so if you need me, I will be at the *Angelina*," said Marco.

David drove to his father's office to meet Frank. He wondered what the plan was that his dad came up with. As he pulled up, Frank was waiting for him at the entrance. He filled Frank in on what his dad told him. He asked Frank to call the Luca brothers. David took the phone but stopped to explain. "It's between the Luca brothers and me."

They walked to the office. Frank rolled the carpet back under the office desk, exposing a large floor safe. Frank asked David, "Do you know the combination to the safe?"

"No" David had a puzzled look.

"You should. It's your birth date," Frank said with a smile.

With the safe opened, they could see the large envelopes with the Luca brothers' names written on them. In the four envelopes, there was a copy and an original. One of the envelops had a note that said, "In case foul play happens to me, send this to Senator Johnson."

"Did you know what was in them?"

"Your father was very secretive about it. All he ever said was he didn't want me involved in his mess. This is my life insurance policy."

"For your own safety, we are going to keep it that way," replied David.

He thanked Frank and told him he would lock up the office. After Frank left, he opened the envelopes that were in the safe. There were photos, tapes, and a ledger with all of the transactions that his father had with the Luca brothers. It was quite evident his father used this information for leverage against the Luca brothers. He then called Al Luca.

"Yea, it's Al."

"Mr. Luca, it's David Ricci. I would like to meet with you tomorrow night at my dad's old boat, *Angelina*, at 8:00 p.m."

"Why there?" asked Al.

"We made some changes in her that you need to know about."

"I think I understand you want to pay tribute to your old man, being on his boat, but don't forget to bring your pen."

David was relieved when Al hung up and the conversation was over. He headed down to the dock where the *Angelina* was. While he was walking to the boat, he received a call from Mary. She said, "I'm waiting for a pregnant walrus with twins to give birth. It could be an all-nighter."

"That's okay. I'm working on the *Angelina* right now."

"Can I have a rain check?" she replied.

"How about tomorrow night at my house?"

"Sure, all I have to do is get the pregnant walrus to cooperate."

"Remember your appointment with John at his office for your retina scan tomorrow."

"Can he do a retina scan if I fall asleep?" she joked.

After saying goodbye, he felt relieved. While all this was going on with the Luca brothers, the safest place for her would be at Sea Land with all the security.

He walked down the gangway to the boat and stepped on board, looking for the best place to set up. Turning on the back deck light, he remembered how his father had taken pictures and documents of every transaction with the Luca brothers. He thought that it wouldn't be a bad idea to record everything in case something went wrong. He found the camera his dad had used and looked for a place to hide it that would show the Luca brothers but not show his dad in the water. He set it up and tested it to make sure it worked at the right angle. Satisfied the test recording was good, he set up a small folding table with three chairs so the camera would not have to be moved. The stage was set. He hoped it would all work. He called Frank to let him know that if something happened to him, he needed to take the envelopes from the safe with the Luca brothers' names and give them to the attorney general and to Senator Johnson.

Later that night, Mary was in the process of finally delivering the twin baby walruses. After giving instructions to Zoe and setting up four-hour shifts to make sure the mother and two babies were all right, she told Zoe to call her if any problems arose and that she would see them in the morning.

As she was leaving, Joe, the security guard, said, "Working late, Dr. Mary?"

"It's twins. Mother and baby walruses are doing fine. I'm going home. Goodnight, Joe."

CHAPTER 15

THEY GOT HER

Pulling up to her townhouse parking spot, she was tired and didn't notice the unfamiliar van parked next to her. As she got out of the car, two men jumped out of the van. One, holding a cloth of chloroform, grabbed her, covering her mouth. The other man slid the door of the van open and pulled her in. They then grabbed her purse, closed her car door, and drove away.

When she woke up, she was blindfolded, tied to a chair, and gagged. Al Luca was standing in front of her and said, "Hey, look; sleeping beauty is awake." She tried to get loose and was yelling, but the mouth gag only let out a muffled plea for help. Then Al said, "We're not going to hurt you as long as your boyfriend cooperates."

That morning after David woke up, he went to the *Angelina* to see if his father was at the boat yet. He was thinking about calling Mary but figured she probably had a late night and was still sleeping. Since it was Saturday and no one would be working on the boat, he thought it was safe enough that he would not be seen by anyone. As he walked down the gangway with the laptop in his hand, he saw his dad pop up out of the water behind the boat next to the swim step. He walked over and greeted his dad. "I'm going to set up the laptop."

Once the laptop was ready, David told his dad about the surveillance video camera he had set up. With Frank's help they found the envelopes with all the tapes and photographs from the safe.

"Good job, David."

David went over the angle so Marco wouldn't be in view of the camera.

Marco said, "I'm so sorry that I put you through all of this. The worst part is that I can't do anything to help you."

"We will get through it together. Is there anything else I should know or you want to tell me about?"

"No, I promise you."

David asked, "What are you going to do?"

"I have to get down in the dirt with them. That's the only way they understand anything. Just remember to keep your cool with them. I'll do the rest." Then he asked David if Mary knew anything about the meeting.

"No, only you, me, and Frank,"

"The less anyone knows about this, the better off we and they are." Then he told David he couldn't bring the police or FBI in on the problem because even if they went to prison, someone else in their family would take over, and they would come after David. "I have to convince them it's in their best interest to let it go. I still have a couple of ideas, but we'll have to play it by ear," he expressed. "David, if you need me, I'll be here all day, and I will see you tonight."

David said he was meeting Mary at John's office for a retina scan at noon. He explained how the

DLP was protected by a retina eye scan so the only people that could access the program would be Mary or himself. That way if it fell into the wrong hands, like foreign governments or the military, they wouldn't have access to it.

"Good idea."

He told his dad that he'd better go because he had a lot to do before the meeting. While he was walking up the gangway, he saw Marco nod his head to say goodbye.

Before David drove away, he texted Mary. "I'm on my way to John's office. I'll see you there." With no response, he thought she was in the shower or getting ready for work. He figured he would get his retina scan first in case Mary was late, and if she had to leave quickly to go back to work, his would be done. When he reached John's office, he didn't see her car anywhere. He asked if Mary had been by.

John said, "No, but we can do yours first. It will only take five to ten minutes for the scan. When Mary comes, I'll do her next."

After the scan, there was still no sign of her. He called her. It rang and rang. Finally, there was a pickup. David didn't give her a chance to even say hello. He said, "I'm at John's office. We were worried about you."

A voice he was not expecting to hear said, "I worry about you too."

David's heart dropped to his stomach. It was Al Luca.

"Where is Mary?" he demanded.

"She's right here. Do you want to talk to her?" Al asked.

"Yes."

After a moment of silence, there was some scrambling. Then he heard her voice say, "I'm all right, David."

Al's voice came back on, cutting off Mary from saying anything more, and said, "I'm going to make you a deal you can't refuse."

"I told you we were meeting tonight and where. Why did you have to kidnap Mary?"

"It's my insurance policy. Now be a good boy, and I'll see you tonight. And David, no funny stuff, or we will send your lady friend back to you in a box. Capiche? And one more thing, David, don't forget your pen." Al then hung up.

David's face turned white. He sat down as John came in from another room. Seeing David's face, he asked, "David, are you all right?"

"I've got to go. Mary won't be coming in today." David stormed out the door.

He got in his car. The only thing he could think about was Mary's safety. He sat, trying to control his emotions before driving. Should he go to the police or the FBI? Time was of the essence, but he knew the best place to go was to his father who was at the boat. His father told him he was going to be there if he needed him. David knew he needed him.

Everything was starting to make sense because Mary said there was somebody outside his house on two different occasions. They were following her and him. Keeping that in mind, he drove to a busy shopping center and proceeded to get lost in the crowd. Going through different stores, he purchased a different shirt and hat, making sure no one was following him. Once he reached the other side of the mall, he called a cab.

Once in the cab, he went to the boat where he got out. Looking around to make sure no one was watching, he ran down the gangway to the boat. He couldn't see his dad, so he turned on the laptop, dropping the mic and speaker in the water, and he called for Marco.

CHAPTER 16

INSURANCE POLICY

When Marco heard David call for him, he popped up next to him. But when he saw David's face, it told him that there was a major problem. "What happened, David?" he asked anxiously.

David's voice creaked, "They got Mary."

"Who got Mary?"

"The Luca brothers." David felt panic as he paced back and forth on the swim step of the boat.

"Okay, slow down and tell me what happened."

"It's all my fault," David moaned. "Mary told me there was a car parked in front of my house when she came to see me. The next morning, the car was still there. When I went out, it was gone. They followed her and now they've kidnapped her until I sign over the business."

"It's not your fault. If anything, it's mine," Marco replied. "They won't do anything to her because they need her to get to you. So has the meeting time changed?"

"No."

"Everything is the same except we have to make sure that Mary is safe, right?"

"Of course." David looked to his father for answers.

"We have to be careful, so we don't tip our hand. You made sure that they didn't follow you?"

David explained how he went to the mall and then took a cab to the boat and stated he would repeat the same process on the way back to the mall.

"David, remember to keep calm. Mary's safety depends on us. We'll get through this together."

He called the cab to pick him up in front of the office at the marina in full view from the boat. When the cab pulled up, he said, "I'd better go, and I'll be back by 7:30 p.m."

He ran to meet the cab. Marco could see the look of concern on his face and how nervous he was about Mary's safety. He could also see the love for her. When they were together, he could see affection for each other in the playfulness they shared and the smiles he had never seen before. Mary's safety was of the utmost importance. Her kidnapping was his fault, and if it came down to it, he was ready to give his life for them. His mission would be carried on by both of them.

David retraced his route back to the mall and changed clothes back to what he was originally wearing before entering the mall so as not to cause suspicion. After getting in his car, he headed to his house to avoid any suspicious actions that might endanger Mary's life. The one thing that kept going through his mind was what his father said about the Luca brothers. At the house, all he could do was pace up and down the floor like a caged animal. Everything he looked at reminded him of her, and he would reflect back on those moments. He was also thinking about what was going to happen. Every few minutes, he would check his watch, wishing the time would go by faster.

Each minute seemed like an hour. His mouth was so dry he went to the refrigerator for a bottle of water. There he saw the eggplant and remembered the dinner they shared together. That was it. He couldn't stay in the house any longer. He grabbed the water bottle and car keys and drove off. Not knowing where to go, he drove to the park near Mary's house where he walked, trying to kill time.

He remembered her telling him she would go running there after work to get relief from the stress of the day. Was that what drew him to the park? To help relieve the stress? After walking in the park for a while, there was a sudden urge of anxiety that came over him. What if on the way to the boat, he was delayed or in an accident? To calm himself down, he made the decision to go to the boat to help calm his nerves. At least he would already be there waiting.

When he reached the parking spot in front of the office, he could see the boat, so when they pulled up, he would be able to see them. Walking down to the boat with the laptop and envelopes, he couldn't see his dad, so once he stepped on the boat, he opened the DLP app on his laptop.

The app started typing. "I'm on the starboard side of the boat." David walked to that side and sure enough, he saw his dad waiting for him. "I couldn't wait any longer at home."

"I understand," Marco said. "Is everything ready to go with the laptop and security cameras?" He was trying to keep David busy so as not to think about what was going to happen.

"Everything is ready to go. All I have to do is turn on the laptop and the security cameras which are controlled by the small credit-card-sized remote that I have in my hand."

Marco said, "I'll be on the side of the boat out of sight unless I'm needed."

"I should go to the back of the boat to not cause any suspicions," suggested David. "I wouldn't want to be seen talking to a dolphin."

That little bit of humor was the first sign that he was calming down. He then went to the back of the boat where he could see his car and any car that would be parked.

The sun was starting to set, and the parking lot light had just come on when a black car pulled up slowly and parked next to David's car. A man stepped out of the car, smoking a cigar, and started walking to the boat. When he reached the gangway, it was obvious it was Al Luca, alone.

David immediately asked where Mary was. Al kept walking and stepped onto the boat and said, "I remember this old boat. Me and your old man made our first deal right here. That's why I agreed to meet here. We had no contract then—just a good old-fashioned handshake. And we knew if anyone broke the deal, there were consequences to pay...if you know what I mean." Al reached over, pinching David's cheek, then lightly slapping his cheek as he blew stinky cigar smoke on his face.

David again asked to see Mary. Al said, "Out of respect for your old man, I will grant you one wish." He took out his cell, called his brother, Max, and said, "Hey, David wants to see his lady friend."

Then the black car's back door opened. Mary stepped out, blindfolded.

Al handed David his phone.

"Mary, are you all right, and did they hurt you?"

"I'm all right."

Max then pushed Mary back into the back of the car.

Al grabbed the phone back and said, "That is enough of that. Did you bring your pen?"

David turned on his laptop and said, "You have to talk to my dad first."

"What is all this? Your old man is dead, and so is your lady friend if you don't sign the escrow papers."

Then over the laptop speaker came the computer voice saying, "I'm alive, you dumb wop." That got Al's attention. No person would dare call Al a dumb wop. That's what Marco would call him when he wanted to get his attention.

"What the hell is this?" Al said.

Marco said over the computer, "David, give Mr. Luca the envelopes."

Al grabbed them out of David's hands.

"What the fuc....! Are you blackmailing me?" he said angrily.

"No, it's my insurance policy, you dumb wop, and it's yours too," Marco told him.

"What do you mean, mine?" Al said.

"The FBI are onto us. I got the tip from one of my paid senators. I staged my death. I made them a promise I would retire from the business and clean up all the hazardous material that we've dumped over the years in return for our immunity. David is

here to make sure it gets cleaned up. We are converting the boats to recover hazardous material
waste and then convert it to clean energy."

"How do I know that this is not a hoax or a set
up?" replied Al.

"Okay, you dumb ass," Marco said, "ask me a
question that only you and I know."

Al thought about it for a minute and said, "Okay,
what were those two broad's names that we banged
in Fort Lauderdale?"

"You mean the two twin sisters, Bridget and So-
phia? Wasn't it Bridget that called you Little Al in
reference to your lower package?" Marco answered.

"All right, all right, it's you," Al answered. "So
why are you talking over a computer?"

"I'll get to that, but first get your dumb ass brother, Max, to let Mary go, and bring her down here."

Al called Max and told him to remove the blind-
fold, untie Mary, and bring her down to the boat.
The car door opened, and she was led out of the car
and down the dock. Halfway to the boat, she was
met by David, who was on a full sprint to meet her.
Holding her in his arms, he kept asking if she was
all right and gave her a kiss and held her tighter.
Confused, Mary asked, "David, what is this all
about?"

"I'll tell you about it later."

Max walked down to the boat and stood next to
his brother.

"You're not going to believe it. Marco is still
alive. He faked his death."

"Why did he do that?"

Al explained, "The feds were on to us. He made a sweet deal with them. He was to retire and clean up his mess. They gave him immunity."

"What about us?" asked Max.

"Yah, what about us?"

Marco told them, "You have two choices. I can try to get you the same deal, or you could run like hell and hope they don't find you. I've seen the evidence. Some of it is in the envelopes if you want to look. They can't prosecute me. I'm already dead. I guess the only ones they can go after are you guys."

"What guarantee do we have? What do we have to do?" Al asked.

"The same as me," he replied. "They wanted proof. First, I staged my own death. I'm sure you can figure that one out. Second, sell all your business dealings. That money will go to the hazmat cleanup in the ocean. Get out of the state, or better yet, out of the country where you can't be recognized by anyone. If you get caught, it will be an embarrassment to the people that I'm working with, and you don't want that to happen. Trust me."

Al asked, "How much will it cost us?"

Marco answered, "About a million bucks each, which will be donated from your estate to the Hazardous Material Cleanup Foundation led by David Ricci and Dr. Mary Cole. That is the kind of proof they want to see."

"What is wrong with this picture?" asked Al. "We are talking to a computer. I want a face to face with you before we agree to anything."

"I'm warning you, what you're about to see will be hard to believe," Marco said. "Remember what I told you would happen if you got caught. I have to live with this the rest of my life. Now go to the starboard side of the boat and take a look."

Just as they both stuck their heads over the boat rail, Marco jumped high enough to knock the cigar hanging from Al's mouth inside his brother's shirt. While Max was busy trying to get the cigar out of his shirt, it ended up in his pants. Al took a look over the rail again. Marco nodded his head up and down. Al could only say, "Son of a bitch."

Marco said, "I was lucky. They wanted me to be a walrus."

Al said, "Make the deal. We will send the money."

They both went running up the gangway to the car, Max trying to pull his pants up. Mary put her foot out, tripping Al as he ran by, followed by Max. They both fell down over each other. Mary said, "Whoops." They waited until the Luca brothers drove off, and then they gave each other high fives before heading down to Marco at the boat.

Marco was watching the whole thing from the water. Mary asked, "What the hell was that all about?"

Marco said, "I'm sorry for what they put you through for my indiscretions. I had no idea what was going on until David told me they had kidnapped you. Please forgive me."

"I was kinda hoping they would screw up. I have a spot for them in the walrus show at Sea Land."

"Did you see Mary trip them as they ran up the gangway?" David asked, smiling.

"Guess you heard some of it, Mary, but to summarize, we won't have to worry about the Luca brothers anymore." Then he explained, "Instead, we'll be receiving a two-million-dollar check from their estate sometime soon. Which reminds me, David. Call Frank and have him set up Hazardous Chemical Cleanup Foundation, so the Luca brothers know where to send the check."

Mary laughed. "That means we'll have more funds for the cove project. Maybe I'll have a couple of walrus pens available just in case the Luca brothers show up."

David, shaking his head, said, "How did you come up with such a plan? I was ready to give them everything to get Mary back. And here we are with Mary next to us and two million dollars for our programs."

"Remember you are overlooking the best part. The shutdown of hazardous material dumping and keeping drugs off our streets that are poisoning our young people." They both nodded their heads in approval. Marco told them, "I have to get back to the cove to Aaron. I'm worried about him. If you need me, that's where I'll be." He said goodbye to them and left.

While they walked up the gangway, Mary stopped and said, "I don't want to be alone tonight."

"I understand. I'll be right here." He kept holding her with occasional extra squeezes if to say "I'm here" without speaking a word.

While driving to her house, all of sudden, she said, "My phone. It's with the Luca brothers."

"We will pick you up another one tomorrow."

"But David, the DIP app is on the phone."

"Was your phone locked?"

"Yes."

"No problem. Those two goombas together couldn't figure out how to turn on your phone, much less how to crack the security code. Maybe you should stay at my house for a couple of days since it has a security system and I have to go back to MIT tomorrow."

She smiled and said, "Do you have coffee and any more eggplant?"

"I've something better than that."

"David, could we stop by my house, so I can pick up my car and some clothes?"

Once at Mary's house, David walked in first to make sure it was safe. While Mary was packing her clothes, David made a call to Frank to let him know how everything went down. He told Frank that the Luca brothers were not a problem anymore and gave him instructions to get started on the paperwork for the new foundation that will be called Hazardous Materials Cleanup Foundation. He also told Frank that the Luca brothers' estate would be sending over a two million dollar check to the foundation.

There was a moment of silence. Then Frank asked, "What the hell happened?"

"My father did something really good, and everyone should be all very proud of him. And he made them an offer they couldn't refuse," expressed David while laughing. I'm going back to MIT tomorrow for the final touches on the hazardous chemical program. I'll have more time for the cove project when I get back. We need to finish the pier in two months because my dad has something special planned. While I'm gone, if you need to reach my dad, call Mary, John, or Nicole. My dad will be in the cove with Aaron tomorrow."

Mary walked out of the bedroom.

"Are you hungry?" David said as he took her bag.

"All I want to do is relax with you...if that's okay with you. I think we both had a very stressful day." They walked to their cars. David followed her to his home. While driving, Mary noticed her handbag and a brown paper bag on her dashboard. She opened it and saw her phone with a note attached to it that said, "Sorry for the misunderstanding." She then called David.

When he saw it was Mary's number, he knew that it was the Luca brothers. *What do they want now?* Not giving them a chance to talk, he said, "What now?"

Mary tried to sound like a mob gangster. "Do you know where I can pick up some fresh sardines for my brother?"

He quickly figured out that it was Mary on the other end. "No, but I know a good veterinarian that can help you."

Mary laughed. "Your dad must have scared the crap out of them."

"Or maybe you did after tripping them."

"That was pretty cool, and it felt so good," Mary said, laughing again.

When they reached David's house, he opened the gate, and they both drove in. Walking into the house, they went straight out to the pool area. They sat in the patio lounge overlooking the ocean view.

"I'll bet by now you're ready for something to drink." He looked over to her.

"I thought you would never ask."

"What would you like?"

"Anything with alcohol in it. I would even consider rubbing alcohol right now," she said jokingly.

He knew what kind of wine she liked, so he poured two glasses of Pinot Grigio. Walking to the pool area, he noticed she had moved to the chase lounge for two next to the pool. He handed her the glass of wine and sat next to her, putting his legs out flat. The first thing she did was to smell the wine. He gave her a puzzled look.

She looked at his face, "I wanted to make sure you didn't take me seriously!"

"I've already learned that."

She then gave him a playful bump with her shoulder spilling his wine on him. "Whoops!"

He quickly jumped up to shake off the drink. He took off his wet shirt. Then he sat back down on the chase lounge next to her. She sat there with a smile on her face. David, not to be outmaneuvered, used one of Mary's sayings and in her same mannerisms. "What?"

"I was wondering how I was going to get your shirt off."

He just gave her a kiss. As the kiss lingered, she set her glass on the table so she could use her other hand to place it on his masculine torso. He felt her cold hand on his chest and did everything in his power not to jump. It was only when she started to laugh that he jumped. "Way to ruin the moment."

"I'll make it up to you later," she said. She then cuddled in his arms, and they just lay there, looking at the stars together. The stress of the day got to both of them, and they soon fell asleep.

When David woke up, he picked Mary up in his arms. She took both her arms and wrapped them around his neck. She gave him a kiss on the neck— the kind of kiss that says "Take me. I'm yours." He carried her to the bedroom, gently laying her down on the bed. She pulled him down on top of her as they rolled around from one side of the bed to the other. She ended on top of David, and before it got too intimate, she said, "Keep that thought. I'll be right back." She gave him a quick kiss.

While she was in the bathroom, he took off his clothes and slipped under the covers in anticipation of her return.

When the bathroom door opened, the first thing he saw was a lean firm leg that wrapped around the door jam. She then slid her leg up and down on the door jam, exposing firm thighs. She had dressed in one of David's shirts and in her deepest gangster's voice said, "I want to make you an offer you can't refuse." She posed with one arm high on the door, barely exposing her butt.

He couldn't keep his eyes off her as she slowly walked toward him with her long, blonde hair flowing off of her shoulders. His eyes grew bigger with each step, with a smile from ear to ear. With every step, David became more aroused. She finally arrived at the bed crawling like a tiger stalking its prey. As she was crawling to him, each movement exposed more of her chest. Once she reached him she pulled back the sheets, straddled him, and said, "I'm glad you are still thinking about me."

He slowly started to unbutton her shirt. Each button exposed more of her beautiful body. When he reached the last button, he said, "I definitely want a piece of this!" He then reached his hands behind her neck pulling her down gently until their lips joined as one. They made love like there was no tomorrow.

CHAPTER 17

SAVING WATER

The next morning, he woke up in a spooning position with her still asleep in his arms. He gently slipped out of bed, not wanting to wake her up as he went into the kitchen. Knowing how she liked her coffee first thing in the morning, he brewed some. Then he went to the refrigerator, pulling out bacon, eggs, and hash brown potatoes. It didn't take long for the smell of bacon and coffee to reach her, which woke her up. She went into the kitchen dressed in the same shirt. "Wow, I'm impressed!"

He handed her a mug and kissed her. "I told you I had something special for you."

She, as usual, had a quick reply, "I thought that's what we had last night."

"That was really nice. Every time I'm with you is special, but last night beyond special."

"Can I help you with anything?"

"Everything is almost done. How would you like your eggs?"

"Scrambled, but not too wet. I like them on the dry side," she said with a smile. Seeing his face, she then said, "What?"

"You're not making it too tough on the cook. No pressure."

While David was scrambling the eggs, she stood behind him, putting her arms around him. She definitely knew how to push his buttons.

"Okay, that's not fair. I can't defend myself. Now please go over to the table. Breakfast is being served."

"Okay, if I have to."

"I'm going to miss my flight." He gave her a gentle pat on the butt, guiding her to the table. While eating breakfast, he told her. "I have to go back to MIT for a couple of days. The recycling unit is done, and with its last test completed, they are shipping it to Florida in order to start recovering hazardous material from the dumpsites...which means no more trips to MIT. I'll be able to spend a lot more time here.

"That's great, David."

After breakfast, he went over the security system with her and gave her the remote to the front gate and garage.

He then started to clean up the dishes. She stopped him and said, "I've got this. I have to earn my keep." She returned the pat on the butt, led him out of the kitchen, and said, "Now go get ready. I've got this."

While doing the dishes, she could hear him in the shower, so she then stopped and headed to the steam-filled bathroom. Opening the door, she said, "I hear there is a water shortage, so to save water, can I share the shower with you?" She grabbed the soap and rubbed it over him so he was completely covered.

He couldn't take it any longer and gave her a kiss, using her body to spread the suds. "I hear there is a shortage of soap too." Then he turned her around, covered her back, and pulled her in close to his body so he could soap the front of her body with his hands.

Mary then used her butt to spread more soap on him until she felt he was ready. She then took the bar out of his hand and dropped it on the shower floor and said, "Whoops!" As she bent over to pick it up, they engaged in lovemaking.

After the shower, she said, "Look how much water we saved. We did our good deed for today."

He answered her by saying, "Every time I hear of water conservation, I'll remember this day." They both started to laugh.

He finished packing and gave Mary a quick kiss goodbye and said, "Now I really need to hurry. Somehow, I had a little delay. I'll call you tonight."

"I'm going to be at Sea Land all day. They're probably wondering what happened to me. If they only knew."

CHAPTER 18

AARON IS SPECIAL

Marco swam into the cove and saw Aaron sitting at the end of the dock, tossing his ball up and down. As he got to the end of the pier, he jumped high into the air so Aaron could see him. He could see the excitement on his face. "Nono!" he yelled out. He threw the ball high so Marco could catch it. It always made him feel good to see Aaron's smiling face. He toned his phone, so Aaron then turned on the app so Marco could communicate easier with him.

"I'm sorry I had to leave. I had to help David on my old boat. But we are done, so I'll be here for a while."

"My dad told me you had something to take care of and would be back soon."

"How are you feeling?"

"I'm great now that you're here."

Nicole come down to the pier. Seeing Marco back brought a smile to her face. "You're back. Is everything all right?" She looked over Aaron's phone for an answer.

"It went better than you could imagine."

"Is there anything that I can get you?"

"A good hamburger, but I don't think Mary would approve of it."

"You're right. Only a seafood diet for you." She chuckled.

He went on to tell her that the construction on the new pier would be starting soon. Then, with excitement in her voice, she said, "Mary asked me to be the coordinator for Make A Wish. I'll be in charge of coordinating all the children to come down to the facility. I'm really looking forward to that. Aaron said he would help me with the kids too. We'll make it a family affair."

It was great to see Nicole so happy after all the stress she had gone through the last month with her son's cancer return.

"Nono, do you want to play catch? Nono means grandfather in Italian," Aaron told his mom.

"I hope you don't mind. I wasn't trying to take anything away from Aaron's grandfather."

"We would be honored. May I call you Nono too?"

"Of course, you can. I'm relieved you don't mind."

"It's time for lunch, Aaron," Nicole said. "I might have a can of sardines in my pantry for you, Nono."

"No, thank you. I prefer fresh sardines since I can't have my hamburger." Nicole and Aaron laughed, and then Marco said, "Aaron, if you have a baseball bat, after lunch, bring it down."

Aaron cheerfully agreed. While they walked up to the house, Marco watched them holding hands and felt like he was once again part of a family. Since it was time for his lunch too, he left the cove to feed.

After lunch, Aaron came running down to the pier with a baseball bat and a ball. Marco said,

"Okay, Aaron, I'm going to throw the ball, and you are going to hit it."

Aaron looked down at the message. "I'm not very good at hitting the ball, but I'll try."

Marco threw the ball, but Aaron swung so hard he almost fell down, and he missed the ball. Aaron ran and got it and threw it back. It happened again and again with Aaron missing each time, but he would chase down the ball and throw it back.

After the fourth time, he put the bat down and said, "I'll be right back." He ran back to the house where he grabbed his mother and said, "Mom, we need you. We need a catcher." Dragging his mom down to the pier, he yelled, "Nono, I got a catcher." He instructed his mother where to stand. After everyone was ready for the next pitch, he missed the ball again and again, but so did his mom. Each time, Aaron dropped the bat and ran after the ball. Finally, he showed his mom how to catch the ball and picked up the bat again.

Marco patiently threw the ball again. Aaron connected and hit the ball over the dolphin's head. When he returned with the ball, he saw Aaron and his mother giving each other a high five. "I don't want you to overextend yourself. Come on in and rest and do your homework while I cook dinner." I haven't even started to get dinner ready. And I don't remember anyone doing their homework yet, so say your goodbyes to Nono."

Marco sent a message to him, saying that he wanted to talk to his mother. He handed the phone to his mom. "Nicole, when John gets home, I would like to talk to him."

The Dolphin In Me   Nick Miraglia

"I'll have him come right down. Thank you for playing with Aaron."

She walked with Aaron back to the house. On the way, Aaron questioned his mother on what was said. Nicole said, "Nono needs to talk to your father so he can do something for him."

"He could have asked me."

"I'm not sure, but I think it probably has something to do with a computer program. You'll have to ask him. Now off you go. Get cleaned up and get your homework done. Maybe when your father gets home, you can get a couple of innings in with a real catcher before dinner."

When John returned from work, Aaron was at the door waiting for him and said, "Dad, guess who is back? Nono!"

"Who's Nono?"

Nicole greeted her husband with a kiss as he walked through the door and said, "Nono is what we call David's father. It means grandfather in Italian. Before you get settled in, Nono is waiting for you at the pier."

John put his briefcase down and went to the office to pick up his laptop computer that he used to communicate with the dolphin. He then headed to the pier where Marco was waiting.

Marco popped up so John could see him. John set up his laptop on the end of the pier.

"Okay, I'm ready to go."

"Thank you again, John, for all your help. I don't know what we would do without you."

John answered by saying, "Every time I see Aaron's smiling face, I want to thank you. Without the

153

gift you gave him, he wouldn't have a chance to live another day. I will be forever grateful to you."

"That brings me to this question. When is Aaron's next doctor's appointment with his oncologist?"

"In two days,"

"Aaron is a very special boy. Without his trust in me, we might never be where we are now. I know in my heart that God has a special mission for him. Why else would his cancer just disappear with no medical explanation unless he has plans for him. The key to bridging the gap between sea animals and humans is with our children. And Aaron is our poster boy that will be carrying the torch for us. I can't believe Aaron would not be there."

"We feel so blessed to have Aaron as long we have, and we're ready for anything that may happen."

"John, I want to give you a heads up on what has happened the last couple of days. As you remember from the other day, the Luca bothers were causing some problems. They ended up kidnapping Mary for ransom until David signed over the business to them. Mary is all right." He went on to explain how they fooled the Luca brothers into thinking they had to pay two million dollars or else they would turn into walruses.

John gasped, "What, are you kidding me?"

"We won't have to worry about them anymore." He then went on to explain that they would be starting on construction on the u-shaped pier soon and that it needed to be completed in two months. He told John he had something special planned, and they were going to need everyone's help when the time came.

"You can count on the whole family. Nicole is excited about working with Mary and also with the kids in the Make A Wish program."

"I need one more thing of you, John. Is there any way to convert my human voice instead of using that computer voice?"

"That's a good question, but we need data of your voice to be able to do that, and you can only speak in dolphin language, so that wouldn't be possible," explained John.

"What if I had recorded voice messages from when I was human?"

John thought a minute and then said, "That might work. If you can get me the taped voice messages that you have, I'll see what I can do."

"I'll need you to call Frank and have him meet me here."

"I'll show Nicole how to use the DLP app on the laptop for Frank, so I don't have to be here...unless you need me."

"John, I have a good feeling about Aaron's doctor appointment."

"Thank you. That really helps." He headed back to the house.

At the house, John made a call to Frank. "Frank, this is John Sullivan. Marco needs you to get voice recordings of him, like voice messages from answering machines, and he wanted to talk to you at the pier tomorrow. Nicole will be there to help you with the laptop to communicate with him."

"Okay, John. Tell Nicole I'll be there at noon."

After he got off the phone with Frank, John asked Aaron, "Do you want to go down to the pier? I have to talk to Nono."

"Yes, can you play baseball with me and Nono?"

"Sure, go get your ball and bat."

Marco could see John and Aaron approaching. He jumped high in the air, showing his approval. Aaron then ran down to the end of the pier and threw him the ball. Then he instructed his dad where to stand. Marco flipped the ball to him and Aaron hit the ball over his head. Pretending he was on a baseball field and hit a home run, he ran around the bases.

They played ball until Nicole came down and said, "No extra innings. Dinner is almost ready."

John said, "I talked to Frank. He'll bring all the tapes from your office tomorrow at noon."

Marco nodded his head.

They walked up to the house; Marco found himself wondering how fragile the family was being held together by Aaron's fight against cancer. He only hoped that his presence there with Aaron would help him in his fight for his life. For the first time in a long time, he said a prayer, not for him nor for something that he wanted, but for Aaron to be free of cancer and never have it come back again.

CHAPTER 19

DAVID'S PLAN

At Sea Land, Mary was greeted with questions from Zoe. They had been trying to reach her. "Is everything all right?" she asked.

"I'm sorry. I lost my cell, and when I found it this morning, I came right to work. Is everything all right here? Thank you for covering for me." To change the subject she then asked, "How are the twins doing?"

"Mother is fine, and the twins are good and both are feeding," replied Zoe.

"If you guys don't mind, I would like to name the twin walruses Max and Al."

"But only one thing is wrong. Did you forget it's a boy and girl walrus?"

Mary put her hand on her forehead and said, "I guess it will be Maxine and Al." They then walked to check on the mother and her babies.

David was at the MIT lab, finishing up all the paperwork and getting ready to ship everything to Florida. He had to make a quick trip back to his house to pick up more clothes and take his car back home. Later that night, he called Mary to see how everything was going.

When she answered, she was sitting on the poolside chase lounge, winding down from a long day at work. "You know I was just thinking about you."

"I hope it's good thoughts."

"Oh yeah, I'm sitting on the chase lounge by the pool. Capire!"

"Your Italian is getting better. Yes, I got it, boy do I get it. Are you feeling safe at the house?"

"Yes, but it would be better with you here."

"I'll be home in a couple of days," he said. "I have to go by my house to pick up more clothes and bring my car back with me. I'd better get going. I'll call with an ETA when I get close."

"Drive safely; I've got plans for you."

"I can't wait," he replied as he said goodbye.

He went back to his house and piled his clothes in his car, trying to figure out what he needed. The weather was so much different from Maine to Florida. He finished packing and pulled out of the driveway. He looked at his sailboat still there, right where he left it when Mary first came to Maine to get him to go come back with her to Florida. How times had changed. If it wasn't for all the work ahead of him when he got to Florida, he would hook up his sailboat and tow it back with him. He could imagine Mary under his arm, sailing off into the sunset.

While he was driving, all the thoughts of times he spent with Mary flooded his mind—everything from their first date where she dropped her keys and they kissed to the last time when they were saving water in the shower. Those were exciting, passionate, and erotic, but what kept him smiling was her quick wit and her sense of humor. She had a way of making a bad day good.

He thought about holding her in his arms as they looked at the stars and when both of them stared at the microwave waiting as she hummed the *Jeopardy* theme song. He loved how she would give him a wrinkled forehead and say "What?"—her favorite expression when she wanted to make a point.

While he was thinking those thoughts, he decided to turn the tables on her. He formulated a plan that had all the elements of what he was feeling— the closest thing he could do without saying "I love you." In his mind, actions spoke louder than words. Words were so easy to say, but when love came from the soul, it meant much more.

CHAPTER 20

LUCA BROTHERS LOST AT SEA

It was noon when Frank came to the front door. Nicole greeted him. He gave her the tapes from Marco's office and then they walked down where Aaron and Marco where playing catch. She set up the laptop for Frank and said, "Let's leave them alone to talk. It's time for lunch." She walked with him back to the house.

"How is it going, old friend?"

Shaking his head, Frank said, "I'm doing fine, but what the hell happened with the Luca brothers?" Frank reached into his briefcase, pulling out a newspaper. He started to read. "Accident takes the life of two prominent businessmen, Al and Max Luca, after their boat capsized offshore while on a fishing trip. The US Coast Guard conducted a search for the men, but failing to find their bodies, they have suspended the search operation and the brothers are presumed dead. The Luca family's attorney announced the brothers contributed a substantial amount of money to the Hazardous Material Cleanup Foundation because of their love of the sea."

He showed Marco a check for two million dollars from the Luca estates and asked, "How the hell did you pull that off?"

"I made them an offer they could not refuse."

Frank shook his head while laughing and said, "I'll bet you did."

Marco asked him if he brought the tape recordings.

Frank told him he gave all the recordings that he could find to Nicole. Frank then gave Marco an update on all of the projects. He said, "David is just about done with converting the boats to recover the hazardous material, and we were able to get grant money from MIT to help, so we're able to divert more money to the cove project. Mary is working with the architect in designing the facility. The most significant update is that Senator Johnson has expedited all the permits needed for the pier and is working on a joint venture with us that will be starting this week."

Marco then told Frank it was important that the pier be finished in two months, the start of the full moon, and that he was planning on something special. He had already told the pod of dolphins it would be in two moons. By using the moons, the dolphin pod would know when to come to the cove. Frank said, "I've been assured by the contractor that it would happen. Everything is running smoothly. I'm getting a lot of response from different organizations that are wanting to help with the cove facility."

"That's great. Good job." Marco could see Frank looking at the computer, still uncomfortable looking at him.

"If anything comes up, I'll be in touch." He packed up the laptop and headed for the house. Nicole greeted him and asked him if he'd like to stay for lunch. He gave her the laptop and told her he had another appointment and asked for a bottle of water instead. Frank told her construction on the pier was going to start within days. Then he said goodbye.

After lunch, Aaron headed back down to the pier. His mother reminded him that he had to go to the lab that afternoon for the test for his appointment with Dr. Bailey the next day. "So don't stay more than an hour with Nono."

"Okay, Mom." When Aaron reached the pier, he told Marco that he could only play for a little while because he had to get the test for Dr. Bailey. Marco nodded yes. As they played ball, Marco could only think of how the test would turn out. After a while, Nicole came down to get Aaron. As she looked at Marco, he gave her a nod as if to say, "Everything is going to be all right." She smiled as they walked away.

CHAPTER 21

THE SURPRISE

As David made the long drive to Florida, he pulled over to answer a message from Mary. He didn't want to talk to her. He was afraid of giving away his surprise by saying something to tip her off.

She texted him back, "If you are reading this while you are driving, then you are in trouble!"

He took the bait and called her.

"I didn't want to distract you while you were driving."

"I pulled off the road, so I wouldn't be."

"That's a good thing. I need you in one piece."

"How is everything going today?"

"You're not going to believe what happened at work. Remember the night when I got kidnapped after delivering the twin walruses? I told Zoe that I would like to name the twins Max and Al. But there was one problem; one of them was a girl. So Max is now Maxine. I'll tell you about that when you get home. Okay, break is over. I need a hug, and the only way that's going to happen is to get yourself home."

"I'm looking forward to that and maybe a kiss."

"Maybe something more. See you soon."

After they hung up, she reflected on what she said about coming home. It sounded so natural as if they were a married couple and she was waiting for her husband to return. She never had a soulmate before. She thought, *Is this what true love is all about? We have a very strong physical attraction and an emotional one as well. It is all happening so fast, sometimes I can't even catch my breath.* She wanted to tell David how she felt, but those three little words stood in the way. She didn't want to scare him away by being the first one to say I love you.

David merged back onto the highway. He also felt security with the relationship. When he heard her say "I'll see you at home," it melted his heart. It felt so natural, and he really felt they were on the same page, not in a physical way but an emotional way. The more time they spent together, the more his feelings were confirmed. She is my soulmate. The surprise he planned could seal the deal.

To avoid driving all night and to keep his surprise by not arriving too early while she was still at home, he stopped at a hotel so he would arrive in mid-morning. After a couple of stops to pick up what he needed the next morning, he was home unpacking the car.

He called Frank to see if he was needed for anything. Frank updated him on all the events, including the Luca brothers being lost at sea.

He started to laugh but gained his composure and said, "I can't believe they staged being lost at sea. Wait until Mary hears how they staged their deaths. She was hoping they would be reincarnated into walruses so she could pay them back."

"I set up the Hazardous Material Foundation trust account. I need you to come by the office in the next couple of days to sign the two-million-dollar check so I can deposit it into the trust account."

After getting everything out of the way so he could concentrate on his surprise, he sent a message to Mary that he was home and that he had picked up some steaks for dinner. He also asked what time she would be home.

"Steaks are good," she said. "Should be home around five o'clock unless something unforeseen happens at Sea Land, or maybe I get kidnapped. I will call you if I'm going to be late."

"If there is any kidnapping, I'll be the one kidnapping you."

She always had the last word. "Whoa, I like the sound of that."

While he was getting everything ready for his surprise, he could not help but notice Mary's clothes in the closet, her perfume filling the room, and other toiletries on the bathroom counter neatly placed on one side.

Everything was ready for her. He kept looking at his watch and checking his cell for messages. When he heard the security system beep that the front gate was opening, he quickly took his position, awaiting her arrival. She stepped out of the car. Seeing his car with Maine plates, the excitement made her heart race. She opened the front door, but when he wasn't there to greet her, she was a little disappointed until she saw the trail of red rose petals leading to the bedroom. She followed the trail, losing one of her articles of clothing every few feet until she was at the bedroom door with only her bra and panties left on.

She took the hair clip from her hair, letting her long, blonde hair flow over her shoulders. The red rose petals led right up to the bed, covering it like a blanket with David lying in wait for her. On the other side of the bed was a pillow with a single long-stemmed rose. She slowly walked over to the bed, slipping one bra strap over her shoulder and the other over her other shoulder and then unsnapping her bra from the back. Next to the bed, she let her bra fall to the floor, exposing her firm breasts, and she picked up two petals, placing them on each nipple. Then without letting the rose petals fall to the floor, she slowly rolled her panties off one leg at a time until they fell to the floor. With a quick kick of her foot, she flipped her panties at his face without losing the rose petals.

Still not a word was spoken as she slowly knelt on the bed, arching her back, trying to see if she could reach without losing her rose petals. After the first movement of her knee, she lost one of them and then the other. "Look, I lost my pasties!" She slowly worked her way up until she was on his chest giving him a kiss. The kiss lingered, and he slowly rolled her over, so he was on top as she was lying face down.

He reached over to the nightstand picking up massaging oil. Putting oil on his hands to warm it up, he started with her neck, working down her shoulders and then down to each arm, only stopping when he reached her fingertips. He then started anew on her neck. He started down her spine, working all the way to her buttocks, only stopping when she would say, "Right there." He massaged each leg, stopping a little longer at the arches of her feet. While he worked his way back to her neck, he couldn't help himself by sliding his fingertips under each breast as he worked back. Once he reached her neck, he kissed her as he gently rolled her over on her back until their lips touched.

Placing his finger on her lips, he said, "Now the fun starts." He reached over to the nightstand again, putting more massage oil on his hands. He started back on her neck, sliding his hands down and massaging each shoulder. Then he slid his hands down to the side of her breasts and gently massaged each one. He kissed each nipple as his hands worked their way down each side of her leg. He could feel her body quivering as his hands moved to the inside of her thighs.

She said, "All right, I give up." She reached up grabbing his neck and pulling him down on top of her. They made love, but it was not an out-of-control lovemaking but a sensual lovemaking.

Feeling each other's emotions and acting upon them, they rolled from one side of the bed to the other, picking up the rose petals as the massaging oil made them stick to their skin like postage stamps. It wasn't until they finished, and their bodies molded into each other's arms that they noticed all the roses on the bed were all over them.

Mary could not help herself. She reached over, picked up the long-stemmed rose lying on the pillow, and said as if they were on the reality show,

The Bachelorette, "David, will you accept this rose?"

"Not until you get rid of all the rose petals." He started laughing and pointed to all of them on her skin.

"Look, I'm blooming." As she settled down in his arms with her head on his chest, she said, "I felt that I was in your soul."

He gave her a gentle squeeze. "I know things are moving fast and we have a physical chemistry that is insane, but we've been thrown into this relationship because of my father's mission. I want to explore outside of all that. I want to know about you and where we're going with this relationship." He held her even tighter in his arms.

"I would like that." She buried her head into his chest.

While they lay there, all of a sudden, her stomach started to growl.

"Excuse me."

He started to laugh. "I'd better feed my lady."

Uncoiling their bodies, they got out of bed and headed to the kitchen. She picked up each article of clothing saying, "Whoops, whoops." Laughing, David continued to the kitchen, and she went to the bathroom. He pulled out steak and lobster tails from the refrigerator and then went out to barbecue them.

As he was cooking, Mary came out, looking as beautiful as ever. Putting her arms around his waist, she said, "What can I do to help?"

"How are you with making a salad?"

"You'll see. By the way, I like my steak medium—not dry and not bloody."

David gave her a puzzled look.

"What? You want to know me." She gave him her cutest smile.

"Like the scrambled eggs...dry but not too dry and definitely not wet."

She winked. "You got it!"

While eating their dinner, he said, "You know all about me and my family, the good and bad. I want to know all about you and your family."

"Well, I'm not a serial killer."

He couldn't help himself. "You might want to talk to the Luca brothers about that....By the way, I forgot to tell you that I talked to Frank today, and he read me the front-page headlines that the "prominent business brothers" were lost at sea and presumed dead. Also, they had left a sizable contribution to the Hazardous Material Cleanup Foundation."

"They'd better hope they don't come back as walruses, or they'll have wished I was a serial killer by the time I'm done with them."

"Sorry, Mary, I didn't mean to sidetrack you." He reached over the table to touch her hand.

"I lost my father about five years ago. He was helping a little, old lady who blew a tire. A car didn't see him changing the tire and swerved to miss hitting a dog running across the road. It hit and killed him.

"I'm so sorry."

"You would have liked my dad. He spent 29 years in the fire department and was planning his retirement when it happened." She wiped the tears from her face as he hugged her. "My mother was devastated; he was her whole life. To this day, she has never dated, and she is a beautiful woman too. She plays golf three days a week with her girl-friends, and the rest of the time she volunteers her time with environmentalists."

"Do you have any brother or sisters?"

"No, I'm pretty much the spoiled brat. We talk all the time. She lives about an hour away. She has been on a month-long cruise with her golf girl-friends to Europe. I told her about you."

"When she gets back, I would be honored to meet her."

"Be careful of what you wish for. My mother is a handful."

David asked, "Who are the biggest influences on your life?"

She thought a minute before saying, "Both of my parents. My dad was a paramedic on the fire de-partment, so on being a veterinarian, I would say my dad. But spiritually, emotionally, and for my love of nature, it's my mom."

"Your mother must be very proud of you."

That brought a smile to her face. "When she calls me at work, she always asks for Dr. Mary Cole." She went on to express how hard it has been to keep their secret from her.

"That's something I love about you. You put eve-rything first before your own interests. I can trust you above all."

After dinner, he told her he had one more sur-prise for her, but she had to wait until the morning.

The next morning, she asked him what she should wear. He told her to dress casually and bring her bathing suit. As they pulled into the marina, he parked the car and pulled a picnic basket out of the trunk. He then took her hand as they headed down to the boat docks. They didn't stop until they reached a thirty-five sailboat. He took her hand, helping her onto the boat. "Welcome aboard, my lady."

"It's my first time on a sailboat."

"I can't believe you have never sailed before."

"My father would either take me fishing, or we would be going water skiing. And at Sea Land, the research vessel is powered.

"Well, I plan to change that."

He started the engine, and without any hesitation, she went right to the front and cast off the line. "Never been on a sailboat, huh?" he said while casting the aft line.

"What? It's a boat!"

He just laughed. They motored out of the slip to the open sea. He then had her steer the sailboat as he set the sails, and they were underway. He turned off the motor, letting the wind fill the sails. He sat down next to her and took over the helm. The only sound was the water hitting the hull and the wind against the sails.

"How relaxing this is," Mary said, leaning back against him.

"I love the ocean. This is what it is all about. Setting the sail and just letting the wind be your guide." David looked at her and gave a quick kiss as they sailed off.

After a while, he opened up the picnic basket, pulling out two glasses. He went down below and came back with a bottle of Champagne. Popping the cork, he poured the two glasses and made a toast. "Here is to your first sailing trip."

She returned the toast, holding up her glass and saying, "Here is to our first but not our last sailing trip." They sailed off into the sunset.

CHAPTER 22

AARON'S CANCER

At Aaron's house, everyone was getting ready to see Dr. Bailey that morning for the result of Aaron's test. Aaron came down to the pier to see Marco before he left for his appointment. Marco told him that everything was going to be all right and not to worry. As Aaron was looking and reading the text from his cell phone, he nodded and smiled at Marco and said, "I don't want to be sick anymore."

Nicole and John walked down to the pier, worry on their faces as they told Aaron that it was time to go. With the three of them together, Marco nodded his head as if to say, "It's going to be okay."

They walked back to the house, John and Nicole holding Aaron's hands. Aaron turned around and said, "I'll be back in a while."

All Marco could do was to tone his cell and text, "I'll be here waiting for you."

At. Dr. Bailey's office, both parents sat in the waiting room, worrying what the test results would show. John was so nervous he couldn't sit still, so he paced the floor. He didn't want Aaron to become anxious, so he sat down again. Nicole was calmer but anxious as well. When the nurse opened the door, she called them to follow her. She didn't take them to an examination room but to Dr. Bailey's office. She then said that Dr. Bailey would be right in to see them.

John and Nicole looked at each other with concern. Nicole's eyes started tearing up, thinking the worst.

When the door opened, Dr. Bailey came in and greeted everyone with a smile on his face. Seeing Nicole's eyes, he knew that he should explain why he had them in his office. "All of Aaron's tests came back negative. I even had them run again with the same results. It's as if he never had the cancer, and I can't explain it either. That's why I wanted to talk to you to help me figure it out."

Nicole could not hold back the flood of tears, hugging Aaron, her husband, and finally Dr. Bailey. "When we came to the office instead of the examination room, we were expecting the worst," she said as tears of joy flooded from her eyes.

Dr. Bailey said, "I'm so sorry. I didn't mean to scare you." He then went on to explain. "I wanted to find out what changes you made in Aaron's daily routine. Eating habits? What changes did you do to help Aaron? In all my years, I have never seen such radical changes from terminal cancer, to remission, to terminal cancer, then to not a trace. If we could find out what was causing that, it would change how we treat cancer."

John said, "Working with the dolphin at Sea Land with Dr. Mary Cole, Aaron got to interact with the dolphins through Make A Wish Foundation. In fact, Dr. Mary Cole is working with the state to provide funds for opening the rehabilitation center for all the sea animals. Nicole is volunteering with the children from Make A Wish. The new facility will be opening within a year, but the kids are getting to work with the dolphins at the new pier adjacent to the center in two months."

"But, were there any other outside influences or diet you used on Aaron?" Dr. Bailey seemed skeptical.

"No, just a steady diet of working with the dolphins," Nicole replied. "I could put you in touch with Dr. Mary Cole. She can give you more detailed information on the study she is doing."

"I would appreciate that. If working with dolphins helped Aaron, I would like to pursue any and all possibilities."

"I will have Dr. Cole get in touch with you."

Dr. Bailey handed Nicole his card.

"Does this mean I'm not going to be sick again and lose my hair?" Aaron asked.

"You'll be like all the other boys," Dr. Bailey said. "Let's follow up in two months just to make sure."

After saying goodbye, Aaron and his family left the doctor's office to go straight back home, and once they reached the house, Aaron took no time to run down to the pier, followed by his parents. Marco could see Aaron running with a big smile on his face that said it all. He jumped high into the air to show the joy he was feeling.

Once Nicole and John reached Aaron, John pulled out his phone and said, "You were right. Aaron is a special boy. All of his tests came back negative!"

Marco sent a message to John's cell. "I know now that God has special plans for him."

"Can I play baseball on a team now?" Aaron asked.

"We'd better practice if you want to make the team. Now run up and get the ball and bat," John said as he patted Aaron's back.

Aaron ran back to the house. John and Nicole thanked Marco again for saving Aaron.

"I believe it was a miracle," Marco said. "I know that Aaron is special and there is more to come that involves him." Marco felt his mission was about to end, but Aaron's was about to start.

Nicole then told Marco that Dr. Bailey asked what changes were made with Aaron's daily habits and diet that made such a dramatic change in his cancer and put it into total remission. "I told Dr. Bailey that we went to Sea Land with Make A Wish, and Aaron got involved with the dolphins in the park. I told him I was volunteering to help with the children from Make A Wish when the new facility opens within a year and that I would have Mary get in touch with him for more details on her study. I hope that it was okay to say that."

"Yes, of course. You did the right thing because I'm planning something special that fits right in with what you told Dr. Bailey. We'll let Mary work her magic with your doctor."

John then told Marco that the voice recognition project was coming along, and they would be ready in a couple of days.

"Great news. That will make it more personal when I talk to everyone—especially Frank because every time he hears the computer voice his eyes get bigger and bigger."

While Marco was speaking with Nicole and John, Aaron came down, carrying his baseball bat, ball, and glove. Then they all played baseball until it was dark.

That night after dinner and when Aaron was in bed, John and Nicole sat in the living room going over all the events of the day from lows to the high points of the day. Then John said, "Did you hear what Marco said that Aaron's mission is just starting?"

"Yes, what is that all about?"

John shrugged his shoulders and said, "I'll talk to him and find out." He reached over to her, giving her a hug. He then said, "We got our boy back, cancer free!"

She nestled into his shoulder, giving her husband a squeeze and nodding her head without saying a word. It was an emotionally draining day, but for the first time, they would go to sleep knowing that their only child would live a normal life. The fear of the cancer coming back was gone. "I know now that God has special plans for him." What those plans were was yet to be answered, but Marco hadn't been wrong yet.

CHAPTER 23

NEW CHAPTER IN MARY'S LIFE

The next day at work after their sailing trip, Mary had a new and excited outlook on her relationship with David. She had an unmistakable glow on her face. Zoe said, "It looks like someone had a good day off."

"A very good day off."

While they were doing her rounds, she pulled Zoe aside and told her that she had a once-in-a-lifetime opportunity to open a rehabilitation center and that she had a meeting later in the day with upper management to tell them she was going to be cutting back on her hours until the rehabilitation center opened.

Mary said, "I'm going to recommend you for my position as the head marine veterinarian."

Zoe stopped in her tracks, overjoyed that she might be taking over Mary's position, and said, "Oh, my God, thank you so much for even thinking of me. I will be forever grateful."

"Because of all the night classes you took to get your degree along with your many years being my right hand, I feel good about your chances." Mary gave Zoe a hug. "I'll let you know after the meeting."

As they continued their rounds, Mary got a call. It was her mother, Elaine. Mary told Zoe to continue and she would catch up with her, expecting the call might take some time since Elaine was back from her month cruise to Europe with her golf group.

"Hi, Mom. How was your trip?"

"It was fantastic—but long—and it's good to be home. I got your message that you're seeing some-one named David. So, how is that going?"

"Mom, every time I'm with him, it gets better and better. How did you know that dad was the one?"

There was a pause, the question catching her mom off guard. "Your dad made me laugh and put up with all my crazy moments, and he knew how to get into my soul. That's when I knew he was my man, but your father had no idea what he was about to get into."

She thought for a moment before asking her mother, "Who said the three magic words first?"

"Your dad, of course. He was the romantic one. I can still remember that day. That is when he touched my soul. Why are you asking these ques-tions? I think we need to have a mother and daugh-ter chat."

"I'll have to call you later, Mom. I have to finish my rounds."

"Okay, Dr. Mary, but we need to talk. Love you. I'll talk to you soon."

Mary let out a big sigh after confirming her feel-ings about David. It was almost scary how similar it was to the relationship that she and David shared compared to what her mother and father had. Walk-ing to catch up to Zoe, her head was filled with thoughts of what her mother said.

She got a message from David that said, "Good morning, beautiful Dr. Mary. How is my sailing mate doing today? The *Angelina* is ready for the first hazardous material recovery. Just a few things left to do. Call you later, beautiful."

"Okay, mate. I'll put another shrimp on the barbie. Why is it when you say sailing mate it sounds like I should be in Australia?"

"What?"

She started laughing as she had no reply for that one. She remembered her mother said her dad made her laugh.

After finishing her rounds, she had the meeting with upper management where she told them she would be leaving Sea Land to pursue her dream. Mary explained the once-in-a-lifetime opportunity to do what she had always dreamed of doing. She told them she would work with them on any animal they could not handle. It was a rehabilitation and education center.

She went on tell them about Zoe's performance during her tenure as her assistant, going to night school to finish her degree, and how they couldn't find a better candidate. She also explained she would work part time until the rehabilitation center was finished and help with the transition to fill her position.

They understood what a fabulous opportunity it was for her and also agreed to promote Zoe to her position.

After the meeting, she called David to tell him what she had done. She said, "I did it, David! I started a new chapter in my life. I told upper management that I would be leaving to start the rehabilitation center but I'd stay on a limited time until the center is completed. I can't thank you and your dad enough for the opportunity to fulfill my dream. And, that being said, can I steal you away for lunch? I'm buying."

"How can I refuse that."

"Of course, it's a free lunch."

He shook his head and laughed and said, "All right, I'll meet you in an hour at that Italian restaurant where we had our first date. That's where it all started."

After talking to him, she found Zoe to let her know about the meeting. Mary could see the anxiety in her mannerisms, so with a smile, she said, "Congratulations, you got the position."

Before she could say another word, she found Zoe hugging her while jumping up and down. "Thank you, thank you!"

"It's just a formality, but they still need to interview you. Keep it under your hat until it is official."

"I will; I promise you." She gave Mary another a quick hug.

"I know you're going to do a great job. Just pretend that I'm at a seminar. At any time, if you need help or just need someone to talk too, I'm only a call away. I'd better go. I have to meet David for lunch."

Zoe, still glowing from the news, said, "Have a nice lunch. Take your time. I've got you covered."

During lunch, David and Mary both received a message from Nicole and John saying that Aaron's tests came back negative and he no long had even had a trace of cancer. They looked at each other and smiled. David texted back, "We're at lunch together. That's great news. We will see you after we finish."

Mary put down her phone, her eyes full of tears. David grabbed a napkin, wiping them away. "Nicole and John have to be overjoyed that Aaron's cancer free and will live a normal life. I can't imagine what a roller-coaster ride of emotions that they've gone through. I can't wait to see them. Can we go over there now?"

"Sure, I'll ask the waiter for our check."

While they waited, David told Mary they needed to talk to his dad to inform him that they will be starting hazmat cleanup the next day. "I'll be at the recovery site for at least two days, and then I'll be back home. Once I get my crew settled in on the recovery procedures, I won't have to be there all the time. I'll be working on the boat tonight and then taking off early in the morning if everything goes according to schedule." As he looked into Mary's eyes, he asked, "What do you have going on?"

"I'm meeting with the architect for the new facility and making the final touches. Then I promised my mother we would get together. She's back from her European cruise. I know my mom will want to stay overnight, so I have to go to the grocery store and buy some food."

David quickly jumped in to say, "You should have your mother stay at my house."

"Thank you, David, but I want my mother to meet you first to see how nice you are before she sees our love shack." While he laughed, she took his face in both of her hands. "God, I miss you already." She then gave him a quick kiss and said, "We'd better leave to go over to see Aaron and your dad."

CHAPTER 24

PIER UNDER CONSTRUCTION

Arriving at the house, it didn't take long before Nicole and Mary were hugging each other with tears of joy running down their faces. David greeted John with a handshake, and they held it together a little better than the girls did. After they dried the tears off their faces, they went down to the pier where Aaron was playing catch with Nono. Aaron saw David and Mary. He ran over and gave them both a hug and then told them that he was going to try out for the baseball team. He asked them, "Do you want to play baseball with Nono? That's Grandfather in Italian. That's what I call your dad."

Nicole said, "Okay, Babe Ruth, someone hasn't finished his homework."

John, Nicole, and Aaron went up for lunch. Mary walked up to the edge of the water and turned Marco over to check him out and then said, "How's my favorite guy doing? Are you feeling okay, and are you getting enough to eat in the cove? I can bring some fresh sardines, or how about a hamburger?"

"What? Are you turning me into a fast food junkie?"

"How are you doing, Dad?" David reached over to put his hand on the side of his dad's head.

David looked at the computer for the answer. Marco said, "Fine, except for the pilings for the new pier they are pounding into the sand for the last two weeks."

Hearing his dad's voice instead of the computer voice was a surprise. "It's your own voice I'm hearing…It's nice to hear your voice again, Dad."

"I had John change the voice to help give a personal touch for everyone, especially Frank."

"Well, here is your chance to get away from the noise for a couple of days," David said. "We're starting the hazmat clean-up tomorrow at the dump site, and I will be there."

"I could use the break, for sure."

"Mary, did you talk to Nicole about what she told Dr. Bailey?" Marco asked.

"Not yet. I'll talk to her before I leave."

"By next full moon, we need all the children from Make A Wish to be at the new pier. I have something special planned. That is why we have to make sure the pier is finished."

David nodded his head. "Okay, I'll make sure it gets done on time. Frank has assured me that the contractor said it will be done, and the state has cut all the red tape to make it happen."

On the *Angelina*, he had put under-water microphones and speakers so they could communicate when they were at the hazmat site without anyone knowing.

Marco told David he had better get going so he could make it on time to the hazmat recovery area.

David then said, "I will be looking for you there, Dad."

"Don't stay in the area too long," Mary said. "Make sure not to eat any fish in that area either. I don't want my first patient in the new rehabilitation center to be you."

"Yes, Dr. Mary."

Mary asked, "What name are we going to use for the Rehabilitation Center?"

"Good question. I've been thinking about The Dolphin In You. Maybe the words will have a symbolic meaning, bridging the gap between the dolphins and humans."

"I like it." David looked at Mary who nodded her head in agreement.

"I have got to go," said Marco. "Say goodbye to Aaron for me. Tell him to practice while I'm gone so he can make the baseball team."

At the house, Aaron had just finished his homework when Mary and David walked inside.

"Nono just left so he could help David at the hazardous site. He said to practice while he was gone so you can make the baseball tryouts," Mary said.

Aaron ran outside in time to see Nono leave the cove and yelled, "Bye, Nono. See you in a couple of days."

David had to go. He kissed Mary goodbye, gave both Nicole and John a hug, and told Mary he would call her later.

Mary sat down with Nicole, asking about what she had said to Dr. Bailey. Nicole told Mary the question Dr. Bailey had asked about any changes in Aaron's diet, habits, or anything else that changed. Nicole said, "I told him we went to Sea Land with the Make A Wish Foundation and he interacted with the dolphins. I told him if he wanted or needed any more information he should call you. He said in all his years, he has never seen a patient go from terminal cancer, to remission, to terminal cancer, and back into remission in such a short time. I hope I didn't say anything wrong."

"No, in fact, you helped by putting the word out that we are planning something special for Make A Wish kids this month." She then added, "In fact, you will be helping me set up everything for that day. I'll talk to Dr. Bailey and let him know what is happening on the medical side. I'll have him call you to set up how many patients he would like to invite. There is a lot of work to get done in a short period of time."

"I'm ready for the chance to help, and Aaron will be helping too. He is our poster boy."

Nicole gave Mary Dr. Bailey's business card as they exchanged hugs.

Mary reached down, kissing and hugging Aaron goodbye.

CHAPTER 25

THREE MAGIC WORDS

On the way to the architect's office to finalize the plans for the new rehabilitation facility, Mary called Dr. Bailey's office and left a message with his receptionist to give her a call regarding Aaron Sullivan.

Mary than called her mother to see if she was free for dinner. Elaine didn't pick up, but texted back. "I'm playing golf with the ladies. I'll call you back when I'm finished."

She texted back, "Are you free for dinner at my house around 5 p.m.?"

"See you then, Dr. Mary."

Mary knew that she was going to be drilled with questions by her mother about David. Also, she hadn't told her about quitting her job at Sea Land to start up the new rehabilitation center. She had to come up with something to tell her mother that made sense without disclosing the truth about David's dad being a dolphin. It was going to be tough.

Mary didn't have any close friends. Most of her time was spent at work or out to sea working on the research vessel. Her mother was her closest friend, and she had a hard time keeping secrets from her. She practiced what she was going to say until she reached the architect's office.

After going over the last final plans, she told the architect the name of the rehabilitation center would be The Dolphin In You Rehabilitation Center. Giving it a name would put some realism to the fact that it was really happening. After leaving the architect's office, the next thing was to get ready for her mom. Everything in the refrigerator was old or out of date because she had been staying at David's house. A quick stop at the store would give the appearance that she was living there and everything was normal.

While Mary was getting everything ready for the arrival of her mom, the doorbell rang. It was her mother with her suitcase, as expected, and a couple bottles of wine. "Hi, Mary." Mary took the wine bottles so she could give her a hug. "It's been a while since we spent some time together, so I hope you don't mind I brought a suitcase to stay overnight."

"Of course. We have a lot to talk about. So much I have to tell you." Mary took her mother's bag. She said, "I'll put your bag in your room, and you open a bottle of wine from the refrigerator."

As they sat on the patio overlooking the water, Elaine said, "Okay, tell me all about David, and don't spare any details."

"Well, where do I start? He is tall, dark, and handsome. He reminds me a lot of Dad."

"In what way?"

"Great wit. He treats me like I'm his best friend, and he makes me laugh." She added, "And, most importantly, he puts up with all my little quirks. We share the same ideals in so many ways that it's scary. He never ceases to amaze me by doing special things that I have to keep pinching myself to make sure this is really happening."

Elaine could see the sparkle in her daughter's eyes—the true joy that she felt for David. "Where did you two meet?" Elaine reached for another sip of wine.

Mary was prepared for that question. She didn't like lying to her mom, but she had no choice. "In Maine, at a small art gallery where David was showing his paintings. David is a gifted artist, and I was looking at one of his paintings went we met. We talked over a glass of iced tea. He told me that his dad had recently passed away in Miami, Florida. He told me he had to settle his father's estate and asked if he could take me out to dinner when he was there. We've been seeing each other ever since."

"His profession is an artist?"

"No, I'm sorry, Mom. He paints on the side as a way to express himself. He's a chemistry professor at MIT and is working on a project that takes chemical waste and turns it into clean energy."

"I like him already." Elaine poured more wine for both of them.

She explained how they found a huge hazardous chemical site off the coast that someone illegally used to dump drums of industrial chemical wastes. "In his will, David's father wanted to start a foundation to clean up an area like that, but David took it a step further by removing the chemical waste and then turning it into clean energy. In fact, that is where he is right now, at the site, recovering the chemical drums."

"You know I read about two prominent businessmen lost at sea that gave a large sum of money from their estate to a hazardous chemical foundation."

"That foundation is David's." She was doing everything she could not to laugh so as not to give away the truth about the Luca brothers. "That is the same foundation that David started for his father."

"You'd better latch onto that boy, or I will. I can tell by the way you talk about him that there's love in the air."

"But that is just the half of it. There is more." Mary then said she would be right back.

When Mary came back, she unrolled the drawing that David drew of the new rehabilitation center. She then told her mother that money from David's father's estate was to open a new rehabilitation center for all marine animals.

After spreading out David's drawing, her eyes filled with tears. She could not hold them back and started crying.

Elaine quickly hugged her daughter and asked, "What's wrong?"

"David filled my lifelong dream—a rehabilitating center for all the sea creatures that are sick or injured. And after they are rehabilitated, then we return them back to the sea not to be exploited. It will also be used as a research center too. I'm going to be running it."

Now both mother and daughter were crying tears of joy. After they both stopped crying, Mary went on to explain what all the different areas of the facility were, showing everything she had designed.

"Your dad would be very proud of you." Mary could only nod her head to keep from crying again.

They were looking over the drawing of the facility, Elaine couldn't help but notice seeing the man looking down from the hillside. "Who is that?"

Still tearing up, she explained that it was David's father looking down on it with his approval.

"The facial expression said it all. You are right. David is a gifted artist. It reminds me of a Norman Rockwell painting. You should have David make a big painting to hang in the facility."

"You should see some of his other paintings. They are just incredible."

"Okay, when am I going to meet him? I promise I will be on good behavior."

"Too late. I've already warned him about you."

"What did you tell him?" Elaine asked with her hands on her hips.

"That you are a handful, and it's because of you that I'm a spoiled brat," Mary replied.

"That was your father's fault. You were his princess," Elaine said as she smiled.

Mary went on to tell her mother about the surprise David did with the rose petals—leaving out all the toe-curling moments—and about her first time sailing with him.

Elaine said as only her mother could do, "Well, did you seal the deal?"

"Mother. What kind of woman did you raise?"

Elaine raised her eyebrows.

"What?" Mary blushed, looking at her smiling mother.

"Okay, it was absolutely wonderful. We have this physical chemistry, like two magnets, as soon as we get too close to each other. But it's more than that. We have bonded our heart and souls together."

"That's why he has a PhD in chemistry." Elaine asked, "How does David feel?"

Mary told her, "When we were on the sailboat, David told me that we have an insane physical chemistry, but he wants to explore the other part of our relationship more."

Elaine said, "Okay, now the earlier conversation makes sense. Who is going to say the three big words first? Sounds like you two have a lot on your plate. Maybe a slow and steady course is the best."

Mary answered, "That is what Dad would say. What would you do, Mom?"

"It's like poker. When you have a good hand, you go all in."

"Are you hungry? I have Chinese for dinner."

After dinner, Elaine told Mary all about her cruise.

Mary's phone rang. It was David. "Your ears must be burning. I'm sitting on the patio with Mom, talking about you."

"I sure would like to be a fly on the wall right now."

"I bet you would." She laughed.

"Is it okay to say hello?"

The request caught her by surprise. "Okay, do it at your own risk." She handed the phone to her mother.

"Hello, this is Dr. Mary Cole's assistant. How may I help you?"

David started to laugh. "Now I know where Mary gets her humor. I just want you to know what a wonderful daughter you have raised and how special she is to me. I'm looking forward to meeting you soon."

David's kindness left Elaine speechless. All she could say was "I'm looking forward to it as well." She handed it back to Mary with a blank stare on her face.

"You've left Mom speechless," Mary said.

"I'll let you go now, so you can get back to your mother. I miss being there with you."

"Me too. I'll call you tomorrow and let you know what's happening out here." She hung up.

Elaine said, "Did he say the magic words? I heard you say me too."

"No, he just said that he wished he could be here."

"He was so nice over the phone. I didn't know what to say. All I know is you'd better set the hook right away on this one. No catch and release on him." She gave a wink as she finished her wine.

"I know, Mom, but I don't want to rock the boat by going too fast."

"It sure sounds like you both are on the same page to me." Elaine raised her eyebrow.

"Would you like to look at the location of the new rehabilitation center tomorrow?'

"Yes, I would love to. Have you come up with a name yet?"

"The Dolphin In You."

Elaine gave her the look of approval. "How did David come up with the idea of the rehab center?"

Mary was not prepared for that question. She needed more time to figure out how to explain David's involvement in the center. She was never good at lying and just making something up off the top of her head. Her mother would know something wasn't right.

"I'm tired, Mom. I had a long day. I'll tell you about it in the morning on the way to the new rehab center. It will all make sense when I tell you the whole story." She reached over and kissed her goodnight. "I'll see you in the morning."

"Meet you at the coffee pot." Elaine headed to her room.

After going to her bedroom, Mary lay on the bed with her hands over her face. She didn't like deceiving her mother, her best friend. She lay down on the bed and came up with a plan. She texted John and Nicole that she was bringing her mother by and gave them a quick idea of what she was going to tell her so that everyone was going to be on the same page.

CHAPTER 26

HAZARD SITE

The next morning, Marco could see the *Angelina* at the dump site already getting ready to start recovering the drums of chemical waste that had been dumped over the years. To not be noticed, Marco went under the boat to see if he could communicate with David. He let out the appropriate tone and clicks. "David, are you there?"

After a couple of attempts, he could hear David's voice say, "Dad, I hear you loud and clear."

"How is everything going?" The underwater communication system was working better than expected.

"Everything is good, but some of the drums are leaking. You'd better not stay in the area too long. Remember what Mary said, Dad. Be careful."

"It looks like you've got everything in hand. There is not much I can do. I feel so helpless, David, just watching you clean up my mess."

"That's okay, Dad. We will be here for a couple of days, making our first load. I will have my assistant trained by the end of the trip on how to handle all the different types and how to categorize them."

"I understand about the leaking drums. I'll return to the cove unless something comes up."

"I think that is best. No need for you to stick around, especially with the condition of the drums. I'm pretty much off the boat after this trip."

"Thank you again, David, for all you're doing. I know if anything happens to me, between you and Mary, the two of you will carry on my mission. I don't know how much time I have left or what is going to happen to me next, but to know you both are there, I will pass in peace."

"It's a team effort, Dad. You'd better get out of here before you get sick."

Marco said his goodbyes; he couldn't help but feel the close relationship that he had developed with David and how proud he was of him. He wished he could have done better with him when he was human.

Making the long trip to see Aaron gave him time to think of what was in store for him next. Was he to remain a dolphin for the rest of his life or when the rehab center was complete, would he just pass in the night? It was so strange to have no control or know what was going to happen next. That was the hardest thing. He had a mission, and his mission was just about over.

CHAPTER 27

ELAINE HEARS ABOUT AARON

That morning after breakfast, Elaine and Mary started to drive to the rehab center. Mary started to explain her prepared answer to her mother's question from the night before. Mary said, "I'll answer your question of who's idea it was for the rehab center. It started out when I was on my research vessel, the *Sea Odyssey*, when we got a distress call from a lobster fisherman who found a dolphin that was attacked by a shark. He told how the dolphin saved a little boy from the shark. When we got there, we were able to keep the dolphin alive and bring him back to Sea Land to rehabilitate him to be used in the dolphin shows. This was a very unique dolphin like I have never seen before. He had a white star on his forehead, and once he was fully recovered from his injury, we tried to put him with the other dolphins in the show. You could talk to him and give him a command, and you would swear he would understand you like he was trained before.

"There was a group of kids from Make A Wish Foundation at the dolphin show. When the dolphin saw the little boy, it went crazy, and for the boy's safety we had to shut down the show. The little boy was crying hysterically, saying that was his dolphin.

"Later on that evening, the same little boy was caught breaking into the dolphin pool, looking for the same dolphin when the security guards found him without his parents. He refused to tell anyone his name until he could see his dolphin. Security called me for help. I made a deal with the little boy. If I showed him the dolphin, he would tell me his name and where we could find his parents.

"The boy's name was Aaron, and he was with the group of Make A Wish kids. Aaron had terminal cancer. Once the boy and the dolphin saw each other, it was like how a dog reacts when his owner has been gone. When the boy's parents came to pick up their son, they told me that Aaron was rescued by a dolphin from a shark. It was the same little boy that the lobster fishermen told me that the dolphin saved. While he was with the dolphin, his cancer went into remission. After the shark attack, he was separated from the dolphin, and his cancer returned. It was by chance that they were there at the dolphin show."

Mary started to fan her eyes, but the tears started to flow.

Mary's mother handed her a tissue and said, "There'd better be a happy ending to this story."

Mary's tears were flowing as she tried to catch her breath. "After a month with the dolphin again. Aaron's cancer went into complete remission." Now both were crying. Mary had to pull over to the side of the road to regain her composure.

"What is the explanation, Mary?"

"We have no medical explanation for this. There have been some studies that show working with the dolphins releases certain hormones like serotonin and endorphins. All of those hormones are nothing more than chemical reactions taking place inside our bodies. Each and every emotion we experience is a result of the release of certain hormones. Some hormones are responsible for making us feel good, some are responsible for making us feel bad, and some others are responsible for the feelings we get when we fall in love with someone.

"Aaron's dolphin is very special, and we are working on a theory that the release of these hormones is fighting the cancer. In fact, part of the rehab center is dedicated to such a study. We are partnering up with Make A Wish Foundation to help kids like Aaron in their fight against cancer. Would you like to meet Aaron?"

"Yes, after hearing the story, you bet I do."

The rehab center is in the same cove that Aaron's home is. I'll give Aaron's mother a call to see if they're home. Nicole is our coordinator and is working with kids from Make A Wish."

Arriving at the rehab center, they could see that the U-shaped pier was under construction. Mary was greeted by the contractor who was overseeing the job. After introducing her mother to the contractor, Mary told him she was amazed how fast everything was coming together. She could see they were already pouring the slabs for part of the center along with dolphin pools. "Yes, we're ahead of schedule thanks to Frank Goldstein's connections cutting out all the red tape," expressed the contractor.

Mary could see it was really happening. She could see the pride in her mother's face too. Her mother said, "If only your father could see what I'm feeling right now, he would be so proud of what you have done."

"I've got the feeling he knows, Mom."

After looking over all the new construction, Mary gave Nicole a call to see if she was home. She turned to her mother and said, "Are you ready to meet Aaron? They're home."

"Yes, I would love to."

After they left the construction area, Mary felt bad in deceiving her mother by not telling her the real story about Aaron, but she had no choice in the matter.

CHAPTER 28

MARCO MEETS ELAINE

When Marco arrived at the entrance to the cove, he could see the end of the pier where Aaron was waiting for him right on cue. He swam over, gave Aaron a splash, popped up next to him, and gave him his patent flip for good measure. He could see Aaron laughing, which made his heart feel good.

"I'm glad you're back. Mom wanted me to tell you that Mary is on her way over with her mother to see us. Mary's mother doesn't know about you other than you live in the cove and play with me. I have to put away the laptop and cell until she leaves." Marco nodded his head to let Aaron know that he understood. Aaron then said, "I have to let Mom know you're back, and I'll bring my ball and bat in case they want to play baseball with us." Marco had to chuckle over Aaron wanting to play baseball with Mary's mother.

When Mary and Elaine arrived at the house, both Aaron and Nicole were waiting for them at the front door. Mary greeted Nicole and Aaron with hugs and introduced her mother, Elaine, to them. As Elaine reached down to Aaron, she said, "I've heard all about you, and it's a pleasure to meet you."

Aaron said, "Do you want to play baseball with my dolphin?"

His request took everyone by surprise, but Elaine said, "Sure, why not? It's not every day I can play baseball with a dolphin." Aaron grabbed Elaine's hand and pulled her out the back door, down to the pier.

While Elaine and Aaron were on their way to the pier, Nicole told Mary that Aaron understood they were coming over to see him and he was not to use the cell phone or laptop until they left. Mary laughed and said, "Okay, like playing baseball with a dolphin is normal." They both made their way down to the water.

Marco was watching the house. He could see Aaron pulling a stunning looking woman down to see him. He assumed it was Mary's mother. He could see the resemblance and knew where Mary got her good looks.

Once they reached the end of the pier, Marco popped up, so she could see him and not be afraid. Aaron introduced them. Marco nodded his head. Aaron encouraged Elaine to shake a flipper. "It's so good to meet you, Mr. Dolphin. I hear that you have some special power."

At that moment, Marco felt her hand and a warm feeling came over his body. Not to spoil the moment, he just nodded his head with clicks and tones that a normal dolphin would make.

Then Aaron said, "Okay, batter up!"

He handed Elaine the bat and threw Marco the ball. Marco could see what a good person Elaine was as she played along with Aaron. She took the bat, swinging it around and around and then pointing to the center field bleachers as if she was in a baseball stadium just like Babe Ruth did when he hit the famous home run. Elaine said, "Okay, Mr. Dolphin, let's see what you've got." So Marco threw her up a nice easy ball, and she blasted it out over his head. As Marco was retrieving the ball, Elaine was already running the bases, giving high fives to everyone. Getting caught up in the excitement and not to miss out on all the high fives, Marco pushed himself out of the water so Elaine could give him a high five too.

Mary said, "You all just got snookered! My mother used to play in a woman's softball league."

Mary got a call from David. She explained that they were playing ball with everyone at the pier. She told her mother that David called and would like to take them to dinner. Mary said, "So I guess we'd better get back to the house and get ready."

Then Elaine said, "Oh, are you coming too?"

"Yes, Mother. He might need some protection from you." After Mary and Elaine said their good-byes, they walked back to the car.

CHAPTER 29

DINNER WITH ELAINE

While driving back to Mary's house, Elaine expressed how wonderful it was meeting everyone and that Aaron was amazing. She said, "What a special boy he is, and the dolphin and Aaron have such a special bond between them. Now all the things that you told me about them makes sense." Mary nodded her head. "Now, where is David taking me for dinner tonight?" Elaine asked.

Mary looked over at her mother, shaking her head and said, "You mean us. He didn't say where he will be taking us, but if I had to guess, it would be somewhere special, and he said he will be by at 7:00."

Then without hesitation, Elaine said, "I didn't bring anything nice to wear for dinner."

Mary looked over at her mother and said, "We're both about the same size. I'm sure I'll be able to find something for you to wear. Preferably it will cover you from head to toe. And by the way, promise me you will be on good behavior."

"Moi?" replied her mother.

On the boat, David was thinking about where he was going to take Mary and her mother. Then it became perfectly clear. David was quite nervous. It was the first time he ever met a woman's mother that he was in a serious relationship with. Mary had already told him about her mom and dad and what a special relationship they had. He wanted her mother to know how special Mary was to him. On the way home, he picked up a nice bottle of wine and stopped at the florist to pick up some flowers to give Elaine.

When he arrived at Mary's house, his heart was racing as he pushed the doorbell, but when the door opened, he saw Mary and everything was calm again. Mary gave him a quick kiss and then took his hand and walked over to the couch were her mother was sitting. Mary introduced him. He immediately handed Elaine a dozen yellow roses and gave Mary the bottle of wine. Elaine was taken aback by the flowers. Her eyes were full. Mary knew what the flowers meant to her mom. Her dad used to give her mother yellow roses. Mary tried to lighten the subject by saying, "I'll take the flowers, Mom. I'll trade you for a glass of wine."

David opened the bottle, and Mary brought three glasses for him to pour the wine in, giving David a hug around his waist to say thank you.

Mary put the flowers in a vase. Elaine was still sitting on the couch when David handed her the drink. "Thank you, David, and thank you for the flowers. They're very special to me."

"You're welcome, and it's a pleasure to finally meet you in person," said David.

By then, Mary joined everyone on the couch. Sitting next to David, she proposed a toast as she held up her glass. "Here is to David's first successful retrieval of the hazardous materials."

David said, "And to finally meet Elaine. Now I know where Mary got her beauty from."

Elaine said, "I guess it's my turn. Here is to David for giving my daughter the opportunity of a lifetime to do something really wonderful. Now let's drink."

"That's my mom."

Not to let her daughter get the last word in, Elaine said, "What? My arm is getting tired holding up this glass, and I'm thirsty."

David laughed out loud as Mary and Elaine both said at the same time, "What?" Realizing what they had done, they started to laugh along with David. After the laughter subsided, David said, "Now I know not only did you get your beauty from your mom but also your sense of humor."

After the laughter again subsided, Mary told David about taking her mom to the new facility and over to meet Aaron and Nicole. Getting off the couch, she demonstrated how her mother held the baseball pose pointing to centerfield and swirling the bat around and around like Babe Ruth did in the game hitting the famous home run over the center-field bleachers. "Then she trotted around the bases giving high-fives even to the dolphin. What my mother didn't disclose was that for many years, she was in a woman's softball league."

Elaine sat there with a sheepish grin on her face like the cat that swallowed the canary. She said, "I saw how special the relationship is between Aaron and the dolphin. You could write a book on Aaron's amazing fight against cancer. Tell me, David, was this a lifelong dream of yours to build the facility and to clean up hazardous waste?"

"Yes and no," expressed David. He went on to explain that he was the messenger. The movement came from his father's wishes. He was working on the theory of how to recycle hazardous waste into clean energy at MIT University. He also explained how his father, who passed away, gave him the funds available to start the facility at MIT. "That's when I met Mary and saw the wonderful work with the dolphins...and how Aaron's story came to my attention. It has snowballed from there. This is what my father would have done if he was still alive. Today marks the first day that we successfully retrieved the hazardous waste from the ocean so we can recycle it."

"Now that's something to toast," Elaine said as she held up her glass.

"I'd better get you ladies something to eat before we have any more toasts. We might not be able to find the restaurant."

Mary asked, "Where are we going?"

"Somewhere very special to me."

They left Mary's house, Mary on one arm and Elaine on the other. They started to walk to David's car when David stopped and said, "Maybe we'd better walk just in case we have any more toasts. Plus, with a beautiful woman on each arm, why would I want to drive?" Both Mary and Elaine gave him a kiss on a cheek.

After about a twenty-minute walk, Mary stopped when she saw what restaurant they were headed for.

She gave David a glance and then David said, "I told you it was a special place."

Mary told her mother that is was where their first date was. And then she said, "Whoops!" Both David and Mary started to laugh.

David said, "That was special too!"

Mary told her mother it was an inside joke. Elaine, not letting that go by said, "You know I didn't just fall off a turnip truck."

"Okay, it was our first kiss," replied Mary.

"Are you sure it was just a kiss?"

"Mother," replied Mary.

David said, "I think we better go get a drink."

After two more bottles of wine and an uneventful dinner with a lot of laughter, they made their way back to Mary's house. Once they arrived at the house, Elaine thanked David for dinner and a wonderful time and gave David a hug and a kiss on the cheek. Elaine said, "I'll leave you two lovebirds alone. I'm going to turn in." Then she said, "Whoops!" giving both of them a wink and a smile as she headed to her bedroom.

Mary shook her head as her mother went by and she watched her mom's bedroom door close. She then turned around with her arms around David's waist. She pulled him in close and gave and him a long, slow kiss. "I've been waiting for that all night," David said as he pulled Mary in even closer.

"I've got more where that came from," Mary said as she looked up at David, giving him a wink.

"I'll bet you do," David said, grinning from ear to ear. "But it will have to wait. I have to go back to the boat tonight. We're leaving early in the morning. Plus, I don't want to give your mom the wrong impression."

Mary said, "Are you kidding me? Did you see her give the wink and say whoops on her way to her bedroom?"

David replied, "You and your mother are so much alike."

Mary pressed her breasts on David's chest, and she got on her tip toes until she reached his lips for a passionate kiss. After the kiss, she said, "Well, if you have to go, this will give you something to think about while you're gone." She knew just how to turn him on.

He shook his head and said, "Wow, that's a lot to think about."

She smiled as she walked with him to the door, gave him a goodbye kiss, patted him on the butt, and told him, "Be safe out there."

After taking a few steps toward the car, he stopped and turned to look back at her. Seeing her in a seductive way with one foot on the door jamb, teasing him, he turned and headed back to her. When he reached her, he gave her a toe-curling kiss that left her speechless. Then he said, "Touché," and headed back to the car.

Mary watched until he was out of sight. Then she walked in the house, shutting the door behind her. She leaned back against the door with a big, "Wow!" When she saw her mother's light on in her bedroom, she walked over and knocked.

Her mother said, "Come on in." As Mary entered the room, her mother asked where David was. Mary told her he had to go back to the boat because they were leaving early in the morning, and he didn't want to leave with the wrong impression of him. Elaine patted the bed for Mary to sit down.

"What do you think of David?"

"Oh my God. He is too good to be true. All I've got to say is, honey, you'd better set the hook on that one. Did you know about the yellow roses?"

"Nope."

"Did you ever mention to David that your dad would always give me yellow roses?" asked Elaine.

"No!" exclaimed Mary. Both of them sat on the bed shaking their heads in amazement. "That's just David," Mary said. "Every time I think I know him, he comes up with something that just blows me away….Just like tonight. I tried to do everything to have him stay over, but he didn't want to leave you with the wrong impression."

Elaine said, "Everything?"

"You want me to tackle him?"

Elaine's farcical expression said it all.

"Really, Mom?" Mary then told her how David started to the car, stopped, and came back to give her a kiss that curled her toes.

"Was it unprovoked?" asked Elaine.

"Well, I might've helped a little bit. I'm worried it might be just a physical relationship….I just don't know. Again, just when I think I've got him figured out, he does something that throws me for a loop."

"I guess the three magical words have yet to be spoken by either one of you," surmised her mother.

"No, that's what makes me feel like it's a physical relationship." Mary's eyes started to tear up when all of a sudden, a text message arrived. "I'm

211

safely at the boat. Looking forward to seeing you tomorrow. XXOXX."

"See what I mean?" expressed Mary as she showed her mother the text. Mary reached over, giving her mother a hug and kiss saying, "I'll see you in the morning. I have a lot to do in two months before the opening up of the pier for the kids."

"Can I help?" asked her mother. "I'll be out of here by the time you set the trap for David tomorrow night."

"We will talk about it in the morning. Goodnight, Mom."

CHAPTER 30

NERVES OR MORNING SICKNESS?

In the morning, Mary's mother was up early to cook breakfast. It wasn't until the aroma of the bacon frying in the pan that Mary woke up. Elaine saw Mary looking like she had not slept all night. "Did you have a tough night?"

"How could you tell?" Mary asked.

"Let me see—blood shot eyes, bags under your eyes, and you overslept."

"Too much vino," answered Mary as she took a sip of coffee.

Elaine handed her a plate of bacon and eggs. One bite and Mary suddenly pulled from the table and ran to the bathroom. Concerned, her mother followed her. Mary began to throw up. The first thing that came to Mary's mother's mind was morning sickness, but she didn't say a word other than "Are you all right, dear?"

She got a face towel wet and handed it to her.

Mary stood up and said, "That's a first. Maybe it's from not getting enough sleep and too much vino."

"Too much vino or too much David."

Mary, wiping her face, said, "I think I'll skip breakfast."

Elaine told her she would clean up the kitchen while Mary got herself together. When her mother left the room, Mary could not help but think what caused the sudden urge to throw up. It had to be all the nerves from thinking about David and the pressure of getting everything ready for the opening of the new pier in a week. Mary's phone rang. It was Nicole asking what time the meeting was. Mary told Nicole that her mother volunteered to help, and they should be there around 11:00. When Mary got off the phone, she told her mother they needed to get going.

Elaine said, "I've been ready. I'm not the one praying to the toilet gods this morning."

"Toilet gods? Really, Mother?"

Elaine didn't let her daughter get the last word and said, "Whatever!"

CHAPTER 31

OPENING DAY PLANS

At Aaron's house, Nicole went out to the pier where Aaron and Marco were playing catch. Nicole told Aaron and Marco that Mary and her mother were on their way and for Aaron to put his computer away until Elaine had left. Then Nicole headed back to the house to meet the ladies when they arrived at 11:00. Aaron told Marco he would be back after Mary's mother left. He then headed to the house too.

Marco was left all alone. He was anxious to speak with Mary to see if everything was on schedule, and he needed to go over a few things with her. He needed to talk to David as well.

When Mary and Elaine drove up the street, Mary noticed a truck on the property next to Nicole's house. As they drove by, the sign on the truck said Florida Architect & Survey Co. That was the same architect company working on their rehabilitation center. Mary told her mother about the coincidence as they got out of the car. Walking up to the front door of the house, they were immediately greeted by Aaron, who went to Mary's mother and said, "Elaine, or is it Babe Ruth? I watched the Babe Ruth story on TV last night and saw the famous home run. Do you want to play baseball with Nono and me?"

"Who is Nono?" asked Elaine.

Nicole said, "That is the dolphin's name."

Aaron interrupted and said, "It means grandfather in Italian."

Elaine answered, "Well, I need to help your mom for opening day of the pier. But afterword, maybe we could sneak in an inning or two."

"That would be great."

Mary asked Nicole what was going on next door. Nicole told her that someone bought the property, and the company was surveying for the property lines. Mary said, "It's the same architect we use for the center. For a minute, I thought they got lost. Do they know about the rehab center?"

"How could they not? The parking is complete, and they're framing and plumbing. They have to know something is going on there. Come on inside. I made lunch. I have a lot of exciting things to tell you," said Nicole.

They sat at the table. Nicole took out of the oven a tuna casserole. Mary said, "That smells delicious, and I'm starving!"

Elaine said, "Sure, I spent this morning making you breakfast you threw up and now you can't wait to eat lunch."

"Are you all right?" asked Nicole.

Mary told Nicole about introducing David to her mother. "I was a little hung over this morning."

"David is such a nice man," said Nicole.

Elaine interjected, "And a hunk too."

"Mother!" exclaimed Mary. "What's the good news you have to tell us, Nicole?"

Nicole said the word had gotten out about the center. They were overwhelmed with requests for children to come to the pier, and it had turned into a nightmare for scheduling. Mary addressed it by saying, "We can have two sessions—a morning session and an afternoon session so we can accommodate everyone. I'll talk to David about it today."

Nicole explained she had great responses from sponsors who wanted to donate wheelchairs and hydraulic lifts so they could lower the handicapped kids into the water. "They will be installing lifts this week before the opening of the pier."

"That's fantastic," expressed Mary.

Elaine interjected, "Is there anything I can help you with?"

"Yes, I want to do some sort of snack for the kids along with something that they could take home with them," responded Nicole.

Elaine asked, "How about if we had some cute, stuffed dolphins for the kids?"

"That would be wonderful," Nicole answered. "We'll need about 200 for this first round. I'll give you our account number so you can go ahead and order them. Make sure we can get them before the opening of the pier."

Mary asked if there were any other issues they needed to deal with.

"No, that's it," expressed Nicole.

"All right, thank you. I'll leave you two to work out the details. I'm going down to the pier and check the dolphin out while I'm here. I'll be back soon." It was a good chance to get away from her mother and talk to Marco.

CHAPTER 32

WHOOPI GOLDBERG

Marco was waiting by the pier. As she got close, he jumped into the air so she could see him. Then he heard her say, "I see you." She took out her cell so she could communicate with him, and if her mother saw her, it looked like she was on a call.

Mary kicked off her shoes and sat on the pier with her feet dangling in the water. Marco popped up next to her, putting his head on her lap. "I don't care if I'm dating your son. You're still my guy."

Her cell phone started to translate what Marco was saying. He asked, "And how is that going?"

"What was David like growing up? It seems like every time I think I've got him figured out, he surprises me with something else. I mean in a good way."

"I'm embarrassed to say that David pretty much was raised by his mother. She had a great influence on his life, and she taught him when you put your mind to it and work hard, you can accomplish anything."

Marco looked up at Mary's eyes. He saw a puzzled look. She said, "I guess you know that I'm smitten with your son. I just don't know how he feels."

Marco could see Mary's concern in her eyes. "When you got kidnapped by the Lucci brothers, I've never seen David more concerned or worried about anything in his whole entire life. What David is short on his words. He makes up for it in

To him, actions mean more than words. And his actions tell me he is also smitten with you."

The smile came back to Mary's face. "Thank you."

"Not to change the subject, but can you have David come down? I need to go over something with you both."

She nodded her head. "Nicole told me response has been overwhelming for the kids. I told her we could split it up into a morning session and after-noon session if that is okay with you."

Marco asked, "Can we do it in two days? Would that work for you?"

"Yes, we'll be able to get all the kids in that are signed up."

"We'll keep doing it every month on the full moon. That way the dolphin pods know when to come to the cove. And we'll keep doing it as long as the children keep coming." Marco looked toward the house. "Your mother is coming."

Mary put down her cell. Aaron was with her.

Aaron asked Mary, "Do you want to play base-ball with us?"

"Sorry, I have to go over to the rehab center and talk with the architect, but I will leave Babe Ruth with you."

Aaron then handed the ball to Elaine and said, "I get to bat first this time, Babe."

Elaine saw Mary sitting with the dolphin next to her and said, "Excuse me, but I have to talk to my pitcher." As she sat next to Mary, holding the ball in one hand and the other reaching out to touch the dolphin, she said, "Go with the fastball right down the middle." Holding the dolphin's face and handing him the ball, she suddenly dropped it. A warm feeling had come over her. She had a flashback of her late husband as if the dolphin was him.

Mary saw her mother's face and said, "Mom, are you all right?" It looked like she was in a trance.

"I'm okay. Let's play ball!" As Elaine got up and went back to her position of catcher, she then said to Aaron, "Okay, let's see what you've got." Aaron took the baseball bat and swung it around and around, imitating what Elaine had done the last time they played. He pointed it to the center field bleachers. Marco then pitched the ball and Aaron hit it over his head for a home run. Mary watched to make sure her mother was okay, giving Aaron a high five as he rounded the bases.

Mary asked her mom again, "Are you sure you're okay?"

"I'm fine. Go play with your architect and pick me up when you're done."

Mary shook her head and said, "Okay."

After a couple of turns at bat, Elaine called time out. She wanted to interact with the dolphin again before Mary came back to see if she would have the same reaction as before. As she walked to the edge of the pier and sat down, Aaron followed her, sitting down next to her. She asked Aaron to call the dolphin over.

"He will come to you. Just call him."

Marco heard the whole conversation and saw the reaction she had to the first time they touched. He was curious to see what she was feeling. He reached her and did the same as he did with Mary, putting his head on her lap.

She touched his head and jumped, and Aaron said, "Don't be afraid. He likes you."

Marco could feel Elaine start to relax as she reached down with her hand, giving him a quick touch on his head as if touching something hot. She said to Aaron, "I can feel a warm feeling and a peacefulness over my whole body."

Aaron reached over and touched his head and said, "Feels normal to me."

Just then, Mary showed up and said, "Hey, quit flirting with my guy."

"Mary, touch his head, and tell me if it feels normal."

Mary, sitting next to her mother, reached over to feel his head. "Oh my god! You're right. It feels like a normal dolphin." Both Aaron and Mary had a good laugh. "Okay, quit molesting Nono. We have to go."

The only ones not laughing were Elaine and Marco. He also felt a warm, peaceful feeling as if he was in her heart when she touched him. *What is going on?* he thought. As they walked away, he could see Elaine glancing back.

After saying their goodbyes to Aaron and Nicole, they headed back to Mary's house. As they were driving, Elaine was quiet as a church mouse. Mary said, "All right, let's talk about what happened back there."

"No," replied Elaine.

"I promise not to laugh, dolphin molester," said Mary.

"See what I mean!"

"Okay, I'm sorry, Mom. Please, you saw me at my worst this morning."

"You promise?"

"Yes, Mom." Then Mary started to worry if she had to explain how David's father was the dolphin. How would her mother react?

Elaine explained when she touched the dolphin the first time, she got a warm feeling, and she had a flashback, seeing her husband's face, and a peaceful feeling came over her. She said, "After you left, I sat down on the dock with Aaron and the dolphin. He came by himself and put his head on my lap. At first, I jumped a little, but then I touched him with both my hands to the face like I used to do with your father, and tears started coming down my face. I again got that warm, peaceful feeling like not a care in the world, but this time there was no flash-back. I felt the power of the dolphin like I was in your father's soul."

Mary listened to her mother. She had to pull over to the side of the road to console her. They both just held each other until the tears stopped. Mary said, "I'm so sorry, Mom. I had no idea what went on."

Her mother took both of her hands, holding her daughter's face and her forehead until they touched, and said, "I know, Mary, but it was so real. It was like your father letting me know that everything is okay, and I felt so at peace."

Her mother was still holding her face. She pulled back to look eye to eye with her mother. "Maybe Dad's spirit was using the dolphin to let you know that he is at peace, and he wanted you to know.

Look what the dolphin has done with Aaron. Where is Whoopie Goldberg?" she said laughing.

"We'd better get going. You have your big date with David tonight, and I have to go home before the traffic gets crazy," Elaine said.

CHAPTER 33

THE TRAP

On the boat, David was supervising the last couple of hazardous material barrels to come up over the deck. He told the crew, "Okay, we'll wrap it up for today. Time to head home."

He received a call from Frank Goldstein telling him that he needed to come by the office because they had gotten a full-price cash offer on his house, and they wanted a thirty-day escrow. "Wow," replied David. He told Frank that the boat's ETA back to the dock was around 6 p.m., and he would be there around 6:30. After hanging up with Frank, he let out a big sigh of relief. One more thing he didn't have to deal with.

He was looking forward to seeing Mary, especially after the goodbye kiss she gave him last. He texted that he would be a little late and explained he had to go by Frank's office and then to his house. He would call her when he had a better idea of what time he would be by to pick her up for dinner.

Mary replied, "To save time, I'll make dinner at the Love Shack. That way we'll have more quality time together without you running around. Plus, I have special plans for you tonight. XXOOXX!!!!!"

"I like the way you're thinking!"

Mary had the last word. "By the way, the O in XXOOXX is not a hug."

That put a smile on David's face as the excitement of seeing Mary intensified. No need to reply to that text.

Mary arrived at her house with her mother. After her mother gathered her things, she said, "I will be back tomorrow to help Nicole with the preparations for the kids." She then kissed Mary and said, "Remember to set the hook tonight!"

"I'm going to snag him," replied Mary.

"That's my girl!" Elaine headed toward the door, giving Mary a wink.

Mary helped her mother to her car where she took one of Elaine's yellow roses and said, "I need one for bait."

Elaine smiled and said, "I've got the feeling David's not gonna know what hit him." Mary gave a quick kiss to her mother and watched her drive away.

Mary had a new feeling of confidence after talking to David's father about what David went through when she got kidnaped.

If action means more than words to David, she was going to give him something to think about. She gathered her belongings together to get ready for the big night.

On the boat, David went over everything with his assistant so they would be able to handle the rest of the hazardous material pick up without him. He had a lot on his plate with the grand opening of the pier and the selling of the house. The last thing he needed was to be out there. Plus, he really missed being with Mary, and since his house had sold, David was confronted with a new problem. Where was he going to live? Traveling back and forth from Maine was not an option. Putting all questions behind him for the moment, his main concern was getting back to see Mary. To save time, David decided to shower and get cleaned up on the boat so when he arrived at the dock, he could immediately go to Frank's and get all the paperwork signed.

Mary stopped at the store to pick up everything for dinner. After arriving at David's house, she made preparations. She had really never cooked for a man before except for David the night she made beef stroganoff for him. She had to try something different. She settled on making spaghetti—something easy and fast. She wanted to spend much time with David and not while cooking. She put all the ingredients in a pot on high. Remembering what David did with the rose petals leading to the bedroom, she planned something similar but with a twist. Instead of rose petals, she put a trail of her clothes. For the final touch, she put on a very sexy nightgown—all white with a garter belt that held up white silk nylons. The top accentuated her body in an elegant but sensual way. Lying on the bed, she held in her hand one of the yellow roses that David had given her mother. As she practiced how she was going to lay in the bed, she fell asleep.

CHAPTER 34

DINNER WAS HOT AT THE LOVE SHACK

David arrived at the dock, immediately jumped off the boat, and headed for Frank's office. At the office, David signed all the papers and noticed that outside of the sale price, they wanted to negotiate the furnishings. Frank told David to make a list of all the things that he wanted to keep. David agreed, thanking Frank, and hurriedly headed home to see Mary.

Arriving at the house, he could see Mary's car parked in the driveway. Just seeing her car gave him the feeling that he was truly home.

Opening the front door, the smells filled the room. But what caught his eye was the trail of Mary's clothing leading to the bedroom. As he followed the trail, he picked up each article—first the shoes, blouse, bra, skirt, and finally her panties. Each time he picked up one, the anticipation and excitement stimulated him. What did Mary have planned for the end?

He entered the bedroom and was taken aback by the sheer beauty of Mary lying on the bed, asleep. The first thing that came to his mind was the movie *Sleeping Beauty*, and, like in the movie, David reached over and gave her a soft, romantic kiss—a kiss to wake up a sleeping beauty.

Mary opened her eyes. She smiled at him, a smile that he had grown to love. Putting her arms around David's neck, she gave him a return kiss.

All of a sudden, the smoke alarm went off. David jumped up and ran to the kitchen to investigate with Mary right behind. The pot holding the sauce was black. David took a potholder from the countertop and put the hot, burnt pot into the sink. He tried to silence the smoke alarm by opening up the doors to the pool.

Looking around for Mary, she was nowhere to be seen. When the smoke alarm finally stopped making the loud noise, he heard Mary in the bathroom throwing up. David knocked on the bathroom door and asked Mary if she was all right.

In between throwing up, she said, "I'm all right. I'm so sorry, David." Then the door opened, and Mary came out.

David put his arms around her and asked, "Are you okay?"

"I got a good hit of the smoke. It went right to my stomach. I wanted this to be so special tonight."

The home phone rang. It was the security alarm company saying that the fire department was on the way. David quickly explained that it was food on the stove and the fire department was not needed.

David hung up the phone. He could see Mary sitting on the couch with her head in her hands. David sat next to her, putting his arms around her. As he moved both of his hands to her face so he could look directly into her eyes, he said, "Mary, I know that you wanted to make this night special, but just being with you is special to me. Seeing you in the amazing negligee was something special that will forever be in my mind. Making love to you is incredible, but being home with you is just as incredible. You and I can overcome anything thrown at us." He gave her a loving kiss and said, "So, that being said, how did your day go with your mother?"

"Are you sure you want to know? It's sci-fi."

"Okay, now you have my attention," he answered with a puzzled look on his face. "Before you start, can we order some food? What sounds good?"

"After trying to burn your house down and then throwing up my guts, let's see, how about holding me and not letting me go?" She gave David a squeeze and kiss.

"I'm here all night, and I'm not going anywhere."

"Okay, how about Chinese?" Mary said with a smile on her face.

"Now that's my gal."

"You order your favorite dish, and you can order shrimp and veggies for me. We can share each other's dish, and I'll know what you like for the next time I order instead of trying to burn down your house," Mary told him.

"You know, the sauce looked really good except for the black char." Mary gave him a punch and told him to go order the food. David got up laughing. He picked up the phone book, looking for a takeout. He rejoined her on the couch. "I'm ready for the story."

She began. "So, I took my mother to Nicole's house for lunch and to go over the preparations for the opening day of the pier. I went to talk to your father on the scheduling for the kids. I had to cut it short because my mother came down with Aaron....By the way, your dad told me that he needed to talk to you. I told him you would be there about 12:00. Aaron and Nicole started to play baseball

229

when my Mom handed the ball to your dad. She went into like a trance, dropping the ball. I was a little concerned about her. She looked like she was in another world with this blank stare on her face. I checked her out and she was fine, so I left her to play baseball with Aaron while I had a meeting with the architect. When I returned, my mother was sitting down on the edge of the pier with your dad's head in her lap. She asked me to feel your dad's head. She got upset at me because I was teasing her."

"That doesn't sound like your mom," he answered with a confused look on his face.

Mary admitted that she called her mother a "dolphin molester" and then said, "When I felt your dad's head, I might have teased more, but Aaron jumped in too."

"Why does that not surprise me?"

"Anyway, on the way home, I got my mother to talk about it. She told me that when she touched Nono, she had a flashback of my father, and he was telling her that everything was okay, and that he is at peace. Because of the way my dad died, my mother really had a hard time excepting it. My mom never complained or showed any emotions about the passing of my dad except one exception, which was when you gave her the yellow roses the other night."

This drew David's attention. "What did I do?"

Mary explained that her dad would only give yellow roses to her mom. "When you gave her the flowers, it stirred up all the emotions. When my mom had your dad's head in her lap, she had a warm and peaceful feeling as if she was with my dad. She thinks your dad is funneling feelings from my dad to her."

"Wow."

"I told you it was a sci-fi moment. Remember the movie *Ghost* with Whoopie Goldberg?"

"So, let me understand. Your mother thinks my dad is like Whoopie Goldberg."

"You got it."

"And what do you think?"

"Now, let's put this into perspective. If I told you your father was a talking dolphin, what would you say?"

"I think we have had this conversation before." She just looked with both eyebrows raised and a smile. "Have you talked to my father about this?"

"No, it just happened." She reached over to hold his hand when a ring came from the front gate, so David buzzed it open and said, "Dinner is being served."

Mary, still wearing the seductive lingerie, got up, saying, "I'd better change for dinner."

"Boo."

Mary grinned and said, "I'll put it back on for dessert."

That put a smile back on his face as he went to the front door to get the food. While he paid for dinner, she set the table, wearing one of David's shirts.

While they were eating, he said, "I got some news today, but it's not as exciting as what happened to you and your mother."

"What is it?"

"My house sold. It was a full-price cash offer. That puts it at the same time as the pier opening for the kids."

"That's great news."

"The only thing is they want a thirty-day or less escrow, and they want to buy the furniture too," David told her.

"Does this mean we are losing our Love Shack? I guess we'll have to relocate to my house if that is okay with you."

"Are you sure? I don't want to impose on you."

"Give me a break. Okay, think of it as if I'm paying you back for your hospitality when I needed a place to stay."

"I don't want to offend your mother."

In a serious voice, she said. "Okay, no sex while you're at my house." She exposed the white lingerie that she was wearing earlier.

"You're not playing fair." He picked up Mary in his arms and carried her to the bedroom.

On the way to the bedroom, she said, "Oh, it must be time for dessert."

He gently laid her on the bed. She reached her hand around his neck, pulling him against her body and turning around so she was on top. Then she started unbuttoning his shirt, exposing his bare chest. Once she finished, she slowly kissed her way down, not missing a spot. She then stepped off the bed, unbuttoned his pants, and pulled them off. She then gave David a striptease dance without the music, starting with the garter belt and slowly taking off the nylons. She then started rolling each shoulder until her top slipped off her body. She then said,

"You'd better get all you can. Remember no sex at my house!"

David said, "Right." He pulled her on top of him and made toe-curling love.

CHAPTER 35

THE TEST

Early that morning, Mary woke nauseous. As she slipped out of bed not to wake David, she ran down the hall to the guest bathroom just in time to throw up in the toilet. After finishing, she washed her face with a wet towel and said to herself in the mirror, "What the hell is going on?" Having been in complete denial of the possibility of being pregnant, she began to think what if she was? She went to the kitchen, looking for something bland to eat that might help with the nausea.

She found some crackers and made a cup of coffee. Looking around, she saw the mess from the fire and began to clean it up. She tried to not think about being pregnant, but her mind drifted back to what to do about the possibility. She came to the conclusion to stop at a drugstore on the way back to her house to pick up a pregnancy test. Once she knew the truth, she would worry about what to do. She walked out to the pool area with her crackers and coffee.

She sat on the patio chair, trying not to think of the possibility of being pregnant, but as much as she tried, she kept going over the course of events. A cold chill came over her, recalling the day she got kidnapped by the Lucci brothers. Her birth control pills were at the house, and she hadn't taken them for two days. If I'm pregnant, I guess they got the last laugh.

David came out of the kitchen with a cup of coffee. "Someone's an early bird this morning."

She told him how she couldn't sleep with the mess she made in the kitchen, so she got up to clean everything. "Except for the sauce pot. It's history. I need to replace it."

"No need. We will be using your pot the next time. I didn't hear you when you got up."

"You were out like a light. Must of had too much dessert last night." She gave a sexy smile.

"All I know is it was delicious." He reached over to kiss her.

She reminded David about the meeting with his dad at 12 o'clock. "I'd better get ready to go. I have to meet my mother at my house today." She gave David a kiss and whispered in his ear, "That was pretty delicious. Maybe we should have seconds later." She walked into the house.

When Mary was ready to leave, she gave David a kiss goodbye and said, "I'll see you at Aaron's house at noon."

She headed straight to the first drugstore she could find to pick up a pregnancy test kit. She then went to the counter where an older lady cashier scanned it. When Mary handed her the credit card, she noticed the cashier glancing down on her left hand to see if there was a wedding ring. Mary noticed it and quickly said, "I'm retaining so much water that I couldn't get my wedding ring on this morning." The cashier smiled and gave her the receipt.

Mary asked if there was a restroom in the store. The cashier pointed to back and said, "Next to the pharmacy."

While waiting for the bathroom to be vacated, she started to read the instructions on the box. Once the bathroom was clear, she entered it, locking the door behind her. She began to follow the instructions. As she waited impatiently for the results, she kept checking her watch. When it changed from white to pink with a plus mark, Mary put her head in her lap.

Still in denial, she went back to the isle and picked up several different brands. She went back to the same cashier, putting four more kits on the counter. The cashier looked at Mary and said, "Is that it?"

Mary quickly picked up a Snickers candy bar from the rack behind her. "You never know if they might have a false positive."

The cashier said, "When I was pregnant, I craved Snickers." Mary quickly put it back on the candy rack, and handed the cashier her credit card. The cashier, with a wide-eyed smile, said, "Have a nice day."

Mary grabbed the bag and went to her car. Once inside, she put her head on the steering wheel and said out loud, "I can't ever go back to that store again."

When she arrived at her house, she went right to the bathroom, using all four pregnancy test kits with the same positive result. Walking back to the living room and sitting on the couch, she began to cry.

It wasn't ten minutes later that the doorbell rang. She was so upset she forgot about her mother coming over. She quickly grabbed a tissue, blotting her eyes before answering the door. It was her mother all right. "Oh, my lord, what is wrong?" Mary walked back to the couch and grabbed another tissue to blot her eyes. Elaine, seeing her daughter in distress asked, "Did something go wrong last night?"

"Let's see. I had fallen asleep and forgot to turn the spaghetti sauce down and almost burned down his house. The smoke made me throw up, and there is one more thing. Oh yes, I'm pregnant!"

Elaine's jaw dropped and her mouth fell wide open. "Are you sure?"

Mary emptied the bag of the five pregnancy test kits all showing positive, except one. "Why five?" asked her mother. Mary gave her a sarcastic look. Elaine, looking over all the test results said, "Oh, look. There is one that's not all pink and no mark."

Mary glanced over. "Oh, yes. That's where I ran out of pee."

Elaine shrugged her shoulders, paused for a moment, and asked, "Does David know?"

"No, I just found out."

"When are you going to tell him?"

"Not until we have the grand opening of the pier. I don't want to spoil that."

Elaine said, "Let's look at this as a positive…"

Mary interrupted her. "Let's not use the word positive." She looked down at the four positive pregnancy tests on the table.

"Good idea…you know, telling him could draw you and David closer together."

"But Mom, I don't want David to feel pressure that he has to marry me. I want him to be madly in love with me and want to get married. Like what you and Dad had. You know David by now. He's like Sir Galahad defending his lady's honor. And by the way, one other thing I forgot to mention. David sold his house and will be staying here for a while."

Elaine's mouth dropped, and she said, "That's a start."

"No, Mom. That just puts more pressure on Sir Galahad. Any way I look at the situation, it just makes things more complicated. We are just starting to really know each other. I want him to say I love you. Now I'll never know if it was honor or love."

"Let me tell you something, Mary. Your father and I thought we knew what love was. Then you came into our lives, and it took our love to a whole other level. To see the love in your father's eyes when he held you for the first time outperformed any wild sex that we ever had, and we had our share."

"I know, Mom, but there will always be that doubt in my mind." She blotted her eyes.

All her mother could do was hold her daughter. No other words could help.

Thinking back, Mary wondered what her dad would have told her if he was still alive. He had a way with words. No matter what the problem was, he could always put a smile on her face.

CHAPTER 36

IS MARCO'S MISSION OVER?

At Aaron's house, Marco could see Aaron coming down to see him. He needed to have a heart-to-heart talk with him. Marco had a feeling that his time was just about done. He needed to explain that he might not be around forever, but Aaron had his whole life in front of him. When Aaron reached the end of the pier with his laptop, Marco told him he wanted to explain something to him and to sit next to him.

He sat down with the computer on his lap. Aaron took his shoes and socks off and let his feet dangle in the water. Marco then swam up to him, putting his head between Aaron legs so he could get his full attention. He said, "Aaron, we've had quite a journey together from the first day that we met right here."

"Yeah! That's when you scared all the fish on top of the dock."

Marco then said, "If it was not for your trust in me, all of this would not have been possible. I was given the opportunity to reverse some of the bad things I have done in my life. Now I feel that my mission is just about done, and I don't know what is in my future. All I know is you are the key to what we are trying to do here. You are the future of how man and nature can live in harmony again. But there are bad people out there who want to take advantage of what we have done. For example, if they ever found out how we can communicate with sea mammals, they could exploit it for military use. It's very important that this be kept as our secret. When you are at school or just hanging out with your friends, the temptation to tell them that you can talk to sea mammals will be great. You must avoid any temptation to do so. Remember, you are key if we succeed or fail."

"I know. My dad told me all about this too. When I grow up, I told my dad I want to be a marine biologist like Mary, and I could work with her at the rehab center with the dolphins. You know, I've got a pretty good resume."

"Yes, you do, Aaron, and I'm sure Mary would love for you to help. Now that brings me to a subject I don't like to talk about. Remember when we were out in the boat and the shark attacked us?"

"That's when I fell overboard and hit my head."

"Yes, and you got sick again," Marco replied. "Just like me, you have been given a second chance in life. One day you will go down to the pier and I won't be there. Don't be sad. That means that I've finally finished my mission, and I have made my peace with nature. But all you have to do is look in your heart, and I will always be there for you."

Aaron put his arms around Marco, giving him a hug, and said, "I love you, Nono!"

It just melted his heart. He then told Aaron that he would be leaving soon to meet with the other dolphins to come for the grand opening. Marco then said, "I need you to help with all the kids on that day. Remember, you are our poster boy."

"Okay. I need to go help my mom get everything ready." Aaron then said goodbye and walked up to the house.

On the way to the house, he met David walking down. David stopped to pick up Aaron and give him a high five. When he reached Marco, David opened up his laptop computer and sat down and said, "Hi, Dad."

"Hello, David."

"The big day will be here in days," David told him. Mary, Nicole, and Elaine have everything ready to go. They all are doing a great job."

"That is why I need to talk to you. I feel my mission here is just about done. I don't know what is in store for me now. We've gotten a good start on bridging the gap between man and sea mammals. I don't know what is left for me to do. Will I remain in this form, or will I be set free from this form and allow to pass in peace? I had a talk with Aaron to not be sad and to always remember I will be looking after him when I'm gone, and he should look no farther than his heart. And David, of all the thinking that I have done, the one thing I regret most was that I was never a real father to you. I hope in your heart that you have found a place for me again."

David said, "I know, Dad. I wish things would have been better too, but we can look back and have our regrets or we can choose to look at the present and remember how at last we became close to one another. Also, we can look forward to what we can do to make this world a better place. Look at what you've already done. The sea mammals now have real hope that a change is coming. Without your powers, Aaron would not be with us. And look, in less than a week, the new pier will be filled with kids with new hopes and dreams. I believe that your mission is not at an end but is just starting."

"Thank you, son, for the kind words. I guess we'll have to wait and see what my fate will be."

"Mary and Elaine are on their way here. I guess you left quite an impression on Elaine yesterday."

"Yes, she did me was well. When she touched me, it was like I looked into her soul. I felt her pain, and then I felt her joy. Her beauty goes right to her soul." Marco told David that he would be leaving about three days before the grand opening of the pier. "I have to meet up with the dolphin pod. That might take a day or two, but we will be there when the kids arrive that morning. I have a big surprise for them."

While waiting for Mary and Elaine to arrive, David went back to the house to meet up with John, Nicole, and Aaron. At the house, David said he had to go to MIT to finish the paperwork, pick up something at his house in Maine, and head back in time for the grand opening. Then David reminded everyone not to use the cell phone or laptop computer to talk to his dad. He then told them, "While the kids are here, the press and TV crew will be there, and we don't want our secret out."

Mary and Elaine arrived at the house. Mary then introduced her mother to John. After everyone went over what they had to do, David pulled Mary aside so her mother couldn't hear. He told Mary what his dad had told him when Elaine touched him and what he felt. "So, I guess there was something that happened between your mother and my dad."

"Wow!"

"It looks like everything is ready to go here, I have to go back at MIT, but I will be back the morning of the grand opening." He then pulled her in close to kiss her. "I'll call you later tonight."

After they walked back to the room to join everyone, David said his goodbyes to everyone except Elaine, who was unexplainably absent and nowhere to be found. "Maybe she's in the bathroom," said Mary. David looked at his watch to see what time it was. Mary said, "I'll tell her goodbye for you. You'd better go now or you might miss your flight." She walked David to the door, giving him a quick kiss goodbye.

When Mary returned, she still couldn't find her mother even after checking the bathrooms. Then, looking out the window, she saw her at the pier.

"There you are. David was looking for you to say goodbye before he left for the airport."

"Oh, I didn't know he was leaving town," Elaine said.

"He had some loose ends to tie up at MIT and will be back in time for the grand opening. What are you doing out here?"

"I was looking for Aaron's dolphin."

"He left to find the dolphin pod. He'll be back for the grand opening with all the other dolphins," Mary explained.

"I was hoping to let your dad know through the dolphin that he was going to be a grandfather."

She gave her mother a hug and said, "I'm sure Dad knows and is jumping for joy." That brought a smile to her mother's face. "Now, we have a lot to do today, so we'd better get going. By the way, could you stay with me until David returns back from Maine? I have to make room for his clothes and things. My place is a mess."

"I know," Elaine said.

"What…it's not that bad."

Elaine shrugged her shoulders, laughed, and said, "But you really need to get organized, and I'm just the one to do it."

"Whatever." She then told her mother that she needed to leave her with Nicole because she'd made an appointment with her gynecologist. She didn't want to cause any suspicion going to a doctor, at least not until she had a chance to talk to David.

"Good idea. You need to be thinking about the baby now. No more wine for you, and more for me. Oh, my god, I'm too young to be a grandmother." That brought a smile to Mary's face as they started walking up to the house.

In the afternoon, Mary returned from the doctor without anyone suspecting where she had gone. When the opportunity came, she was able to talk to Elaine alone. By the look on her face, her mother already knew that nothing had changed, except a due date. Mary then said, "It's official, Grandma!"

Her mother, excitedly clapping her hands, said, "Sorry, not every day you get a chance to be a grandmother."

"I know, Mom, I just wish it would have been better timing."

"When is your due date?"

"Let's just say you will know what to get me for Christmas." She could see the happiness in her mother's eyes.

"When do you plan on telling David?"

"I don't know. I have to find the right time, but I know it won't be until after the grand opening. We'll talk about it tonight. We'd better get back and help now."

CHAPTER 37

WHAT WOULD DAVID SAY?

While driving home, Mary and her mother had a better chance to talk about the pregnancy without worrying about someone overhearing them. "Do you know what you are going say to David?"

"No. I'm scared to death what his reaction will be. What if he says 'Oh!' Or he just gives me a blank stare. I just don't know." Elaine could see sadness in her face. "I would rather raise the baby by myself than to be with a man that only married me because I was pregnant."

Elaine tried to comfort her daughter by saying, "I don't think David is that type of guy."

"He has never said that he loves me either."

"Just give it some time."

"Do you think he's not going to notice?"

There was nothing she could say at that point to calm down her daughter. She tried to change the subject. "What should we have for dinner?"

"All I keep thinking about is what that lady in the drug store said to me. All she wanted was a Snickers candy bar when she was pregnant. And you know what, that sounds pretty good right now."

"You know you're going to have to watch what you eat now."

"I have some stuff at home. I don't want to go anywhere but home and get into some comfortable clothes."

That night when David called, she did her best to act normal, like nothing was wrong, but inside her stomach was turning. She so badly wanted to tell him, but it had to be done in person—not over the phone. After she got off the call, she sat on the bed alone, trying to put her mind at ease so she could get some sleep. There was one day left to prepare for the grand opening. So many people were counting on her that she had to pull it together and not worry about what was to come.

CHAPTER 38

THE BIG DAY

The day finally arrived with all the preparations completed. Mary and Elaine arrived early that morning where they were greeted by Aaron, John, and Nicole. It wasn't ten minutes later when David pulled in from the ride from the airport. The first bus arrived with all the kids. David greeted everyone and said that his flight was late and asked if there was anything that he could do. Mary gave him a hug and said, "Everything is ready. We just need to get all the kids ready down at the pier and set up for the ones that need special accommodations."

When everyone was in place, Mary used a megaphone to welcome all the kids. She told them to look out over the ocean and there would soon be a special surprise for them. As all the kids watched, the TV crews set up their cameras, waiting for the big event. As everyone waited, Mary looked over to David, shrugging her shoulders as if to say, "Where is your dad?"

David reached out, putting his arms around Mary, giving her support. "Don't worry. He'll be here."

One of the children shouted out, "What is that?"

Mary and David turned to look. There was a wall of white water headed into the cove. Mary picked up the megaphone. "Okay, everyone, your surprise is on its way to see you." As more and more of the children saw the white wall, the screams of joy got louder and louder. Then, as it reached closer, they could see what was making the wall of water.

A large school of dolphins was headed to the pier, jumping and spinning as they approached. Once at the pier, the dolphins broke off, going to each of the children, letting the kids touch them as they interacted with each child. Mary ordered the lowering of the hydraulic lift so the handicapped children could interact with the dolphins too.

The only thing missing was Nono. Aaron was holding a baseball in his hand, watching for Nono to show up. As he looked up at David and Mary, he could see the concern on their faces. Aaron said, "Where is Nono?"

Tears ran down his face. Both Mary and David went over to comfort him. David held him and said, "Remember what Nono told you? That one day if he's not here, just look in your heart. He knew that his mission was done, and now it's up to us to continue his work."

Aaron was so upset he dropped the ball in the water. He said, "But not now."

Both Mary and David held Aaron. Out of nowhere, a wet baseball rolled back on the pier, hitting Aaron on the leg. Aaron looked down at the baseball next to his leg and turned to see Nono looking up at him. Aaron shouted out, "Nono!" Mary and David turned to see as Aaron ran over, hugging Nono. Mary and David joined the joy of Nono's return.

As all of this was going on, seeing how the children were responding to the dolphins, David turned to Mary, held both of her arms, and said, "Mary, without you, all of this would not be possible. I've been waiting to tell you from the first day that we met that there was something special about you and that I wanted to know you more. The more I knew you, the more you found a home in my heart. You are my soulmate. You make every day special to me. I don't want to let another day go by not letting you know that. I have fallen head over heels in love with you. Mary, I love you."

David got down on one knee and asked, "Mary, will you spend the rest of your life with me?" He let go of Mary's hand and reached out over the water. His dad came out of the water, holding a box in a waterproof bag. David said, "Thank you, Dad." He opened the bag exposing his mother's wedding ring.

Mary got on her knees. Her hands were shaking, and she said, "Close your eyes."

David was surprised and said, "Mary, not here."

Mary reached inside her purse, pulling out the pregnancy test kit and placed it in David's hand and said, "It comes with a package deal. You can open your eyes."

When David opened his eyes, he was puzzled until he read the label He then looked up at Mary, who totally lost it. "You mean we're going to have a baby?" The joy filled his face.

"All Mary could do was nod her head yes. "Whoops!" Both of them were on their knees, hugging and kissing.

David took out the ring, putting it on Mary's shaking hand and said, "This was my mother's wedding ring, and she told me when I find the love of my life, to give it to her. Not only did I find the love of my life, but I found my soulmate. Mary, please, will both of you marry me?"

"Yes, yes, yes!" Mary exclaimed.

They both got off their knees and looked around. Everyone cheered.

"I almost forgot, there's one more thing I need to do." He took Mary's hand, walking her over to where John, Nicole, and Aaron were standing. "I want to introduce you to our new neighbors," David told her. With a puzzled look on Mary's face, David pointed to the house under construction next to John, Nicole, and Aaron's house. "I thought you might want to be close to work."

Mary looked at David with tears of joy still flowing like a faucet from her face. She then gave David a hug and kiss and said, "You have made me the happiest person in the world. All of my dreams you have made come true. I love you with my whole heart and soul."

Mary, still filled with emotion and her hands still shaking, turned to Nicole, gave her a hug, and said. "Did you know?"

"I swear to God I didn't!" Nicole answered. Then John stepped in to give Mary a hug. Aaron was jumping up and down with excitement.

As all of that was going on, David went over to Elaine, who was so filled with emotion that she was kneeling on the dock with her head buried in her lap. David knelt down next to Elaine and reached out with his hands to lift Elaine's face up until she was looking at his eyes.

Once she saw it was David, she reached over and hugged him, saying, "That was so beautiful how you proposed. My husband would've been so proud and happy."

"I would like to ask your permission for your daughter's hand in marriage."

Elaine joked, "Let's see, you first knocked up my daughter and you proposed to her without my permission. Now you want my consent?" She looked him straight in the eyes. He was surprised and didn't know what to say. Then Elaine said, "Sure, why not!"

When she started to laugh, all David could do was to shake his head and say, "Boy, you really got me!"

He helped Elaine up. Mary came over, and her mother said, "I told you it would work out."

"What! There was no way you could have figured this one out." Her mother just shrugged her shoulders and smiled.

Everyone was celebrating, but Marco could only watch. The only thing that went wrong with the proposal was he showed up a little late to the cove with all the dolphins. And in all the excitement, David slipped up and said, "Thank you, Dad." But with all the clapping, Marco didn't think anyone heard what he said. His job was to act like a dolphin and not to cause any attention.

Marco stayed near the pier and saw Elaine walking up to him. She sat at the edge with her feet in the water and called Nono over to her. When he got close, he put his head on her lap. She reached over with both of her hands. "Our little baby is getting married, and you are going to be a grandpa." He could feel the power of her emotions as he tried to keep his head clear so not to interfere with what she was feeling. He could see that she definitely was feeling something special. He could see the emotions on her face.

After a couple of hours passed and the children were given lunch and their gifts to take home and the last bus left, Mary used the megaphone to tell everyone that they had one hour before the next group of kids would arrive. She thanked all the volunteers for all their help. "The catering truck is providing lunch."

While everyone was having lunch and getting ready for the next group of kids, Mary was surrounded by TV news crews that were filming the event for the evening news. Mary answered their questions about the new facility and how the dolphins interacting with the children had a beneficial effect on them. The next question came about David's wedding proposal. Mary explained it was a complete surprise, but it did cap off a beautiful day which included the grand opening for the kids.

After the last team of kids had left and everyone was still all together, Mary thanked them for making the day very special for the children. She turned to David with her arm around him and said, "I mean very, very special day."

Nicole and John invited everyone up to their home to celebrate. David told everyone they would meet them at the house but first he wanted to show Mary the new house under construction. When the coast was clear, David pulled out his phone so he could talk to his dad. Holding Mary tightly, he walked to the end of the pier, looking around and listening to make sure no one was there. He then said, "Thank you, Dad, for helping pull this off. How does it feel that you're going to be a grandpa?"

"David, I'm so happy for you both. You have something very special together that only comes along once in a lifetime. Being a grandfather is just as special. I only wish it could have been better timing before I became a dolphin."

"If the course of events were any different, then David and I would have never met," said Mary.

David added, "Look how close we've become. You're going to be a grandpa, and that would have never happened either."

While Marco listened to them, he realized they were right. The only reason they found each other was because of his bad behavior. The curse of being turned into a dolphin ended up as a blessing. Not only did it bring David and Mary together, but it gave Aaron a chance to live a full, cancer-free life. So his penance for his sins against nature and humanity was a badge of honor, and whatever became of him, he proudly accepted. He then told them, "You'd better get to the house before everyone wonders what happened to you. And, David, you need to show Mary her new home."

"I'm so excited about the house. I'll be able to keep an eye on you," said Mary.

"Love you, Dad," David said as he reached down, putting his hand on the side of Marco's face. Mary gave him a kiss on the top of his head.

He watched them walk together to the new house, Marco's heart was full of happiness. For the first time since David was a small child, he said to his dad, "I love you." He never knew how much those three little words could touch his heart.

Reaching the new house, David picked up Mary in his arms, carrying her over the threshold of the framed house and only stopping to give her a kiss. "Welcome to your almost new home," he said to her. Showing her the plans for the house which were in the framing stage, he told her, "If there are any changes you want to make, just let the architect know."

Mary looked over the house plans. "I wouldn't want to change anything except maybe a couple of extra bedrooms. I want to fill them up with children." With a smile from ear to ear, she asked, "If that's okay with you?"

"I already told the architect to make provisions for room additions," David answered. As he opened up the next page of the plans, it showed a great room that could be converted to bedrooms. David, holding Mary tighter, asked, "When do you want to get married?"

"While I still can get in a wedding dress and before you change your mind," Mary said as she laughed.

"That is never going to happen," David told her. "Sorry, you're stuck with me for life....When are we going to have our first baby?"

Mary said, "Like I told my mother. I know what I'm going to get her for Christmas."

David smiled. "I am so ready to be a dad. I can't wait to share that with you. You have made me the happiest man alive."

"You have no idea what you have done for me," Mary replied. "Just to know that you feel the same way is what makes it so special. I was so worried what your reaction would be. I wanted you to marry me because you loved me and not because I was pregnant and it was the honorable thing to do. You have no idea how happy you made me by proposing before you found out we were going to have a baby together....Hey, I could stay here all night, but we have everyone waiting for us next door."

When they reached the house, everyone started clapping for the newly engaged couple. Mary's mother greeted David and Mary and asked, "How was the house?"

"I wouldn't change a thing."

"I hope there's a bedroom for grandma."

"Of course," replied David.

"When are you planning on getting hitched?"

"As soon as possible, before I won't be able to fit into a wedding dress," said Mary.

"Oh boy, we have to go shopping!"

"I'd like you to help plan the wedding," Mary said. "I know where I want to have it. At the new pier overlooking the water. If that's okay with David."

David smiled, knowing that way his dad would be able to attend. "I would really like that."

Nicole said, "I'd be honored to host the wedding reception afterward. Mary reached over and gave Nicole a hug. "Thank you."

After all the arrangements were settled for the wedding and everyone said their goodnights, Mary and her mother drove back home where David would meet them after he went back to his house to pick up some clothes.

While Mary and her mom drove, there was a difference in the conversation. It was uplifting and cheerful as they made plans on what they were going to do. Once at Mary's house, Elaine said, "I need to go home to leave you two love birds alone. I'll meet you back in the late morning after you throw up your breakfast."

"Very funny, Mother." Elaine, with a smile, gave her daughter a kiss goodbye.

While Mary watched her mother drive away, she got a call from David asking if he could take her and her mother out for dinner. Mary told David her mother had already left to go home, and after a long emotional day, all she wanted was to curl up in his arms. David reminded her she needed to have something to eat because she was now eating for two. "How about Chinese?" he asked. "The same as before?"

"Yes, but hurry. I need some hugs," answered Mary.

"No worries. I have plenty of those. Love you. I'll be there soon."

Mary hung up the phone and sat on the couch, thinking what a difference a day made. Just that morning she was worried what was going to happen when she had to tell David she was pregnant. Now she was engaged and heard I love you come freely from him. She rubbed her stomach and said, "You have a pretty special father."

After David reached home, he found Mary sound asleep on the couch, wearing her night gown. David quietly put the food in the refrigerator, went to the couch, picked up Mary, and put her in bed. They both fell asleep in each other's arms.

That morning when Mary finally woke, she found him still in his clothes, holding her. He was sound asleep, and she didn't want to wake him. Like clockwork, she headed to the bathroom, throwing up. When she finally came up for air, there was David holding a wet towel. Mary said, "I'm so sorry. Thank you, David. I have it from here."

David left her in the bathroom, went into the kitchen, and made coffee. When Mary showed up, she wrapped her arms around his waist. "Thank you for being there." She took David's hand and led him back to the bedroom. "We have unfinished business to take care of," she said.

After the most sensitive love making they had shared, Mary said, "I never want to leave my man hungry."

David just said, "Wow."

"What's for breakfast? I'm hungry. I know…let's have leftovers." She bounced out of bed.

He was still a little drained but followed her into the kitchen where she took out the dinner David had put in the refrigerator the night before. David asked, "What can I do?"

"You can pour the coffee, and I'll heat up the Chinese food."

After a comfortable breakfast, Mary looked at the clock and said, "My mother will be here shortly. I've got to jump into the shower. I would ask you to join me but we both know what that would lead to."

He nodded in agreement. While she was showering, he cleaned up the dishes and went to the other bathroom to get cleaned up. By the time he arrived back in the kitchen, Mary had already poured two cups of coffee in a thermal container. The front doorbell rang.

"That's my mom." She greeted her and David gave Elaine a hug.

"Well, did she throw up her breakfast?" Elaine asked.

"Nope."

Mary went to get the coffee. David said, "No, it was before breakfast." Elaine winked to let him know.

"I heard that, David," said Mary. She kissed him goodbye and said, "Tattletale." David shrugged his shoulders.

She handed her mother the coffee. Her mom handed her a Snickers bar. "Really, Mom?" Mary exclaimed. Elaine started to put the candy back in her purse, but Mary sighed, quickly grabbed it, and stuffed it into her own bag.

That afternoon, they went to five different stores, trying to find the perfect wedding dress with no luck. The frustration was setting in when her mother said, "I've got one more place."

"All I want is to find a dress that when David sees me in it, he'll never forget that moment and the day we got married. How hard can that be?" As they got back in the car, Mary exclaimed, "I'm done! Maybe I should wear my birthday suit."

"I'm sure that will get his attention along with everyone else."

After driving for about 45 minutes, Mary asked, "Where are we going?"

"We're almost there." When they turned into her mom's driveway, her mother got out of the car and said, "I have to get something. Come inside with me."

Mary sat on the couch while her mother went into her bedroom only to return back holding her wedding dress. "Try it on for me."

She looked at her mother's face and said, "Are you sure, Mom?"

"Yes, now go try it on," Elaine said. "I'm getting a glass of wine. Can I get you some water?"

"Yes, thank you."

When Mary came out of the bedroom, Elaine's eyes got full seeing how beautiful she looked in the dress. The dress had lace from the neck to her breast, then flowed down, with a long train behind her, clinging to her body like a glove. "Mother this is perfect! What do you think?"

Her mother answered. "You look stunning. I think you will achieve the reaction you were looking for from David without taking off your clothes." They both laughed.

"And it fits perfectly! I don't need to alter a thing," Mary replied in an excited voice.

"For now, but not for long," her mother said.

"Why didn't we just come here first instead of going all over town?"

"I don't know," her mom replied. "For the free wine at the bridal shops? I wanted you to pick out your own wedding dress and not feel any pressure from me."

"Are you sure it's okay? This was special for you and Dad."

"Nothing could be more special than to see you walking down the aisle wearing it. It's just magical," Elaine responded. "I only wish your father could see you. "

Mary went over the course of events with David, telling him that she couldn't wait for him to see her in the dress. "When did you want to get married?"

"Whenever you want to."

"As soon as possible while I can still fit in the wedding dress."

"You just let me know, and I'll be there."

"You'd better," she said as she poked him in the ribs.

CHAPTER 39
I DO'S

The big day was at hand. All the arrangements were done. All that was left were the "I do's." When David saw Mary coming down the pier wearing her wedding dress, his expression was priceless. She had her hair up, which gave her an elegant look, and the trail of her dress flowed with every step she took. The sun reflected beauty off the water as Marco swam alongside her as if he was walking her down the aisle.

David was so overcome with the beauty, it showed on his face and in his eyes. He reached out, holding Mary's hands and taking a deep breath to compose himself. "The first time we met I knew there was something special about you. But how special I didn't know until I really got to know you from the inside out. Your beauty comes from the inside, and the outside isn't bad either. You are my soulmate. I feel your every emotion, your thoughts, and your dreams. You make everyone around you special, and you have made me the happiest man alive today and for every day of our lives."

Mary, with her hands shaking, said, "I feel like Cinderella, and you are my Prince Charming. You make me feel like I never want the day to end. And now it doesn't have to end because you will be next to me every night when I go to bed. And when I kiss you goodnight, you will be the first person that I kiss good morning. I can't wait to see what the next phase of our life together will bring. Soon we will have a little bundle of joy to share together. You have made my fairytale dream come true. I love you with all my heart and soul."

After the ceremony, everything was set up outside so Marco could be a part of it. To see David and Mary share that special moment made Marco feel very special too. He thought if God were to take him, he would be at peace knowing David and Mary had found each other. The only sad part was not knowing if he would be around to see his grandchild. As everyone was milling around, David and Mary found time to reach out to Marco to let him know how they felt.

Elaine walked over and said, "Go find your own dolphin. This one is taken." Elaine sat down on the end of the pier with Nono. "Dad would have been so proud and happy, Mom."

"Yes, he would have. Now you two honeymooners run along. I need some time alone with my dolphin."

David had made plans for a short honeymoon to Maine. That was where it all started, and it was a fitting place to start their new life together. Saying their goodbyes to everyone, they had barely enough time to go home, change, and catch a plane. Elaine gave them both a hug and said, "Don't forget to stop at the store and pick up some Snickers."

CHAPTER 40

IS IT A BOY OR GIRL?

Returning back from their honeymoon, it was back to work, getting everything finished at the aquarium center and overseeing the house construction. Both David and Mary were busy. Every full moon the pod of dolphins would return to the cove where the children would be waiting. In fact, it became over-whelming. The response for the program was so good, they had to add another session. Instead of only having a morning and afternoon session, they also had to add an evening time to accommodate all the children. The only break was going to the doctor for checkups to see how the baby was doing. David was by her side at every visit.

On one visit, the doctor asked them if they want-ed an ultrasound to see if it was a boy or girl. In unison, they said, "Yes."

They positioned Mary to get a clear picture, and it was confirmed to be a boy. They couldn't wait to let the grandparents know. On the way to tell Marco, they called Elaine. Mary told her mom she had a new baseball player for her team.

Arriving at the pier, they walked down to where they could see Marco looking at the construction of the facility. He saw them and swam over as David pulled out his cell phone so they could talk to him. David told him, "Well, Dad, you are going to have a grandson." They both smiled from ear to ear. As they listened to the cell phone, they could hear the joy in his voice.

Marco said, "I'm so happy for you two. It's a boy. Aaron will have a catcher now. Did you let Elaine know yet?"

"Yes, on the way over here," David told him. "We're going to see Aaron play his first baseball game and tell him along with Nicole and John."

CHAPTER 41

HANGING THE PICTURE

The months went by. Aaron would come down to the pier all the time except when he had a baseball game, and then he would tell Marco all about the game and how he did. His team was going to the state finals. The only sad thing was Marco could only listen to what he had done, and to not see him play was depressing.

Marco could only watch as David and Mary's new house was completed and the new rehabilitation center neared completion. Mary would come by to see him, and he could see each time that her stomach was getting bigger and bigger, but everywhere else he would be hard pressed to tell she was pregnant. She was getting close, but she never complained. Marco would put his head on her stomach to feel the baby kick. Mary would say, "I swear sometimes it feels like he is running the bases at a game."

When the new house was done, Elaine helped Mary get organized and helped hang pictures. When Elaine came across a picture, she asked Mary about it. She explained, "This is my favorite picture. It's such a powerful message...man against the sea."

"Who is the artist?

"This is the picture I told you about. This is the only picture of his father." She deliberately left out that David didn't have a face on the painting because of the falling out they had and how she talked

David into painting his dad's face. She asked her mother where to hang it.

They looked for an appropriate, visible place. Mary stopped and said, "Whoa, big guy." She held her stomach.

Elaine asked, "Is everything all right?"

"The baby is really active today, and he kept me up all night. For a while, though, I thought he was coming for a visit. I think he hit a home run and is running the bases again." She started to laugh. "Hold up the picture right here. I think it might look good."

Elaine held the picture up and said, "That's perfect."

Mary reached to mark the spot with a pencil but accidentally dropped it.

Elaine said, "It's right next to your feet."

"Mom, I haven't seen my feet in a month!"

Laughing, Elaine put down the picture, picked up the pencil, and marked a spot on the wall. Mary went to her little toolbox, looking for a picture-hanging hook.

"Let me guess. You can't find anything to hang the picture with."

"I wanted to hang it before David got home tonight. Let's go to the hardware store."

"I'll do it for you, so you can get some rest."

"Thank you, Mom."

After Elaine left, Mary decided it was a perfect time to go down to see Marco while her mom was away.

CHAPTER 42

WHAT JUST HAPPENED?

Marco watched Mary slowly walking down to the pier from the house. She took out her phone so she could talk. While she was walking and dialing up the app, Marco noticed Aaron's bat laying on the pier. He quickly began making noise to warn her, but all he heard was her saying, "All right. What's going on now?" She tripped on the bat and fell onto the pier, her cellphone landing on the dock and her head hitting a metal dock cleat.

Mary lay motionless on the dock, and Marco could see blood coming from the side of her head. He never felt so helpless. He had to do something. He made as much noise and splashing in the water as he could do, but no one was around. Aaron was at his baseball game with John and Nicole. Then he spotted Mary's cell phone on the dock. Concentrating on her cell, he tried to get a dial tone, but nothing was happening. Finally, he heard it tone, so he tried to reach 911. After several attempts, he heard a voice come over her phone saying, "911 emergency. Do you have an emergency?" He made as much noise as possible, trying to get the attention of the operator.

The phone's dial tone came on, so he toned 911 again. Again the operator said, "Do you have emergency?" Marco made as much noise as possible. He then heard the operator say, "Are you having trouble talking? Hit any key on your phone. We have units on the way. I will stay on the line with you. Help is on the way." Marco toned a key, relieved that help was on the way, but seeing Mary lying motionless on the dock sent chills up his spine. All he could do was pray and put his head next to her, letting her know he was there.

The fire department arrived at the house. Elaine saw the fire truck as she was driving down the street. She quickly ran to the house as the fire department had already made their entrance, not finding anyone home. Elaine quickly entered the house. The fire captain saw Elaine and asked, "Elaine Cole?"

Elaine, recognizing the fire captain who worked with her late husband, said, "Randy, it's Mary's house. Where is Mary? She's pregnant and is due any time."

Randy said, "Don't worry. We'll find her."

Elaine explained how she only went to the hardware store and wasn't gone very long. Randy called the fire department dispatch, asking if they still had the caller on the line. When Elaine saw Marco making all the splashes, she saw Mary lying on the dock. She quickly yelled out, "She's on the pier! Please hurry."

The firemen ran down to her. Elaine, seeing her in a pool of blood, broke out crying. One of the medics asked Elaine how many months along Mary was. Elaine, trying to compose herself, said, "She's due any time."

The medics started an IV, put her on a backboard, on a gurney, and into the waiting ambulance. Elaine rode in the ambulance with her daughter to the hospital. On the way, she called David, trying to compose herself before talking to him. When David answered the phone, Elaine explained, "There was an accident on the pier. Mary is unconscious and a laceration on her head. We are on the way to the hospital. I'll see you there." She held Mary's hand, saying over and over, "Hold on, baby. We are almost there."

Once the ambulance arrived, Mary was rushed right into the ICU unit. Elaine was waiting outside the waiting room to hear from the doctor when David came in. She grabbed David's arm. Composing herself, she said, "They took her inside the ICU, and I'm waiting for the doctor."

The doctor came out and introduced himself. "I'm Dr. Allen. We need to do a C-section to save the mother and baby. The mother lost a lot of blood, and we have to relieve the pressure on the brain. She is not out of the woods because of trauma to her brain due to the injury she sustained from the fall. I have to get back into the operating room. Sorry, I'll get back to you as soon as I can."

David asked, "Can I see her?"

"No, I'm sorry, but time is of the essence," the doctor replied. All David and Elaine could do was hold each other and pray.

CHAPTER 43

WHY MARY?

At the pier, all Marco could do was watch as the fire department trucks pulled away, following the ambulance with red light sirens wailing. The helplessness he felt had turned to anger. He thought, *Why Mary? Please take me! I'm the one to be punished, not her and my grandson. I have done everything to make things right.*

A flash of light came over Marco as he found himself lying on a sand beach. While he tried to push himself back in the water, he felt something different and strange. Marco looked at his fin. He found a hand instead. He could hear people yelling at him. "Hey, buddy, this is a public beach." He began to sit up and noticed he was nude. Someone threw him a towel. He looked up and could see two police officers standing over him.

One officer said, "Okay, sir. Will you please stand up? This is a public beach. You need to come with us." As they put him in the police car, all he could think about was how he was going to get to the hospital in order to find out what happened to Mary and the baby.

Once at the police station, they booked him and put him in an interrogation room. They questioned him, but all he would say was "I want to talk to my attorney, Frank Goldstein." He knew if he said anything, they might think he was crazy and put him in the psycho ward. He knew the law. They had to allow him to make a call, and he didn't have to answer any questions without legal counsel. He called Frank and said, "Goldie, it's me. I'm at the police department, and I need you to bail me out. Go by my office and pick up my suit, shoes, and everything that I had stored away in case of an emergency."

"Is this a joke?" asked Frank.

"No, it's really me!" said Marco. "And hurry!"

Marco was in his jail cell when Frank arrived. He was holding his suit and shoes. As they opened his cell door, he walked over to Frank, shook his hand, and said, "I will explain everything in the car."

Once in the car, he explained how Mary fell and that they needed to get to the hospital.

"What hospital?" asked Frank.

"Call David. But don't say anything about me." There was no answer, so he tried Elaine.

When Elaine answered, Frank got the name of the hospital. "l got it," answered Frank. He then told Marco he told the police his name was Joe Ricci.

"Good...If you need to introduce me, say I'm Marco's brother, Joe."

Frank asked, "How did you come back?"

"Frank, I don't know, but there must be a reason."

The Dolphin In Me   Nick Miraglia

CHAPTER 44

MARY, PLEASE COME BACK

At the hospital, the doctors finally came out of surgery and spoke to David and Elaine. Dr. Allen said, "The baby is doing fine."

Dr. Allen introduced Dr. Chang, the neurosurgeon who operated on Mary. "I was able to relieve the pressure on her brain, and she's off life support and breathing on her own, but there is a chance she'll never regain consciousness. I'm so sorry," said Dr. Chang.

Elaine, trying to hold it together, held David tightly. "But there is a chance?" David asked.

"If she regains consciousness, there's a strong possibility of brain damage." Dr. Allen said, "I wish I had better news, but you have a beautiful baby boy waiting to see you."

"When will we be able to see Mary?" David asked.

"In about an hour, but you can see the baby now." Both David and Elaine headed to the nursery to see the baby, stopping only to catch their composure before seeing him.

David said, "There he is." The name tag said Ricci. While they looked at every move the baby made, it was the only joy that stopped the tears from flowing.

David looked at his watch. "I'm going to see Mary."

"I'm going with you."

273

When they reached the waiting room, John, Nicole, and Aaron were there. Aaron was still in his baseball uniform.

David gave them the information the doctor had given him. He also said, "But we're not giving up. We need your prayers and support now. We're going to see Mary right now, but you can see the baby in the nursery." David and Elaine went into Mary's room.

Before they entered, David told Elaine they both had to keep it together. "We don't want her to hear us crying." Elaine had to put her hand over her mouth when she saw Mary lying on the bed with her whole head wrapped in bandages. She waved for David to talk to her while she tried to regain her composure. He was strong even and was able to talk to Mary without emotions taking over his voice.

Finally, Elaine regained her composure. "Hi, baby, it's Mom. We just came back from seeing your baby. He is so beautiful. Come back from where you are and see him for yourself." She held Mary's hand while talking.

"He is the biggest and the loudest baby in the whole nursery. You are going to have your hands full," said David.

They talked to her over the next two hours without a sound or any movement from Mary. Elaine then told David she needed a break and was going to go to the nursery to see the baby. When she left the room, she was immediately greeted by Nicole, John, and Aaron. Elaine told them, "Nothing new. She's still unconscious. I'm going to see the baby now. If you want to see Mary, go on in. David could

use a break. Keep it cheerful as much as you can."
One by one, they went in to see Mary.

Marco and Frank arrived at the hospital and went
right to the waiting room where Nicole and John
were waiting for Aaron to come out of Mary's
room. Frank introduced Marco as Joe, David's uncle. John updated them about Mary's condition. As
Aaron came out of the room, John quickly
introduced Aaron to David's Uncle Joe. Aaron
shook his hand and said, "Glad to meet you, Uncle
Joe." That put a smile on everyone's face. As Aaron
shook his hand, he felt a warm feeling come over
his body as if he already knew him.

Marco went down on one knee to look eye to eye
with Aaron. He said, "I've heard so much about
you. I hear you are pretty good at baseball."

"Can you wake up Mary for us?" asked Aaron.
Marco smiled and walked into Mary's room alone.

Marco saw David sitting in a chair next to the
bed, holding Mary's hand and talking to her. As he
turned to see who came in, he looked shocked. It
was his father holding out his arms with tears running down his face.

"Dad, is that you?" David said as he quickly got
out of the chair. All Marco could do was just nod
his head as he embraced his son and they held each
other tightly. "How did you come back?" asked David.

"Honestly, I don't know. All I know is that there
must be a reason that I'm here." He looked at Mary
lying motionless on the bed.

"Talk to her, Dad. Bring her back."

"It's not me that she wants to hear from. It's her new baby boy she needs to hear and feel," replied Marco. "Go to the nursery and bring her boy back so she can hear and hold him. And David, I'm your Uncle Joe."

For the first time, David felt a ray of hope. He left the room and asked everyone to say a prayer. David went to the nursery and saw Elaine looking at the baby through the glass. As she looked up, she could see the hope in David's eyes. David knocked on the glass to get the nurse's attention so he could take the baby to see its mother. The nurse told David and Elaine to go to the room and she would bring the baby to them.

While David was gone, Marco sat down on the chair, holding Mary's hand, and with his other hand, he placed it on the side of her face just as she would do with him when he was a dolphin. "Mary, this is Marco. I know it's hard to believe, but I'm here, sitting next to you as a man, not a dolphin. I was sent here to bring you back to David and your new baby boy. I know how beautiful it is where you are now, but you have unfinished business here. You have to remember there are people here that love you very much, and David needs you to help him bring up that beautiful baby boy."

While Marco prayed over Mary's still body, David and Elaine came back into the room. David said, "They are bringing the baby to the room."

"Did you hear that, Mary? The nurse is bringing your son to see you."

When the nurse brought the baby to the room, she handed him to David. Marco got up out of the chair so David could sit next to her. Elaine went to the other side of the bed so she could be close to her daughter.

David put the baby on her arm and supported the infant's head with his hands and said, "Mary, look. It's our baby boy." She remained motionless on the bed. All hope was starting to fade as there was no response, so Elaine reached out, putting Mary's other hand on the baby's hand and then to his face. There was still no response.

After about 45 minutes, the nurse said, "I'm so sorry, but I think we'd better return the baby to the nursery."

She reached over David to pick up the baby. He started to cry, and Mary moved her hand as if she was grabbing for the baby. Then her eyes opened ever so slowly until they were wide open. David took the baby out of the nurse's arms and put him back in Mary's. Everyone in the room was crying tears of joy. She smiled, looking at the baby and her family and friends in the room.

The nurse called for the on-call-duty doctor to come to the room. Dr. Allen entered, looked over at Mary holding her baby, and said, "Sleeping Beauty has awakened! Now, I'm sorry, but all of you have to leave the room, except the father, so I can check out mom." When the nurse went to pick up the baby, Mary gave her the stink eye. Dr. Allen said, "The baby can stay, but the father has to hold him until I finish my examination." That brought a smile to Mary's face. When the doctor was finished, he asked, "How are you feeling?"

"I'm feeling good now that I saw my son. Just a little headache. When can I go home with him?"

The doctor shook his head and said, "Mary, you are lucky to be alive. You have defied all the odds." Dr. Allen asked, "What do you remember?"

"I remember going down to the pier, tripping on a baseball bat, and falling. That's it until now."

The doctor said, "Dr. Chang, the neurologist who operated on you, will be visiting you in the morning. He will be surprised to see you awake. We will be running an MRI to make sure there isn't any more swelling or damage, but the fact you can recall what happened is a good sign. You need to get a lot of rest. Your body has gone through a lot of trauma. I will see you tomorrow."

"I'm Mary's mother, Elaine."

"I'm David's uncle, Joe." Elaine reached out to give him a handshake. When their hands touched, she felt the same warm feeling that she did when she touched the dolphin. Hiding her feelings, she said, "It's a pleasure to meet you."

"My pleasure," replied Marco.

When Dr. Allen exited Mary's room, he was immediately surrounded by everyone in the waiting room. He told them, "I'm totally amazed how she came back. The odds on her regaining consciousness were not good. She's not out of the woods yet. She needs to get as much rest as possible."

"Dr. Allen, can I see my daughter for just a minute."

"Just a quick goodnight."

When she entered the room, Mary was holding the baby with David by her side. It was a magical moment, seeing them all together. She walked to the other side of the bed, kissing Mary and the baby. "Dr. Allen said I could only stay long enough to say goodnight, but I will see you first thing in the morning."

Mary nodded her head and said, "I love you, Mom."

"I love you too." Then she blew a kiss to her.

The nurse came in to take the baby back to the nursery. She said she would bring him back in the morning so Mary could feed him. That brought a smile to Mary's face. After the nurse was gone with the baby, David told her he was going to say goodnight and thank everyone for coming, but he would be right back, and he would be spending the night right next to her. He didn't tell her about his dad. He reached over to give her a kiss and said, "Don't go anywhere. I'll be right back."

David went to the waiting room where everyone still gathered. He started to introduce Elaine to his father as his Uncle Joe.

"Too late. We already met," Elaine answered.

He gave thanks to everyone for their prayers. He turned to his dad, hugged him, and whispered in his ear, "You did it, Dad,"

"No, your son did."

David was so filled with emotions all he could do was nod his head. Regaining his composure, David told everyone that he was going to stay in the room with Mary. He asked if Elaine would take his Uncle Joe home to his house.

His dad said, "No, I'll stay with Frank."

Elaine said, "You are family, Joe. Plus, I could use the company instead of being in that big house alone. But I have no car. I came in the ambulance with Mary."

Frank said, "No problem. I can take you two back to the house."

David said, "I need to get back in with Mary. I'll keep you all updated as soon as I hear anything. Thank you all again."

When he walked back in the room, Mary was asleep. Worried she might have fallen back into a coma, he reached to hold her hand. When she opened her eyes, relief came over him, and he said, "Go back to sleep. I'll be right here." Mary smiled and lightly squeezed his hand.

CHAPTER 45

I NEED A DRINK

Walking out to Frank's car, there was a sense of relief, knowing that Mary was going to be all right.
As they reached the car, Marco opened the front
door for Elaine. Elaine said, "I can sit in the back."
Marco said, "No, it's all right. I can stretch out in
the backseat."

Driving to the house, Elaine said that David never mentioned he had an uncle. Marco said, "I have-
n't seen David in a long time. Frank told me about
all the wonderful things that David is doing for the
kids. I heard he got married. I was in Florida, so I
wanted to surprise him, but I wasn't expecting what
just happened." Trying to not go into detail, he
quickly tried to change the subject by saying,
"Frank, I'm expecting the airline to give me a call.
They lost my luggage, and I gave them your number."

Frank, picking up on where he was going with
the story, said, "As soon as they call, I'll pick up
your bags and bring them by the house."

"Thank you, Frank."

Arriving at the house, Marco quickly got out of
the car to open the door for Elaine. It had been a
while since a man opened the door for her. Her late
husband did it all the time when he was alive.
Elaine was flattered with all the attention. She gave
a smile to Marco and to Frank for the ride home.

They walked into the house. Marco was impressed by what David and Mary had done to the inside. Elaine gave him a tour, even showing him what they had done to the baby's room. Walking in the room, Marco saw that all of the walls were done in a seascape with whales and dolphins painted on them. And on one wall was a lone dolphin with a white star on his face, looking down on the baby crib. Marco held back the tears. Elaine, seeing how it was affecting him, told him that David did all the artwork. She then said, "I know. Every time I come in this room, it gets to me too."

"It is incredible."

Walking out of the room, Elaine said, "I don't know about you, but I could use a drink."

"I know what you mean. What a stressful day. Sure sounds good to me."

They walked downstairs to the kitchen. "Would you like a glass of wine, or would you like something stronger?"

"I'll have whatever you're having," Marco answered.

Elaine opened the refrigerator and took out a bottle of Pinot Grigio wine and pulled two glasses out of the cabinet. Opening up a drawer, she pulled out a bottle opener. Marco offered to open up the bottle and poured out the two glasses. Elaine said, "Let's sit outside."

Sitting on the patio overlooking the water, Marco held up his glass to toast Mary's recovery and to meeting Elaine. Elaine smiled and said, "I'll drink to that." Marco slipped back in the chair, enjoying the flavor. It had been a long time since he was able to enjoy a good glass of vino.

"It's obvious you have a close relationship with David," Elaine said.

Marco felt bad that he had to lie to her, but he had no other choice. He told Elaine he and his brother had a falling out, but he had always kept in touch with David. He told her, "David was there for me when I lost my wife years ago." Trying to change the subject, Marco asked, "Where were you when Mary fell?"

Elaine went through how she went to the hardware store to pick up picture hangers for a painting she wanted to hang on the wall before David got home. And while she was gone, Mary went down to the pier, and that is where they found her. Elaine said she felt responsible for not being there.

She finished what was left of her glass and poured another. Marco finished off what was remaining of his, trying not to make her feel like she was drinking alone. Elaine poured him another glass too. Marco said, "It wasn't your fault. It was an accident. There wasn't anything you could have done."

"I know, but I still feel responsible." Elaine said, "Thank God someone saw her lying on the dock and called 911, or she might not have made it. I would like to know who made the call to thank them for saving her life, but why didn't they help her until the fire department paramedics arrived?"

Marco didn't like where Elaine's line of questioning was going. He tried to convince her it was someone who was afraid of getting involved, or maybe it was someone who had a legal problem.

Elaine, with a puzzled look on her face, said, "You're probably right." She finished her wine. She got up and opened another bottle. She poured hers and poured Marco another one as well. She proposed a toast, "Here's to meeting Uncle Joe." They both took a gulp.

Marco, not to be outdone by Elaine, proposed another toast. "Here is to Grandma Elaine."

"Oh my God, that's right…a drunken grandma," laughed Elaine. They both took another sip.

She asked, "Are you hungry? With all the excitement of the day, I haven't eaten. How about you?"

Marco replied, "I could use a little something."

"Good, I'll see what I can find in the refrigerator," Elaine said. When she reached over to pick up her glass and the empty bottle, she knocked the bottle to the floor. Both Marco and Elaine tried to catch it. They bumped heads enough that it knocked her to the floor.

Elaine said, "Whoops." She lay back on the ground and started laughing again as tears of joy and relief from the events of the day came pouring out.

Marco, not having any alcohol in a long time, was affected in the same manner. He got up and walked over to help Elaine up. As he reached over to pick her up, he tripped over her feet and fell next to her. Lying on the floor next to her, he said, "Whoops!" They both started laughing again.

Elaine reached over, putting her hand on his chest and asked, "Are you all right?" As she touched his chest, she felt the warm, peaceful feeling again. As Marco went to help her up and put her in the chair, he told Elaine to stay there and he would fix something for them to eat. "That is a pretty good idea," she said as she started to laugh again.

Marco, feeling the effects of the wine, picked up the empty bottle and headed over to the refrigerator. He wasn't much of a cook. He just stared into the refrigerator, trying to keep from weaving back and forth. He then spotted a box of Snickers bars. He took two out of the box and staggered his way back to Elaine. He said with a smile, "I apologize. I'm not much of a cook."

"That's probably a safe choice." She started to laugh. She took the candy bar, peeled the wrapper back, and then held it up as if she were toasting. "Thank you for a gourmet meal," she said.

While they talked, the time went by fast, and Elaine felt at ease with Marco. Then she happened to look up at the clock. It was past midnight. She exclaimed, "Oh my god! Look what time it is." Marco also felt comfortable with Elaine and didn't want to end the evening. Elaine said, "I'd better get your bed ready."

By then, the wine had lost its effect, and she could walk without falling. She took him to the guest bedroom and showed him the bathroom. Elaine thanked him for dinner.

Marco said, "The pleasure was mine."

Elaine then gave him a hug. As she did, that warm, peaceful feeling again came over her body as she held him tightly. She didn't want to let him go. It lasted so long that Marco didn't know what to do. It turned into an embrace, pulling her closer into his chest. Elaine, out of nowhere, gave him a kiss on his neck and said, "Goodnight, and I will see you in the morning." All Marco could do was nod his head.

Elaine entered her bedroom, shut the door, and then lay down on the bed, thinking to herself what she had just done. What was she thinking? What did she just do? But it felt right. The feeling that she had holding him felt natural, and when he returned it into an embrace, she knew he felt something too.

After Elaine left the room, Marco felt the same feeling Elaine was feeling. Holding her felt good, and feeling her body next to him as they melted into one—and when she kissed him on the neck—sent chills down to his toes. He wanted to kiss her, but realizing what he was doing, he didn't. Was she feeling her late husband, or was it him? Was he just a medium for her husband? How long would he be there and would he become a dolphin again? It wouldn't be fair to Elaine to start something and disappear.

CHAPTER 46

WHO MADE THE CALL?

The next morning, Marco got up early. As he walked downstairs, he saw the painting that David painted of him looking out to the angry sea. It hit home as to what he had done in the past and brought reality to his mission and for the future. He walked out to the patio which overlooked the bay and the pier. As he looked at the pier, he saw Aaron. He knew Aaron was looking for him as a dolphin, so he walked down to talk to him.

Aaron kept calling out, "Nono!" As Marco walked up, Aaron saw him and said, "Hi, Uncle Joe. Have you seen a dolphin with a white star on his head?"

Marco sat down on the pier and asked Aaron to sit down with him. "Remember when the dolphin told you one day he might be gone and that you have to start your own life?"

Aaron answered, "Yes, but how do you know that? I was alone with Nono when he told me, and I didn't tell anyone."

"That's because I told you."

"You mean that you're not a dolphin anymore?"

Marco replied, "For now. Not to say one day I might be a dolphin again, but just like I told you before, that is our secret, and at the right time, I'll tell your mom and dad."

"I understand," Aaron said and gave him a hug. "I knew that there was something special about you

287

when you touched me in the hospital, and I told you to wake Mary up, and you did."

Marco said, "No, Aaron, the baby did. I might have given David the idea."

"So, I can't call you Nono, but Uncle Joe." Marco nodded his head yes. "That means you can come to my baseball game," Aaron said.

"I wouldn't miss it for the world, but I don't know how long I will be here or what is next. I will be here for you always in your heart. You understand it's not in my hands."

Aaron, holding him tight, said, "I want you to stay."

Back at the house, Elaine got up and was making coffee when she saw Uncle Joe and Aaron at the pier. She decided to visit them. "Good morning, you two," Elaine said as she handed Joe a coffee mug. "I hope you like a little cream in it."

Marco took a sip. He said, "French vanilla." Elaine gave him a smile and a wink. She asked Aaron if he had introduced Nono to Joe.

"No, he's not around this morning. Are you going to take Uncle Joe to my baseball game?"

Elaine was surprised at the question and asked, "Did you ask Uncle Joe if he would like to go?"

"He already said yes."

"I guess we'll be there."

"I'd better go back to the house. Mom is cooking my breakfast. Oh, I found Mary's phone on the dock." He handed the phone to Elaine and said, "Goodbye, Aunt Elaine and Uncle Joe."

Elaine turned to Marco and said, "You made quite an impression on Aaron."

Marco smiled and asked, "Have you heard from David this morning?"

"Not yet. They're running tests this morning. I'm sure as soon as David knows something, he'll call. Now, how about some breakfast?"

"That would be wonderful," Marco replied.

Once at the kitchen, Elaine went right to work, making eggs and bacon. Marco asked if there was anything he could do to help.

"I saw you in the kitchen last night. You looked like a lost puppy dog looking for a bone he buried and couldn't remember where he buried it."

Marco laughed and said, "I found the Snickers, didn't I?"

Elaine rolled her eyes. She asked him when was the last time he had a homemade breakfast.

Marco told her, "I'm on the road a lot, and I eat out quite often."

Elaine asked, "What do you do for a living?" Marco had to make up a story but tried to keep it simple.

"I sold my business a couple of years ago, and I'm kind of a freelance environmentalist."

"What is a freelance environmentalist?"

"I volunteer to help when there is need, like oil spills or some environmental accident."

That got Elaine's attention, "I sort of do the same thing but on a smaller scale. We do a harbor clean-up twice a year. If everyone would just pick up their own trash, it would really help."

"Amen to that." Marco nodded his head in agreement, trying to think of how to change the subject. "Are you sure I can't help you?"

"No, thank you. How do you like eggs?" Elaine asked.

It had been so long since he had a real breakfast, he paused for a second and then replied, "Whatever way you cook them will be fine."

"I like my eggs scrambled, but I add my French vanilla coffee creamer in with it."

Marco felt at ease with her. "Hey, there is a box of Snickers as a back-up in the refrigerator." She started to laugh and gave him a smile that would light up a room.

Marco told her he would at least set the table. She told him where the dishes were and to set the table in the patio overlooking the water.

She was finishing the bacon when the phone rang. Marco could hear Elaine talking to someone on the phone named Randy. She told him what had happened and that Mary and the baby were fine. She asked Randy if he knew who had called 911 so she could thank them. He said he'd look into it and call her.

When she finished her conversation, she started the scrambled eggs. Marco walked into the kitchen, and she told him she just got a call from a friend of her late husband. "Randy was the fire captain who worked on Mary the day of the accident. He wanted to know if there was anything he could do."

Marco knew it was going to be a problem when she found out the call came from Mary's cell.

They sat down for breakfast when Elaine got another call. It was Randy again, calling her back with the information. Marco heard Elaine say to Randy, "Are you sure that was the number?"

"That is what dispatch said, and the 911 call came from her address."

"That's Mary's cell number."

"I don't remember seeing a cell near her."

Elaine explained that Aaron, the boy next door, found it on the pier. "Could Mary have called for help?"

Randy replied, "It's possible, but not probable. Her head injury was so severe I don't think it's a possibility, but the dispatch said they could hear strange noises in the background, almost like a dolphin noise you hear at a dolphin show."

Elaine thanked Randy for all the help. As she hung up the phone, she turned to Marco and repeated the conversation that she had with Randy. She said, "How could Mary have called anyone in her condition?" Marco tried to convince her Mary must have called while she was on the pier. She said, "I'll ask Mary when I talk to her, but something doesn't make sense."

Marco quickly changed the subject. He said, "You know, these eggs are really good. The creamer gives it that extra kick."

That brought a smile to Elaine's face, and she said, "It's been a while since I cooked for a man. Ever since my husband's death, I've lost any desire to date anyone. I don't think I could ever find a man like that again. How about you?"

That question caught him by surprise, and he pondered a moment. "I was not the best of husbands. I put my work before my family, trying to get ahead, and I lost what life is truly all about. I wish I could do it all again. I would be a much better husband."

Elaine asked him if he had children. He felt bad about lying to her, but he had to keep it simple. It would open up more questions, so he said no. He told her how wonderful it was that she now had a grandson.

That put a smile on Elaine's face, and she said, "I can't wait 'til they bring him home so I can start to spoil him." Just then, the phone rang again. Elaine answered it and said, "It's Frank. He needs to talk to you."

Frank told Marco they had a problem. When the police booked him for being nude in public, they automatically ran his fingerprints through the computer and found out he wasn't who he said he was. In fact, it came in as Marco Ricci, deceased. They wanted him to come down to the station to talk to them. Marco understood and said to Frank, "I'll have to get back to you on that."

Frank knew that Marco couldn't talk and said, "I understand, and I will try to delay them until you call."

"Thank you, Frank." When he hung up, he told Elaine the airline still couldn't locate his bags.

CHAPTER 47

BRIGHT LIGHT

At the hospital, Mary woke up to find David all curled up in a chair next to her bed, still holding her hand. She squeezed his hand slightly. David quickly woke up to Mary smiling at him. He gave her a kiss and said, "You know you scared the crap out of me. I thought I lost you yesterday."

"I'm so sorry to have put you through that. I remember falling, and I remember being in the most beautiful place in the world. I could see a bright light that just drew me to it. When I got closer, the feeling became stronger to go to the light. I could hear voices calling me back, but I kept telling them how beautiful it was, and I can't come back. I could hear your voice and then Mom, and then I heard your dad's voice telling me that it's not my time and I had unfinished business here. I stopped and turned around, and I heard our baby crying. The light faded away, and I woke up holding our son." Mary said, "I'm never going to leave you again."

The door opened to their room and the nurse, holding their son, said, "I have someone who wants to see you." She handed the baby over to Mary and a bottle of formula to David and asked, "Are you planning on breastfeeding?"

Mary looked over at David and said, "I think so."

The nurse said, "I'll check with the doctor to see when you can start."

David asked, "Can I hold the bottle?"

When they were done, the nurse came back into the room. She said, "The doctors will be here shortly. I'll bring him back after they run some tests."

They took Mary to get an MRI. David waited in the room. It was a good chance to get everyone caught up on Mary's condition. He texted everyone that everything was great. Mary was getting tests and when he got any news, he would let everyone know.

When all the tests were done, Mary returned to the room where David was waiting. The nurse asked if she would like some breakfast. "Yes, that would be wonderful...and coffee," Mary replied.

After breakfast, the nurse came into the room to take the tray away. She said, "I haven't seen such commotion in this hospital in a long time. You've got every doctor lined up to see you, gal."

The first doctor to pay a visit was Doctor Chang. He introduced himself by saying, "I'm the neurologist who worked on you last night." Then he asked how she was feeling and if she had any headaches.

Mary answered, "I'm feeling fine and had a good night's sleep, not like someone else." She pointed to David, who was yawning.

Dr. Chang asked, "What do you remember about what happened?" Mary told him what she had told David earlier. Then the doctor unwrapped the bandages around her head. He was looking and feeling her head with a puzzled look on his face. "I can barely see where your injury was. Your body has remarkable healing abilities. Your MRI shows nothing to indicate that you even had a head injury. In all my years, I have never seen anything like this. By all medical findings, you should still be in a coma with that kind of trauma. And that you can recall up to the time of your fall is remarkable to say the least.

Mary asked, "When can I go home?"

The doctor replied by saying, "As far as I am concerned, you can go home tomorrow, but you need to check with your OBGYN. While you're here, I'd like to run some more tests on you to find out why your healing process is in hyperdrive. This could be a breakthrough in treating others."

Mary replied, "Sure, anything I can do."

Dr. Chang said, "There are some other doctors waiting in the hall to see you. You caused quite a bit of excitement."

Each doctor came into the room, and all left shaking their heads over what happened and how fast Mary was healing. After the last doctor came in and Mary and David were alone, David said to Mary, "Do you remember the voice you heard. You said it was my father. He was sitting in this chair talking to you."

Mary answered, "He is not a dolphin anymore?" Mary's eyes got bigger. "Oh, my god."

"He's staying at our house, and he got a chance to see his grandson." David continued. "He is Uncle Joe to everyone, and the only people who know is Frank, you, and me. I have to think that there is some higher intervention going on."

"I can't believe it. I can't wait to get to meet your father in a human form. Did he say what happened?"

"No, all he said was there was a reason why he is here, and it was his idea to bring our baby into the room. He said it was the baby's voice you needed to hear." David shook his head. He reached over, holding Mary tightly.

"I really need to see your dad and thank him."

"We'll have to wait for the right time to talk to him. I feel bad keeping your mom in the dark, but I don't know if my dad is going to be returned into a dolphin or retain a human form. The reason he came back was to use his powers to save you, and now that you're safe, what will be his fate?"

Mary, still in disbelief of how she was saved said, "We need to talk to your dad to find out what we should do."

David agreed.

CHAPTER 48

KEEP THE SECRET

At the house, Elaine got a call from Mary. "Hi, Mom."

"Baby, how are you feeling?"

"We got the okay from the neurologist, but we're waiting to find out from the OBGYN if we can maybe be home tomorrow. If you and Uncle Joe would like to come today, it would be fine." She didn't go into any detail on how fast she was healing and about all the doctors that came by.

Elaine was surprised she and the baby might be coming home. "Are you sure it's not too early?"

"Have you tried this hospital food?"

She heard her daughter start to laugh. "That's what I'm talking about."

"Could you bring some clothes for me to wear when I leave the hospital? How are you and Joe getting along?"

She could tell the excitement in her mother's voice when she started talking. When Mary was finished talking to her mom, she asked if she could put Uncle Joe on the phone because David needed to talk to him.

She passed the phone off to David. When Marco answered, David immediately told him to be careful so Elaine wouldn't know what they were talking about. The first thing David asked his father was if he could talk without Elaine hearing. His dad replied, "No." David told him they needed to talk to him as soon as possible alone. Marco said loud enough for Elaine to hear, "Just a change of clothes."

"Good job, Dad. Just bring some Levi's and a shirt," David said. "Make sure Elaine doesn't know what we're talking about. Call me back when it's safe to talk."

"Yeah, I know."

After the call ended with Mary and David, Elaine said, "I'd better get ready so we can go to the hospital. I'll pick up some clothes for David along with Mary's clothes."

Marco said all David needed was a shirt and a pair of Levi's. As Elaine went to get ready, it is was a perfect opportunity for Marco to call back to the hospital and talk to Mary and David without Elaine hearing.

When Marco called back to the room, Mary was using the restroom, so David answered the phone. Marco said, "David, it's Dad. I just have a moment to talk while Elaine is getting ready. I want to give you a heads up on what was happening here. Aaron found Mary's phone on the dock and a paramedic who worked the call was a friend. Elaine wanted to thank the person who called 911 for saving Mary's life. They traced down the phone number to Mary's cell. The paramedic friend said that Mary was in no condition to make the call."

"Who made the call?" David asked.

"I did, David. I'll explain later."

"Okay, but we have another situation. A stream of doctors have been shuffling in and out of here all morning, trying to find out how Mary's healing process is in hyperdrive. We need to keep Elaine from talking to the doctors."

"I understand the problem. I'll do my best to keep her away from everyone. I'd better go now before Elaine comes down."

When David ended the call, Mary was just getting back from the restroom. He relayed the information his father told him.

Mary said, "We can't keep changing our story because then no one will believe us. Trust me. Once we get home, my mother will be so wrapped up with the baby she'll forget about it. But keeping her away from all the people here will be tough."

"My dad said he will try to keep her away from everyone at the hospital."

CHAPTER 49

THE JOKE

At the house, while Elaine was still getting ready, the front doorbell rang. Marco answered. It was Aaron, dressed up in his baseball uniform. "I have an all-star game today and wanted to know if Elaine and you could come."

"We have to go to the hospital to drop off some clothes for Mary and David. The baby might be coming home tomorrow. But I'll find out when we get to the hospital, and we could probably make it. Are both of your parents home?"

"Yes."

"I'll be right back." He went upstairs to let Elaine know that Aaron was downstairs. "He wants to show me his baseball collection."

"I'll meet you at Aaron's house. I'm almost ready," she replied.

It was a perfect opportunity to let Aaron's parents know he was back in human form and give a heads up on what was happening. He went back downstairs where Aaron was all smiles, knowing he didn't have to keep the secret from his parents any longer.

When they reached Aaron's house, Marco didn't know exactly how to let them know what had happened, but with what they all went through with Aaron's cancer remission, he was sure they would understand. Together they walked into the house. Aaron told Marco he would be right back. "Mom...Dad...Uncle Joe is here."

John immediately went to shake his hand and said, "We really didn't get a chance to talk much last night at the hospital. It was so crazy."

Marco replied, "I know. That's why I'm here."

Nicole went to shake his hand when a warm feeling came over her that made her say, "I have a feeling that we have met somewhere before."

Marco replied, "We have, but not in this form."

They all had a puzzled look on their faces except for Aaron who said, "It's Nono." Nicole and John were speechless. Marco nodded his head as Aaron said, "I kept my promise. I'm sorry, Mom and Dad, but I couldn't tell you."

Marco didn't even get a chance to finish what he was about to say when Nicole rushed into his arms. "Thank you for saving Aaron's life. I could never give you a proper thank you when you were a dolphin. John also thanked him for giving Aaron a chance to live a full life.

Marco said, "I need to tell you what is going on before Elaine comes over. I know you have a lot of questions, and in time, I'll try to answer them, but for now, we need to keep this a secret from Elaine. At the right time, we'll let her know everything, but now is not the time." He went on to explain everything that had happened from when Mary fell to what was happening at the hospital.

He was finishing up as Elaine arrived at the door. Nicole let her in, and Elaine noticed the mascara that had smeared from Nicole's eyes. "Is everything all right?"

"Joe just told a joke that had me almost wet my pants laughing," Nicole said. Marco jumped in to explain how Aaron had an all-star game, and he wanted them to come later that afternoon. He explained they had to go to the hospital to bring some clothes for Mary and David. He asked, "What time is the game?"

"It's at three o'clock, Uncle Joe. Please, please come!"

"I'm pretty sure we can make it." He looked over at Elaine.

"Sure, we should have plenty of time. Text me the address."

Aaron went over to give Elaine a hug and said, "Thank you, thank you."

"We'd better get going. I need to see my grandson." Walking out to the car, Elaine said, "Boy, you sure know how to make an impression on Aaron." Marco smiled and shrugged his shoulders. Elaine gave him a playful punch in the arm. "I want to hear the joke you told everyone that almost made Nicole wet her pants."

"Maybe," he said as he opened the driver side door for her.

"Why, thank you."

He got in the car. He looked over at Elaine's stunning beauty, and she smiled at him. "You'd better buckle your seat belt."

"Thank you."

She gave him a playful look and said, "What is it going to take for me to get you to tell me that joke?"

"I'll let you know." He knew it was getting to her, but at least it was keeping her mind off what happened to Mary. To keep her from finding out what was going on at the hospital was the next challenge.

CHAPTER 50

MARY, MEET UNCLE JOE

At the hospital, Mary was still being interviewed by more doctors. The last doctor to visit was a pediatrician who was more interested in the new baby, telling them it would be in the best interest for the baby to stay one more day. It was the hospital's protocol that Cesarean-section babies and mothers stay a minimum of three days. Also, it was important for the bonding of the parents and the baby before the relatives arrive. Both Mary and David agreed that it was best to listen to what the pediatrician said no matter how badly they wanted to go home.

When Elaine and Marco came in the room, Elaine immediately went to her daughter's side, giving her a hug and kiss and asking her how she was doing. Mary explained what the pediatrician had told her.

Elaine said, "What do the doctors know about bonding? That's just an excuse to get more money." That got a chuckle out of David and Mary. "All he needs is to have Grandma hold him."

Mary winked while replying, "That is why we need this time alone with him." The whole time, she kept glancing over at Marco.

"By the way, have you come up with a name yet?"

Mary looked over to David and said, "Marco William Ricci." They could see how honored Elaine was that they picked her late husband's name.

"When is MW coming up again?" asked Elaine.

"MW? Seriously, Mom."

"You got it."

Mary shook her head and said, "He just went down for a nap. They took him back to the nursery." She continued to glance over at Marco.

Elaine asked, "Would you mind if I go see him now? We promised Aaron that we would go to his all-star baseball game today."

"Sure, Mom, but no kidnapping Marco out of the hospital."

Elaine gave Mary a kiss goodbye. She said, "Thank You, David, for taking such good care of Mary and for thinking of my late husband in your son's name." Elaine asked Joe if he wanted to go with her to see the baby.

"I'll meet you there. I need to talk to David."

"Go get the car ready, Joe. I'll be coming out of the nursery, holding a little bundle of joy." Elaine gave a wink and a smile as she left the room.

Mary shook her head. "Mothers."

After Elaine was safely out of sight, Mary got out of her bed, walked over to Marco, and gave him a hug. Holding her hand to each side of Marco's face as she did when he was a dolphin, she said, "I finally get to meet you and thank you for saving my life and for all the wonderful things that you've done."

He looked her in the eyes and said, "No...thank you for saving my life and trusting in me. Without you, none of this would have happened, and I wouldn't have a grandson." Marco said, "I know that you two have a lot of questions to ask, but I don't have answers. I'm living each day as it comes. I've told Aaron, Nicole, and John. I feel bad about keeping this secret from Elaine, and I'm planning on telling her when the time is right, which I need your help with. But for now, I'd better go so she doesn't get suspicious or someone from the hospital starts talking about your recovery to her. We'll talk soon." He gave Mary a kiss on the forehead and David a kiss on his cheek. "Thank you both for giving me something to live for...my grandson," he said as he left the room.

Marco quickly walked down to the nursery to meet Elaine, a sense of pride coming over him. Seeing Elaine looking at her grandson through the glass gave him a feeling of having a family again. It made him think of Christmas, Thanksgiving, and all the holidays. It gave him the courage to do what needed to be done and tell her the truth, but that would have to wait until Mary and David got home and the time was right.

He walked over to Elaine. As she looked up at him, the twinkle in her eyes was spellbinding. She caught him staring at her and then said, "What?"

"Being a grandmother is a special time in your life."

"I know. I'm still too young to be a grandma, but how could you not want to be after seeing him." She then put her arms around his waist and her head on his chest. Marco put his arm around her shoulder and his head on her head as they stared at their grandson sleeping. He felt so at peace with her in his arms that he didn't want to move.

A nurse came by, seeing them together, and said, "I love coming down here and seeing all the families looking at the babies. Which one is yours?"

"Marco William Ricci," Elaine replied.

The nurse said, "Then you must be the grandparents. That baby and the mother has got this hospital turned upside down. They are truly a miracle."

Marco interrupted the nurse before she said any more and said, "This is the grandmother, and I'm the uncle."

"Oh," the nurse replied. "I thought you were both the grandparents."

"That's all right. I'm sorry, but we'd better get going to Aaron's baseball game."

Walking out to the car, Elaine put her arm around his and looked up at him with a smile. "Thank you for being here with me, Grandpa."

"You're welcome, Grandma." If only she knew how true that statement was.

CHAPTER 51

LAST INNING

When they reached the baseball field, they could see Nicole and John waiving to them from the stands. Aaron was warming up out on the field.

The game started, Aaron batted for the first time, and Marco could see him looking for them in the stands. He stepped into the batter's box. With the first pitch, he took a rip so hard he fell down. The next pitch was the same. On the third pitch, he was called out. Marco could see he was trying too hard to impress him. The next time he was at the plate, it was the same nightmare with him striking out again. To make things worse, he dropped a ball that allowed the other team to score the go-ahead run.

It was the bottom of the last inning and the last chance for Aaron's team. Marco told everyone he had to go to the bathroom and he would be back before Aaron got up. When he was out of sight, he turned to the dugout. He could see through the chain-link fence Aaron had his head down. Marco called out to him. As he got his attention, Aaron walked over so he could talk. Aaron said, "I'm sorry I'm playing so bad. I really wanted to show you what I can do."

Marco could see the frustration and said, "Aaron, everyone is already proud of you. You don't have to prove that to anyone. Look at what we have done together and everything you have done by yourself. Just get up there like we used to do when we would play baseball with Elaine on the pier. Just relax and have fun."

While they were talking, Aaron's team got a walk, putting the tying run at first base. It was Aaron's turn at bat. Marco quickly ran up to the stands where everyone was cheering that the tying run was on base.

Aaron started up to the plate. Marco saw him look over at them and nod at them. As he stepped up to the plate, he took his bat and pointed it to center field. This took everyone by surprise, especially the pitcher who had struck Aaron out two times. The first pitch was a strike. Aaron then again pointed his bat to center field. The second pitch again was a strike, and the pitcher smiled at Aaron. Now it was two strikes and two outs and the pitcher was smiling at Aaron and shaking his head. The next pitch Aaron crushed over the center field fence for a walk off home run that won the game. Everyone jumped up and started cheering. Elaine was so excited she gave Marco a kiss that about knocked him off his feet. She said, "I taught him that!" As they all cheered for Aaron, all of his teammates tackled him when he hit home plate. Everyone went down to the field to see him.

John and Nicole were the first ones to give him a high five. Elaine asked, "What made you point to center field and then wait until you had two strikes against you?"

Aaron answered, "Uncle Joe told me to relax and pretend I was on the pier, hitting balls."

Elaine looked at Marco and said, "Had to go to the bathroom? Ha!"

"Whoops." He put his hand over his mouth.

Nicole asked, "Why don't you guys come over for dinner tonight?"

Elaine looked over at Marco and said, "Sure, that would be wonderful. What can we bring?"

"Nothing," Nicole replied. We are just having a barbecue with hamburgers—Aaron's favorite."

CHAPTER 52

OKAY, WHAT IS THE JOKE?

On the way back to the house, Elaine stopped by the liquor store. "I know what kind of wine Nicole and John like," she said as she picked up four bottles.

Marco rolled his eyes and said, "Are you sure this is enough?"

"We're celebrating, and I'm going to get you drunk so you will tell me the joke you told Nicole that almost made her pee her pants."

Getting home, Elaine took one of the bottles and took two glasses out. She then said, "It's wine o'clock. Would you care to join me?"

"Of course," Marco replied. We have to make sure it's good enough to take over to Nicole and John's."

"I like your way of thinking," she said. They sat on the couch, and she put her hand on his leg. "What a day. I got to see my grandson and watch Aaron hit the walk-off home run to win the game. Thank you again for sharing that with me. It's been a long time since I've had a day like this." She raised her glass up for a toast. "Here's to a fun day with you."

He replied, "Many more to come."

"I would like that."

Sitting next to her, he wanted to kiss her and hold her in his arms. He was feeling things with Elaine that he hadn't felt in a very long time. She was working her way into his heart. He knew that he needed to tell her the truth about himself, but without Mary and David's help to support what he would say, and the timing being not just right, he would have to wait. They needed to get ready for the barbecue at Nicole and John's house.

"You know, I'd better change and freshen up before we go over to the barbecue," Elaine said as she walked upstairs to her room. Marco couldn't keep his eyes off her. He loved how she carried herself, elegant but still being fun to be around. Just before she walked in her bedroom, she turned her head and smiled at him. She knew that he would be looking.

It wasn't long before he could see Elaine walking down the stairs looking stunning in a halter top summer dress that showed off every bit of her figure.

"Wow, you look great."

"Why, thank you, Grandpa." As he handed her a fresh glass of wine, they sat there just talking until the smell of the barbecue got their attention.

Walking along the beach to the barbecue, Elaine stumbled and started to fall. He reached out to catch her, holding her hand until she regained her balance. She stopped, took off her jeweled sandals, and said, "Good catch. Thank you. These fancy sandals are not made for walking in the sand." She then laughed.

They walked hand and hand to the patio where John was cooking the food. John greeted them as Nicole and Aaron came out the back door. Marco handed the two bottles to Nicole as Aaron ran over to greet him. Elaine said, "Hey, where is my hug, Louisville Slugger?"

Aaron gave Elaine a hug and asked, "What is a Louisville Slugger?"

Elaine explained that it was the number one bat all the greats like Babe Ruth, Ty Cobb, and Lou Gehrig swung.

"We could smell the hamburgers all the way from the house. I haven't had a hamburger in a long time."

Elaine gave him a puzzled look and asked, "Why not?"

"I've kinda been on a seafood diet," Marco replied as everyone started to laugh except Elaine.

Elaine said, "I'm sorry. I don't get the joke."

He quickly thought of something to say. "You know, see food, eat food?"

Elaine was still not convinced. "Okay, who is going to tell me the joke that Joe told you?" she asked.

Marco quickly stepped in to say, "Don't say a word. I told Elaine she would have to earn it."

Everyone put their hands to their mouths to zip them shut. Elaine said, "This is a conspiracy." Everyone nodded their heads yes and then started to crack up.

CHAPTER 53

THE JOKE WAS ON MARCO

After eating, laughing, and talking all night and the last of the wine was gone, it was time to go. Everyone said goodnight. Marco said to Elaine, "It's a good thing that we only have to go next door, or we would have to Uber." They went back to the house, holding each other up from falling down.

About halfway home, they tripped over each other, and Elaine landed on top of him as they fell in the sand. There was a brief minute of silence. Their lips touched which turned into a long, passionate kiss. Feeling the warmth of her body sent chills through him. When the kiss stopped, Elaine said, "Okay, I'm going to try to stand up." She started to laugh and couldn't get up.

He reached over, looking into her eyes while they were both kneeling in the sand. He pulled her in tight until they formed a single entangled body.

Unable to stand, they started crawling on all fours, laughing, until Elaine said, "Stop it. I can't breathe." Marco reached down to pick her up and carried her into the house with her arms around his neck. She went limp and passed out in his arms. Marco carried her up to her bedroom and placed her on the bed. She didn't even move a muscle; he gave her a quick kiss on her forehead and quietly shut the door.

He went to his room and jumped in the shower to get all the sand out of his hair. He knew that she had as much as he did, and he felt bad leaving her clothes on.

After the shower, he lay in bed thinking about what had just transpired and how much fun it was just to be with her. The kiss and feeling her body next to his was a moment he would never forget. He knew that she was working her way into his old heart. Lying there, he kept going over in his mind how he was going to tell her about himself and everything that had happened. How would she take it? One thing he knew was Mary and David had to be there or else she would never believe him.

He drifted off to sleep but was suddenly awakened by a warm body lying next to him. He could feel her naked body and her breasts against his back. Was he dreaming or was it really Elaine? When he turned around, Elaine gazed into his eyes. He started to speak, but she put her finger to his lips and gave him a toe-curling kiss. She rolled over on top of him as it lingered and got more passionate. She straddled him and put her hands on his chest. She gave him another passionate kiss that aroused him, and then they made love. She looked so beautiful. He was totally taken aback as her eyes never left his during the whole time they made love. The whole time, she never said a word.

They both lay there in the bed, coiled like a snake that just captured its prey. Her head buried in his chest, Elaine said, "Does that qualify as earning it? So now you have to tell me the joke."

"Well, maybe."

She playfully punched him. She said, "What do you mean, well maybe?"

He answered, "I meant maybe we should try it again."

That caused Elaine to laugh, and she said, "It's been a long time for me, but they say it's like riding a bike. You never forget."

"Trust me, you never forgot a thing." As he reached over and kissed her, they started all over again.

After the second go 'round, they both lay there in each other's arms until they fell asleep.

In the morning when he awoke, Elaine was not in bed with him. He could hear the shower from her room. He got dressed and went down to the kitchen to start the coffee.

The phone rang. Marco picked it up, thinking it might be David. It was Frank warning him that the cops came by, looking for him, and they had a warrant. He asked Frank, "How much time do you think I have before they come here."

Frank said, "Probably within the hour or less."

"Okay, Frank, I'll get back to you, or I'll have David get in touch with you. Thanks, old friend."

Elaine came down the stairs, putting her arms around him, giving him a kiss. He quickly tried to put a game plan in place that would not involve Elaine. He told her, "I was just going to bring you your coffee and then head down to the pier for a quick swim."

"I wish I could join you, but I just washed my hair. I'll get breakfast started while you're swimming." He gave her a kiss that he would remember for a long time. "Wow, you sure know how to please a woman." He smiled and ran upstairs to change into one of David's bathing suits.

Going down the stairs, he blew a kiss to her and ran down to the pier. As he got ready to jump in the water, he could see Elaine looking at him from the patio. He waved to her for the last time. Marco could see a police car coming down the street as he jumped into the water. While he swam away, he could see the police car stop at the house and saw Elaine walk back inside. He kept swimming when all of a sudden, he was swimming at such a speed he could not see his hand. He knew what was happening. He was back as a dolphin again. His life was changed again, but he accepted his fate. Mary was safe, and he got to see his grandson. His only regret was not being able to hold Elaine in his arms and wake up next to her. That would only be in his dreams.

CHAPTER 54

WARRANT FOR HIS ARREST

At the house, Elaine went to the kitchen to start breakfast when the doorbell rang. Opening the door, she was greeted by two police officers who said, "Good morning, ma'am. I'm Officer Jones and this is Officer Mack. We are looking for Joe Ricci. Is he here?"

Elaine said, "Yes. Is this about his luggage?"

Officers Jones replied, "No, we just need to talk to him."

"He just went for a swim in the ocean. He'll be right back for breakfast."

Officer Mack went to the backyard to go down to the pier. The other officer asked to come in the house. By then, Elaine got defensive and said, "You can wait outside unless you have a warrant."

Officer Jones then handed Elaine the warrant as he walked in the house.

Elaine went right to the phone and called David. She was very upset as he answered. "David, the police are here looking for your Uncle Joe. They have a warrant for his arrest."

"I'll call Frank, and he'll be right over. We'll be home shortly."

Officer Jones came down from upstairs as Officer Mack came in from the pier, holding a towel. Jones said, "No one is upstairs."

Mack said, "I only found this towel. Ma'am, is this your towel?"

"Yes, like I told you, he went for a swim."

Officer Mack said, "I'll check out the other end of the bay where the aquarium facility is, and I'll call for back up. Ma'am is he a good swimmer?"

"I don't know. I guess. He jumped in the ocean," Elaine said sarcastically.

The officer called dispatch for a helicopter and a harbor patrol boat and explained how he was working his way back, walking along the beach.

"Ma'am, was Mr. Ricci acting strange this morning or depressed."

"No, what is this all about?"

The officer responded, "Sorry, ma'am, I cannot discuss this matter with you." He continued asking her questions. "What day did he come in, and where was he staying?"

Elaine said, "Sorry, officer, I cannot discuss this matter with you."

Jones said, "Maybe you would like to answer these questions downtown."

Just then, Frank entered the house and introduced himself as Joe Ricci's attorney and said, "I will answer any questions you need answered. Elaine, where is Joe?"

"He went for a quick swim, and I was making breakfast."

Frank said, "Instead of scaring this lady, you might think about a rescue operation. You know that there was already a shark attack in the cove this year, and I know Joe has some health issues."

Officer Jones answered, "We already have a heli-copter on the way, along with a patrol boat."

Frank went over to Elaine, who was sitting down with both hands on her face. He tried to console her, not knowing that Marco was safe and was hiding out, waiting for the police to leave. If it was the plan, he would do his best to make it as convincing as possible.

Mary and David arrived at the house with the baby along with Nicole, John, and Aaron. Distraught, Elaine ran over to Mary. Mary handed off the baby to David to comfort her mother. "Easy, Mom. What happened?"

Elaine told her daughter how they went over to Nicole and John's house for a barbecue and they got really drunk. She whispered in her daughter's ear how she and Joe had slept together. Then she said, "This morning he went for a swim, and now they can't find him. I didn't know he had health issues or that there was a shark attack in the cove this year."

Elaine started to cry, which woke up the baby. David told Mary he was going to put the baby to bed away from all the commotion.

David motioned to Frank to come upstairs. He put the baby down for a nap and asked Frank what happened.

"When your dad was arrested on the beach, nude, they automatically ran his fingerprints through the computer and found out it was Marco Ricci, deceased. I told your dad they wanted to talk to him, but he had so much going on, I assume he forgot. So they put a warrant out for him. They came by my house, looking for him, so I called your dad and warned him. I think your dad is faking his own death. Elaine told the police he went for a swim. I told the police that he had some health is-sues, which I assume he does going from a human to dolphin back to human again."

"Could you have Mary come up here?" asked David.

When Mary came into the nursery room, he was watching over the baby. Mary saw the baby was asleep and asked David, "What the hell is going on?"

David told her the whole story. "...The police wanted him to come in for questioning."

"That's not all. My mother told me they slept to-gether...twice. And my mother said it was pretty physical, and now my mom thinks that she caused him to drown."

"Are you kidding me?" exclaimed David.

Mary replied, "That's what I said. She's really upset. We need to tell her everything. If she is upset now, wait until she finds out we didn't tell her the truth right away when we should have."

"I'd better get back downstairs and see what's going on," said David.

He was greeted by Officer Jones. "How long has your uncle been here at the house, and are you aware of your uncle's health issues?"

While David was talking to the officer, Frank came over to help. David told the officer, "I was in the hospital with my wife. She had an emergency operation and then had our baby. Uncle Joe came by the hospital and the subject never came up. Frank, who is his long-time friend, would be able to an-swer that better than I can."

Officer Jones asked, "Frank, what kind of medical issues did he have?" Frank told the officer he would pass out, and he couldn't drive because of it.

Frank spoke to the officer, explaining a call came over the radio from the police helicopter that was searching the water in the cove. They reported nothing in the water except a single dolphin swimming next to the pier. Immediately, Frank and David knew it was Marco back as a dolphin. Jones told David the harbor patrol boat with divers was on the way to aid in the search party and that he would keep him posted.

David walked outside where Elaine was sitting in a chair with her head in her lap. He walked over and looked out toward the pier where he saw his dad in the water. It was bittersweet knowing his father was safe.

He knelt next to Elaine, putting his hands over her hands. She looked up with tears flowing from her eyes. David asked, "Do you trust me?" Elaine nodded her head yes. David said, "Uncle Joe is all right." Elaine stopped crying and a smile came over her face. Then David put his finger to his lips and said, "Trust me. As soon as all the police leave, I will tell you all about what has transpired. We need to keep it low key. If you are up for it, could you watch the baby and ask Mary to come down so I can talk to her?"

She got off the chair and asked, "You're sure he is okay, and you're not just trying to make me feel better?" David nodded his head yes.

Elaine went upstairs to the baby's room where Mary was sitting in a chair next to the crib, watching the baby sleep. "He looks so beautiful and peaceful."

Mary got up from her chair to give her mother a hug. Elaine said, "David told me Joe is okay and that he couldn't talk now, but as soon as everyone leaves, he will tell me everything. What is going on?"

Mary didn't want to lie any more to her mother, so she said, "Let me go down and find out. Can you watch the baby? But let me know if he wakes up. It will be time to feed him."

"Of course," she said.

Walking down the stairs, Mary was taken aback by all the police walking around with their radios on, talking to other police officers. Then she spotted David talking to Frank. When David saw Mary, he waved her over to the outside patio where they could talk without anyone hearing them. David put his arm around her as if to console her with bad news and explained what he was doing. Mary tried to look concerned. Then David went on to explain that when Marco jumped into the water to get away from the police, he turned back into a dolphin. "He's okay. We can see him in the water."

"I was hoping somehow your dad would remain in a human form." Her voice started to crack. "The sad part is we lost our baby's grandfather and all the normal family ties that go with having grandparents."

"I know. I feel the same way."

"Also, how is this going to affect my mother? My mother wouldn't sleep with someone without having special feelings."

David explained, "I told Elaine that Uncle Joe was okay and I would tell her everything when everyone left."

"We have to tell her together."

David agreed.

The day wore on, the search intensified with divers in the water and the helicopter in the air, covering the whole cove. Everyone patiently waited for the search to end, trying not to cause any suspicions.

It was starting to get dark when Officer Jones came over to David and gave him the latest update. Jones said, "The helicopter had to go back because it was running low on fuel, and the rescue boat had to return to port. We had a dog check out the beach on the cove with no result. We had the U.S. Coast Guard conduct a search outside the cove with the same result. We will be back tomorrow. I'm sorry, but the chances of finding him are not good. So tomorrow it will be a body recovery search."

Elaine came out of the nursery holding the crying baby. Mary ran upstairs, took the baby back into nursery, and asked her mother to go with her. As soon as she started to breastfeed the baby, he stopped crying. Elaine noticed that Mary's mascara was running down her face, and she asked, "What's going on down there? You've been crying?"

Mary replied, "It was part of the plan to get the police out of here."

"What the hell is going on?" asked Elaine.

Mary said, "Mom, I'm a little busy right now. When I'm finished, David and I will explain everything."

"I'm sorry, honey. I didn't mean to upset you. It's just that I feel guilty about what happened. I'll go downstairs."

"No, just stay with me until the police leave. Joe is okay. Trust me."

CHAPTER 55

THE TRUTH

While in the water, Marco could see all the police walking along the beach in the cove. He could see the helicopter overhead. It was pulling out from its pursuit to find him.

He could keep out of sight except to take a breath of air. Then he saw David looking at the pier. At that point, he jumped in the air so David could see him. He could tell David saw him and knew he was okay. A higher power looked after Marco, for sure. The ability to change back and forth from a dolphin to a human was hard to understand unless there was more work to be done. Marco remembered telling Elaine what he did for a living—a freelance environmentalist who would go to different places where they needed help and volunteers. He wondered if that was his new mission, and could he control the change from dolphin to human? Those were the things that he would have to figure out, but it would also come at a price. It would be very dangerous for him if someone were to find out and try to exploit it for a military use or if terrorists would use it. He was sure his questions would all be answered in time, but he would have to lay low and let David handle the situation. Once the police left, he would let Elaine know everything. *She must be wondering if I'm a fugitive running from the law.* He couldn't imagine what must be going through her mind after spending such a romantic evening with her, and then all of a sudden, he was gone. He knew that when the right time came, David and Mary would tell her.

After all the police had gone and the baby was asleep, Mary and Elaine came downstairs where David, Nicole, John, and Frank were talking. David stopped talking to Frank and went over, asking Elaine to sit down. Mary sat next to her for support. David sat on the other side. Mary took the lead by saying, "Mother, what I'm about to tell you will seem impossible and defies all scientific logic. I held the truth back from you. I'm truly sorry. When I first met David, it was at his home in Maine. I went there to try to convince David to come back to Florida to talk to his dead father who was a dolphin."

Elaine exclaimed, "What the hell are you trying to say!"

David said, "My father and I had a strained relationship because he was involved with some shady people that caused some serious impact to the environment. When he passed away, because of what he had done, the higher powers turned him into a dolphin for his penance. And, after seeing what he had done, he began his journey to communicate to the humans and make them aware of what they were doing to the environment. That's when he met Aaron, who had terminal cancer, and it was being with my father that put his cancer into remission. When the shark attacked, it was my dad that saved Aaron's life, and in the process, he was badly injured. That is where Mary met my father, who was being treated for the shark bite. And when Aaron's parents brought him to Sea Land because his cancer had come back, that is when Aaron showed Mary how he could talk to the dolphin, my dad. That is when Mary came to tell me what we are trying to tell you. And I didn't believe it until I saw and heard it myself."

With a puzzled look on her face, Elaine said, "What does that have to do with your Joe?"

David said, "Uncle Joe is not my uncle but my father."

"Are you telling me that Joe is your father and is a dolphin?" asked Elaine. Elaine looked at David, then Mary, and then finally Frank, who all nodded in agreement. She then put her head in her lap and said, "You mean I slept with a fish?"

Mary replied, "No, technically speaking, he is a mammal."

Elaine lifted her head, gave Mary the evil eye, and said, "Really? I need to see this with my own eyes."

"All right," replied David. He grabbed his laptop computer and told Elaine that she would be able to ask any questions she wanted.

She said, "You guys are really serious?" She looked at everyone. "Okay, let's find out."

Mary asked Nicole if she would watch the baby, and she gave her the intercom remote for the nursery room.

Marco could see everyone walking down to the pier and knew they had just told Elaine and were coming down to prove it to her. As they approached the pier, he swam over so the light from the pier would shine on him. He could see when Elaine saw him, she stopped. He then began to send communication to the laptop she was holding. Marco could hear his voice being repeated on the computer. Her face said it all. Marco said, "I know it's hard to believe what you are seeing and hearing. I've had a hard time believing it myself. I was going to tell you last night, but then you passed out in my arms."

Elaine said, "Okay...I believe it."

He told her that for her own safety, she was kept in the dark, and there simply wasn't a good time to tell her with everything that was going on. Elaine looked over at Mary, who nodded her head. She then turned back as he continued to tell her that if anyone would find out, the consequences could be dire. He then said to Elaine, "I felt so bad not telling you, but I hope you understand after you think about it."

Elaine asked, "So that was the joke?"

Marco answered, "Yes, and no. It was the first time Nicole, John, and Aaron saw me as a human. The crying was Nicole thanking me for helping Aaron with his cancer. The supposed joke was to cover her tears of joy."

Elaine asked, "Can you come back as a human again?"

Marco answered, "I don't know. All I remember after Mary fell is that I was praying to save her and the baby. The next thing I knew, I was on the beach being arrested for being nude. When I was booked, they took my fingerprints, and later when the police ran them, they came back as Marco Ricci, deceased."

David gave everyone a heads up. "The police told me that the rescue had turned into a body recovery. Frank told them there was a shark attack in the cove earlier this year."

Mary interrupted and said, "Well, let's give them some evidence. I have a set of shark jaws back at the Rescue Center. We can use the jaws to tear bite marks on the bathing suit. They're coming back again tomorrow. Let it float on the water so they can find it. I'm going to check on the baby, and I'll go to the rescue center with the bathing suit."

Aaron, along with his father, walked over to Elaine, who was holding the computer. Aaron said, "I was hoping that you would stay as Uncle Joe."

Marco replied, "I know, Aaron, but we figured that this was temporary—and more importantly that we had to keep the big picture in mind. Remember, I will always be your Nono."

David told his father that as soon as Mary finished preparing the bathing suit, he would bring it down to the pier so he could place it where the police could find it.

Frank told Marco, "If anything comes up, have David call me."

Marco replied, "Frank, you're my rock. Thank you again, my friend."

Elaine was the last one still on the pier. Marco said, "I want you to know that the short time we had together will get me through the long, lonely nights. Being able to see our grandson was something I never thought possible, and to share that with you was special."

"I want to thank you for saving Mary's and Marco William's lives. You were the one who called 911 from Mary's cell phone when Mary fell and hit her head, weren't you?"

"Yes, I tried to warn her, but she was walking, looking at her cell phone and tripped on Aaron's baseball bat. It was the worst feeling to see her laying on the pier, bleeding, and I couldn't help. I used her phone she dropped to call 911."

"How could you call 911?"

"Aaron and I first used the cell phone to communicate with each other. I believe a higher power has special plans for Mary and our grandson. I'm just the messenger doing his bidding." Elaine had tears running down her face as she listened to his voice through the computer. "I wish I could hold you in my arms to comfort you."

Elaine said, "I had only slept with one man in my entire life, my late husband. It felt so right being with you these last couple of days. I felt we had something really special. I never felt such strong feelings. I felt like I could look into your soul. And now you are in a dolphin. Can you come back to us?" The words came out broken from the emotion.

"Elaine, when Mary was lying on the pier, I prayed to God that he could do anything to me but please spare both of them. And he did. And now I'm living up to my part of the bargain. He has a plan, and I do his bidding. I have no control over what happens. I'm just thankful that Mary and our grandson are safe. I wish I could hold him in my arms at least once, but you will have to do that for me."

Elaine put the laptop down and walked over to him. She put one finger on her lips and then kissed him on top of his head. Then she walked away.

Marco watched until she reached the house. She was greeted by David, who was bringing down the bathing suit. Holding the laptop that Elaine gave him, he walked to the pier. David said to his dad, "Elaine is taking it hard...as we all are."

"I had a nice talk with her, and I was hoping to comfort her, but I don't know if I accomplished that. We have a special bond and feeling for each other, and I don't know what's next." Marco could see the sadness in David's face. He told David how wonderful it was to at least see his grandson. "I only wish I could have held him in my arms in a human form."

David, feeling all the emotions, could only hand his dad the bathing suit and say with a broken voice, "I'll see you tomorrow, Dad."

Marco stared at the house until all the lights went out. He then sank down under the water but would come back up again, looking back at the house. Every once in a while, he would see the lights come on. He knew the baby was crying and either Mary or David was up.

He sank into the dark water, wondering what Elaine must be thinking. All that she went through and how she handled it was remarkable. That really showed what kind of person she was. Marco only wished there was a way he could have told her before all the trauma that she had to go through. He didn't even finish his thought when all of a sudden, he was back on the beach, nude, and in human form again. "Thank you, thank you, thank you!!" he yelled as he ran up to the house.

He entered the keypad code to let himself in. He grabbed a towel from the bathroom and quickly walked up to Elaine's room. Opening the door, he could see Elaine curled up in a little ball as if in the fetal position. She was still crying.

She heard the door open and said, "I'm sorry. I didn't mean to wake you." She never moved or looked up. Marco slipped into her bed, putting his arms around her. That warm feeling came over her, and she knew it was him. She quickly turned around, looking at him. He put his finger to her lips. She gave him kisses over and over again, not letting him say anything.

Finally, Marco said, "I don't know what happened. All I know is I could not see myself without you. I guess you're a part of the master plan."

They curled up together. Every once in a while, she would look at Marco and say, "I hope this is not a dream. If it is, I don't want to wake up." He kissed her and held her tight. He felt her go limp. She had to be exhausted. She fell asleep in his arms.

CHAPTER 56

WHAT JUST HAPPENED?

Marco stayed with Elaine until almost daylight. He then wrote a note, leaving it on the pillow and crept out of bed without waking her. He went into the nursery to see his grandson as he slept. He knew he had to get back in the water before the police returned. He was confident he could return as a dolphin and still come back as a human. He knew there was a new plan for him, yet he had no idea what it was.

As soon as Marco entered the water, he could feel the change come over his body. He took the bathing suit that Mary prepared and put it in a place where the police could see it. He swam around, feeling wonderful. He kept thinking about holding Elaine in his arms and how at peace he felt. He knew Elaine was going to be a part of whatever was to come.

When Elaine woke up that morning, she assumed she had been dreaming. The happiest she felt during the dream quickly turned into depression then she noticed the salt and sand in the bed. Then she saw the note. It said, "See you at the pier. Don't worry. I'll be back." She quickly got out of bed and ran to the window. She could see Marco from the window as she changed her clothes. She ran down to the pier where he was waiting. With both of her hands on her hips, she stared at him sternly and said, "You don't leave a woman in bed without a goodbye kiss." He splashed her with water. She sat on the end of the pier and kissed him. Marco then put both of his fins around her waist and pulled her off the pier, turning her around and around as if they were dancing. The whole time she was laughing. He felt the total trust she had in him. He turned over on his back and gave her a fast ride as he returned her back to the pier with her still laughing the whole time.

At the house, David was making coffee when he looked out the window and saw Elaine in the water with his father. He quickly went upstairs where Mary was changing the baby. David took over and said, "Look outside at the pier."

Mary saw her mother dancing in the water with David's dad wrapped around her. She said to David, "Are you kidding me? My mother has really adjusted to your dad being a dolphin."

David sadly shook his head and said, "I finally reached a point in my life with my father that we were true friends and we could do things together with our son. That's all I've wanted, and now it's gone."

Mary put down the baby, put her arms around him, and said, "Look at my mother out there with your dad. You can still share the same things, but it might have to be in the water. Who else could go 22 MPH on the water and pull you around. Just think of our son playing with his grandfather."

He gave her a kiss. He whispered, "That is what I love about you. You make a bad situation seem good. Now I'm going to get the baby ready, and we're going to join them on the pier. It's about time our son meets his dolphin grandpa."

While they were walking downstairs, the front doorbell rang. It was Officer Jones. David invited him in. The officer asked, "Can you identify this bathing suit?"

He handed David the suit Mary had prepared. David took a look and told the officer, "Yes, it's mine, and I let my Uncle Joe use it. But it wasn't all ripped up."

Mary introduced herself as Dr. Mary Ricci, marine biologist. She said, these aren't rip marks. They are bite marks, and from the looks of it, a bull shark." She grabbed David's arm, and that started the baby crying, so Mary excused herself.

"That was the same conclusion we came up with. I'm sorry for your loss. We found it at the far end of the cove near the newly constructed pier." He went on to tell them they were posting do not swim signs in the cove. They were also ending the body recovery search for the obvious reason. "We noticed someone in the water at the pier. Please let them know of the posting," he said. "I have to go next door and notify them of the posting of not to swim."

After the officer left, Mary said, "I think I should get an Academy Award for that performance."

David, looking at her with a frown on his face, said, "Don't quit your day job."

"I think I did a pretty good job," replied Mary.

"Yes, dear."

As they were walking down to the pier, Elaine was sitting on the edge with Nono's head in her lap. David opened up the laptop so everyone could hear him and said, "I just had the police at the house. They told me they found the bathing suit, and they concurred that you were killed by a shark. They are posting do not swim signs in the cove and closing the investigation."

Mary said, "I sold it!" David rolled his eyes. By then, Aaron, Nicole, and John made it to the pier to join everyone.

Elaine said, "It's official. I'm a new member of the group, and I have some good news. But I'm going to let Marco tell you."

"You are doing just fine. Go ahead," said Marco.

Elaine was so excited to see David and Mary look at each other with a puzzled look.

Mary asked, "Did you start wine o'clock this morning? I saw you two dancing out in the water."

Elaine said, "No, but I did have a visitor late last night who spent the night with me."

Everyone's mouth opened wide. Mary said, "You mean you slept with Joe? I mean Marco again?"

Elaine answered, "No! Get your mind out of the gutter. He was quite the gentleman. He held me in his arms until I fell asleep."

Nicole put her hands over Aaron's ears. Marco said, "Okay, I think I'd better finish the story. I felt bad about what Elaine had to go through, as all of you did. But poor Elaine was unmercifully hammered all at once yesterday. We have a special bond. I feel her soul inside me. I prayed for guidance, and the next thing I knew, I was on the beach in my human form. Early this morning, I returned to the water as a dolphin before the police arrived. So, I'm able to go back and forth as needed."

Elaine interrupted Marco by saying, "The only drawback is you come back in your birthday suit. So we might have to leave a set of clothes out for you, or maybe not."

"Mother!" said Mary as she gave her mother a disapproving look.

Elaine responded, "I'm sorry."

Marco said, "As I was saying, I have a mission to bridge the gap between humans and the sea mammals but having a way to go back and forth as needed now brings a whole new opportunity. Look what we have done here with the children and the dolphins. The children are the key to getting that message to the next generation and convince the old generation we can live in harmony again. We can do the same thing we have done here to other parts of the country and to the world. I'm hoping Elaine will join me in this adventure, and along with your help, we can make a difference."

No one was aware a drone overhead had been watching the house for weeks, videoing everything. All of the videos were sent back to Key West Navy Base and the Seal Team Special Forces Command Center. The Navy Base Commander asked one of his captains. "Do you have all the videos edited from the last couple of days?"

The captain answered, "Yes, sir."

While the commander looked at the video, he saw Marco diving into the water as a human, transforming into a dolphin, and returning to land as a human. After seeing all the videos, he said, "Son of a bitch, the Luca brothers were right. Do you know what this means to our Seal team? They could travel at 20 MPH in the water and dive 300 plus feet without any breathing equipment. We need to get our hands on Marco Ricci and that computer."

The captain asked, "How are we going to get him if he can change back and forth from dolphin to human? He will be impossible to catch."

The commander answered, "That's why we aren't going after Marco Ricci, but his son, wife, and his girlfriend."

Unaware of what was about to happen overhead, everyone at the house was excited that Marco found a way of transforming himself from a dolphin back into a human form and how much easier it would be to communicate with him without having to use the computer. He could just appear as a man and speak to them. Of course, the change of clothes and a towel would be needed.

Everyone began to leave, going back to the house as if they had just lost someone to a terrible accident. Then Marco said to Elaine, "I will see you tonight." That brought a smile to Elaine's face. She blew a kiss as she walked up to the house.

Once they were gone, Marco left the cove. He knew that the pod of dolphins would be close because it was coming up on a full moon. When he found the pod, he let them know everything was okay and that he would be gone from time to time but to keep coming to the cove every full moon to interact with the kids as usual, even if he wasn't with them.

Aaron, Nicole, and John went back to their house, leaving Elaine, Mary, and David alone while they were still talking over the events of the day. All of a sudden, the house was surrounded by a group of Navy Seals with guns drawn. A helicopter landed, and a base commander entered the house along with his captain. The commander told the group of Seals to stand down. "We don't want to scare these fine folks. All we are looking for is Marco Ricci."

David said, "There must be a mistake. My father is dead."

The commander walked up to David, looked at him in the eyes, and said, "We've been watching the house for weeks. We know that your father is not dead and that he goes in and out of the water in different forms." He gave David a wink.

"I want to speak to my attorney," replied David.

"You're not under arrest. We're just moving you to a secure area for your protection. This is a national security matter now." The commander then ordered his men to get all the computers and to get everyone packed up and ready to leave.

Mary replied, "I just had a baby. You can't just force us to relocate with a baby."

"I'm sorry ma'am. We have everything you need, and if there is something else you need, we will provide it. Now, all of this can be prevented if you tell Marco Ricci to turn himself in to us."

Both Mary and David looked at each other, and David said, "I told you my father is dead."

The commander then said, "Okay, move it out."

CHAPTER 57

THE GAMBLE

That evening, Marco returned to the cove under cover of night so not to be seen by anyone. He dried off and put on the clothes that Elaine had left for him at the end of the pier. A smile came over his face because of the excitement of seeing everyone, especially Elaine. Then he saw Aaron running down to the pier, followed by John and Nicole. The excitement quickly changed to concern as if something was not quite right. He heard Aaron say, "The military came and took everybody away."

John and Nicole arrived and explained how a military helicopter landed a group of Navy Seals who surrounded the house and took Mary, David, Elaine, and the baby. As they all went into the house, Marco found the note that the commander had left for him. His worst fear was realized. He looked up at John, Nicole, and Aaron.

He told what the note said. "I have no choice but to turn myself in." He called the number on the note. When the commander answered, Marco said, "All right, the first thing is to return my family now, and we will talk."

The commander said, "For national security reasons, we need you in a secure location, and if you cooperate with us, we will release everyone. You have my word."

Realizing there was no other option, Marco agreed. The commander told him that a helicopter would be landing shortly, and he would be brought to a secure location and united with his family.

A helicopter landed in the back yard, and a group of Navy Seals entered the house with guns drawn. Marco quickly raised his arms in the air and told them who he was. In just moments, he was hand-cuffed and led to the helicopter. It all happened so quickly that he didn't have a chance to say goodbye to Aaron and his family as he left the house.

While they took off, all that was going through Marco's mind was his family's safety. He had no plan or knew what he was going to say. All he could do was hope that the commander would honor his word and let his family go.

They landed on an airport runway. He was quickly unloaded into a military transport and brought to a building where he was put in a room with a table and two chairs. His hands where hand-cuffed to the table and his ankle chained to the floor. Then he was left in the room all alone. So many things were running through his mind it was all he could do to remain calm. He knew they were watching him.

The door opened. Marco saw a military officer walk into the room with an armed guard next to him. He sat in the chair across from Marco and in-troduced himself as Commander Cook in charge of the Navy Seal team. He turned to the armed guard who was in the room and told him to leave them alone. Marco guessed that was his way of making him feel better. Marco then raised his arms up, showing him his handcuffs and raised his eyebrows. The commander stopped the guard and told him to first unshackle Marco. The guard released Marco from his restraints and left the room.

The commander said to Marco, "Let's not beat around the bush. We have been watching you for weeks. We know you can change from human to a dolphin at any time you want. So, you can realize that if you got into the wrong hands that would be a national security problem. Are you from another planet or another solar system?"

He said, "First, I want to tell you that I'm not from another planet or an ET. I'm a human man just like you, but, before we go any further, I want to know my family is safe and that you lived up to your word and let them go home."

The commander made a call on his cellphone. He said, "Lieutenant, put on David Ricci." He handed the phone to Marco.

When Marco heard David's voice on the other end, it was a relief. He asked, "Is everyone safe, and are they treating you well?"

David answered, "We are all fine. We are more worried about you."

"Everything is going to be fine. They will release you, and I will join you soon. The commander and I have to work out a few things first. I'd better go. I love you, David." Marco handed the cell phone back to the commander and said, "What I'm about to tell you is going to be hard for you to believe, but you already know that I can change from human to a dolphin, so it may be easier for you to understand." He went on to tell the commander he thought his transformation from human to a dolphin was a curse for his sins against nature and humanity. Marco could see by the expression on his face that he then had gotten the commander's attention.

After Marco finished his story, Commander Cook asked, "How do you transform from human to dolphin?"

Marco paused, looked at him, and said, "I'm not sure how it happens. Maybe it's because I'm just a messenger and the message is to bring man to understand what he is doing to the oceans around the world. Maybe one day, man will understand what they're doing to the ocean that the sea creatures have to live in. That is what we started here at the foundation with the handicapped children, and it's that new generation of children who will be the bridge so we all can clean up our oceans."

Commander Cook asked, "Are you like a Messiah?"

"No, I was the worst of the worst. I did some terrible things, and this is my curse or penance."

"You know what would happen if the wrong people got ahold of you?"

"Yes, that is why I need your help. I believe that we can work together to make this a better world. What if you had an army of dolphins at your service to help you protect our ocean's borders and help you with rescues at sea or assist in an intelligence gathering? I can help train your Seal teams with my dolphins, but they are not to be involved in any suicide or dangerous missions." Marco could see he had gotten the commander's attention. He then said, "In return, I need your help in advancing my mission."

"What would that be?" asked the commander.

"In the Sea of Japan, there is an island where they drive dolphins into the bay and slaughter them with baseball bats. They are still practicing this inhumane method today. I need the United States' influence with the United Nations to stop these practices, and in that bay, install a foundation like we have here where the children come to the bay and see the dolphins and interact with them instead of being killed. Secondly, again, I need the United States' influence with the United Nations to start to clean up the Great Pacific Garbage Patch, also referred as the Eastern Garbage Patch, which is roughly mid-way between Hawaii and California. It is a soupy collection of marine debris, which is mostly plastic, that has formed a floating island the size of Texas. My son, David, can show you what can be done to recycle this waste like what he has done off the coast of Florida. There is so much we could do together for the good of the country and the world.

Commander Cook responded, "This is quite a big order to fill. I'll have to consult with the White House."

Marco asked him, "What is an army of dolphins worth? You already have hurricane warning systems in place that the dolphins can use to give you information in real time—like foreign ships and submarines that enter our waters undetected. And the priceless savings in cost and manpower that I can provide with my dolphins. What is the budget to patrol the country's borders? In the billions of dol-lars, I'd guess."

Commander Cook was deep in thought. "How do we know that you can deliver on what you're telling me."

Marco told him in a couple of days, a pod of dolphins would be in the cove at the foundation for the monthly visit with the handicapped children, and he would demonstrate what could be done with the dolphins then. He then told the commander, "Bring anyone you need to convince there, but no military presence. Make sure everybody that comes is in street clothes. Now please release my family, and I will see you at the foundation cove." Taking a gamble that he could teleport back to the cove, he put it all on the line. If a higher power was letting him teleport at his will, that would be a game changer. That would definitely make his point. Marco left Commander Cook with a lasting impression by disappearing right in front of him.

CHAPTER 58

DID THE GAMBLE PAY OFF

When Marco found himself back in the cove, all his questions were answered. He was able to teleport when he wanted to, and he had a new mission. But it was enough to convince Commander Cook he could follow up on his promises.

He saw a helicopter landing at the house, and his family was home. He knew the gamble paid off. He quickly changed from a dolphin to a man standing nude as the helicopter hovered overhead. A big smile came over Marco as he dried himself off. He looked up at the house. He could see Elaine come running down to the pier. Wrapping the towel around him, he was greeted with a kiss that knocked the towel off from around his waist. They lost their balance and landed on the dock with Elaine on top of him.

Elaine said, "What a way to impress a lady. What the hell did you tell the commander?" Marco smiled as she kept kissing him. The kisses became laughter. "I think we may have to increase your pier attire, but I kinda like this look." She gave him a sexy smile.

It didn't take long for the rest of the family to reach the pier. Marco quickly got up and put the towel around his waist. He was greeted by everyone. And, of course, Mary was the first one to say something.

"You guys need to get a room!"

At the house, Marco held his grandson for the first time and gave everyone a heads up on what had happened and that the military would be back at the cove for a demonstration of how they can use the dolphins for good things like assisting in rescues, reconnaissance, and patrolling the borders. However, the deal was the military was not to exploit them or put them in danger.

Elaine came down the stairs with a fresh set of clothes. As she handed the clothes to Marco, she whispered in his ear, "I still like the pier attire best." She gave him a sexy wink.

Elaine walked to the refrigerator and pulled out a couple bottles of wine. Handing the baby back to Mary, Marco helped her by getting the glasses, and then she poured the drinks. David made a toast. "Thanks, Dad. I don't know how you pulled it off again. We are just so happy to have the family back together and safe again. We love you!" Everyone touched glasses.

Not The End, Just The Beginning.

One month later, the rescue center was finished, and Mary got a call from Zoe from Sea Land. She had a couple of walruses they were having trouble with, and she wondered if Mary would be interested in them. Mary had a flashback to the Luca brothers and started to laugh, but she agreed.

Late the next day, Sea Land delivered the two walruses to the center. They were put in a large pen. Mary thanked everyone for staying late to help. Locking up, she walked by the walruses' pen and noticed that both of them were in the corner, shaking. She kept walking when her cell phone toned. The message was 7777-666-777-777-9999. She cleared it, but it toned again 77777-666-777-777-9999. She looked to see if anyone was around. She remembered Aaron's code with Nono, so she pulled out a pen and paper. The code spelled out "Sorry."

She turned to look at them and started to walk over to the pen. Both of them were trying to hide behind each other. Mary then made a call to David, who was babysitting, and said, "Hi, hon. I'll be a little late. I have a couple of loose ends to tie up here." She hung up with a big smile on her face.

Made in the USA
San Bernardino, CA
18 January 2020